THE FOREST GODS' FIGHT

THE
FOREST
GODS'
FIGHT

*Book Two of
the Forest Gods Series*

A NOVEL

ALEXANDRIA HOOK

New York

THE FOREST GODS' FIGHT

© 2016 ALEXANDRIA HOOK.

Published in New York, New York, by Morgan James Publishing. Morgan James and The Entrepreneurial Publisher are trademarks of Morgan James, LLC. www.MorganJamesPublishing.com

The Morgan James Speakers Group can bring authors to your live event. For more information or to book an event visit The Morgan James Speakers Group at www.TheMorganJamesSpeakersGroup.com.

Shelfie

A **free** eBook edition is available
with the purchase of this print book.

CLEARLY PRINT YOUR NAME ABOVE IN UPPER CASE

Instructions to claim your free eBook edition:
1. Download the Shelfie app for Android or iOS
2. Write your name in **UPPER CASE** above
3. Use the Shelfie app to submit a photo
4. Download your eBook to any device

ISBN 978-1-63047-739-4 paperback
ISBN 978-1-63047-740-0 eBook
ISBN 978-1-63047-741-7 hardcover
Library of Congress Control Number:
2015913641

Cover Design by:
Chris Treccani
www.3dogdesign.net

Interior Design by:
Bonnie Bushman
The Whole Caboodle Graphic Design

In an effort to support local communities, raise awareness and funds, Morgan James Publishing donates a percentage of all book sales for the life of each book to Habitat for Humanity Peninsula and Greater Williamsburg.

Get involved today, visit
www.MorganJamesBuilds.com

Habitat
for Humanity®
Peninsula and
Greater Williamsburg
Building Partner

Dedicated to

my parents,
without whom none of this would have happened.

THE FOREST GODS

The Monster Watch:

Athena .... Ashley

Zeus .... Zach

Poseidon .... Luke

Apollo .... Connor

Other gods:

Aphrodite .... Becca

Hermes .... Josh

Hera .... Alicia

Artemis .... Camille

Hephaestus .... Shane

Dionysus .... Jack

Demeter .... Maddie

Hestia .... Haley

Hades

Persephone

Pan

Part One

THE CALM BEFORE THE STORM

Chapter 1

MONSTERS AND A MOVIE

People always talk of the "calm before the storm." As I looked anxiously into the deep blue eyes of Poseidon, the god of the sea, that phrase came to mind. The urgency in my tone had silenced him and now he was just studying me, trying to guess exactly what type of storm was coming and what type of damage might be left in its wake. He could afford to stand unaffected in the middle of the street for a few moments, but I couldn't. In the metaphorical sense, there is no calm before the storm for those who know it's coming, the ones who are more or less responsible for it. You see, in this case, *I* was the storm. I, Athena, the reincarnated goddess of wisdom, was for the first time in my life the most responsible for the trouble at hand. I'd never felt so much like Zeus.

"I—I think Aphrodite's in the woods," Poseidon stuttered quietly, finally realizing that something was very wrong. My sudden return to Washington from Kentucky—nearly two weeks early, in fact—should've been the first clue. I released him from my tight grasp, then turned on my heel and took off in a dead sprint, heading straight into the forest we called home. I didn't even bother to fill him in, or Apollo, or Zeus, none of whom had shared my recent haunting visions of the dead goddess of love and beauty. It wasn't part of the Oracle of Delphi's prophecy—not even the part they didn't know about.

What was happening now, the deterioration of our reign over the forest and our hometown of the Woods, was entirely my fault. No, really. It was obvious to me that Hades, lord of the dead and our current enemy, meant to harm Aphrodite because she represented love, not because he was retaliating after some specific action of hers. He was sending a message. Somehow he knew that Alec, my young hero and destined savior of the war, had feelings for me—and that I maybe had feelings for the Knowing boy, too.

You shouldn't have let Alec stay here, I told myself angrily for probably the hundredth time since he'd stumbled into our woods a few weeks earlier. He was the first human with the Sight (the knowledge that the Greek myths were true and the ability to see monsters for what they really were) any of us teenaged gods had ever come across and he'd told us of a faraway camp filled with people just like him—the Knowing. But his real reason for finding us, he had claimed, was that the Oracle sent him. Zeus, my best friend and Mr. King of the Gods, had given me the final say in the matter, and I'd told Alec he could live under our protection, simply because I would have felt guilty about letting him die on his own in the forest. I should have known not to get attached. I should have let him perish alone, rather than let him build such a dangerous friendship with this generation of Greek gods. Here's the simple truth: I thought I would have more control than I actually did.

But at least for right now, Alec's presence couldn't screw anything else up; he was still back in Kentucky, readying the Knowing army to fight Hades.

As I raced onward, I heard the sound of Zeus, Poseidon, and Apollo frantically running to catch up with me. I threw down my black backpack at the edge of the trees and didn't pause to pick up any weapons when I raced by the hollow, moss-covered logs where our makeshift armory was; there was no time for that, so the metamorphic rock/sword and my pocketknife would have to do. The guys must not have had anything at all with them, however, because I could no longer hear them panting behind me, so I assumed they had paused to grab the master lightning bolt, trident, and bow with a leather quiver full of arrows.

Glaring ahead in determination, I made a hard right, now heading north along the same winding path as in my dream, a route I had taken hundreds of times before. Low-hanging branches smacked my face as I raced along the uneven path and jumped over any old, fallen trees or boulders in the way, but I ignored the stinging sensation spreading across my face and ran faster. I had to make it in time. I had to.

When I heard shouting in Greek coming from behind me, I knew that the other gods had caught up again. The branches of the pine trees reached out across the overgrown path like arms trying to grab the four of us as we sprinted single file along the narrow trail, with me in the lead, since I was the only one who actually knew the complete story of what was going on. I heard a girl's terrible, bloodcurdling scream coming from farther along the trail and knew that we were close, but the question of whether we would make it in time to save her still remained.

I took a deep breath before pulling out all of my energy to run faster than I had ever run in my entire life. Time never seemed to be on our side.

Grumbling to myself in frustration, I jumped over a huge, mangled log and turned left, keeping to the trail from my vision. The trail that I knew would lead us to Aphrodite, whether she was dead or alive. I felt the tickle of the long, lush green ferns at my feet slowly fade away as we four—the gods of our town's so-called Monster Watch—burst into a familiar tiny clearing in the thick trees, but we were not alone anymore.

I had only a few seconds to survey the situation as I tried to slow my breathing and concentrate: the meaty, monstrous Minotaur had the gorgeous Aphrodite pinned against the rough bark of a pine tree, with his thick, furry, black hand slowly starting to close around her petite throat. Aphrodite's eyes were rolled back and her thin arms were flailing around wildly as she tried to gasp for air, but to no avail. The fragile goddess of love who happened to be wearing expensive heels and a white miniskirt (don't ask me why she would come into the forest like that) was obviously no match for the mighty Minotaur in this situation.

Knowing that Aphrodite's precious life was about to be crushed right before my eyes if I didn't do anything, I shouted out, hoping the others would somehow understand my desperate plan. I would have saved her myself, but throwing my own sword at the gigantic Minotaur was too risky; I might accidentally hit Aphrodite and then coming all the way back to Washington from Kentucky would have been useless, not to mention the fact that I would be losing a fellow goddess and friend. So I screamed one word: "Poseidon!"

Then I dove to my left, hitting the forest floor hard. I glanced behind me just in time to see Poseidon's perfectly toned and tanned muscles ripple from stress as he struck the earth with his golden trident humming with power and everything around us started to shake. Sighing in relief that Poseidon had understood what I was trying to tell him, I quickly covered my head and hoped he hadn't caused a big enough earthquake to make the trees topple.

I looked up to see the Minotaur stumble and reluctantly let go of Aphrodite as it tried to regain its balance while I sighed again in relief. The greatly weakened Aphrodite fell to the ground, coughing and sputtering, her luscious golden hair now in unruly tangles from the struggle with the horrifying monster that had reemerged from the mysterious Underworld.

But by then, the giant tremor in the earth had finally stopped. The Minotaur was grunting unintelligibly and stumbling through the coarse grass toward Aphrodite yet again, its red eyes gleaming with even more hatred and anger than before. Aphrodite, on the other hand, was still collapsed in the grass by the tree, her blue eyes glassy due to oxygen deprivation. She was in no condition to defend herself. Meanwhile, Poseidon was readjusting his grip on his trident and, strangely enough, Apollo was having trouble fitting an arrow into his wooden recurve bow properly. Either someone or something had tampered with his weapon of choice, or he was just abnormally shaken up from the quake.

Regardless, glaring at the hungry monster, I forcefully pushed myself up without hesitation and readied myself for a quick battle by pulling the small, gray rock from my pocket. The shining silver blade immediately popped out.

But I shouldn't have even bothered, knowing Zeus was with me, because just then, I was blinded by a flash of white-hot light I knew immediately was lightning and felt a strong burning sensation on the entire right side of my body as the bolt whizzed by me like a rocket. I blinked rapidly, trying to regain my vision as the smell of fire filled my nostrils.

Color seeped back into my sight just in time to see a now stiff Minotaur with singed black fur crumble into a small pile of dust, which then sank slowly into the muddy soil on its way to the Underworld once more. As I took a deep breath, I squeezed the hilt of the sword, turning it back into a rock, and stuffed it in my jeans pocket. Next, I checked the right side of my body to make sure it wasn't burned too badly and was relieved to find that my skin was only slightly warmer and redder than usual. Zeus had learned to control his powers well.

Once I was sure I was unharmed, I hurried with Zeus, Poseidon, and Apollo to meet Aphrodite, who was finally lifting herself from the grass. Her blue eyes simply widened in terror as her body began to shake from both stress and fright, but I still sighed in relief, regardless of her current state. All that mattered was that she was alive. In fact, I was just thinking that Aphrodite was keeping herself composed very well for a girl who had almost been strangled to death when she suddenly broke down. Without saying a word, Aphrodite used the rest of her energy to pull all four of us in for a group hug, as only she could get us more insensitive gods to do, then let out a huge sob as she began to cry into Zeus's dirty white T-shirt. I knew Aphrodite had never been so close to death before. None of us had.

"Just let it out. It's okay," Zeus muttered to her in his most comforting tone, closing his stormy eyes for a sentimental moment. "You're okay."

After about five minutes of Aphrodite crying into Zeus's shoulder, we silently helped her up and headed southwest toward the small meadow where our emergency supply kit was kept at the edge of the trees. We rushed as much as we could to avoid running into any more monsters, but Aphrodite still hadn't gained much energy back after her near-death experience so it was slow going for most of the way. Not to mention she still hadn't uttered a word to any of us, though on the other hand, that gave me time to tell everyone about the vision I'd first experienced the night before.

By the time I finished my explanation, I decided she had recuperated well enough to offer her own. "Hey, Aphrodite, what were you doing in here anyway?" I asked her curiously, because truthfully, Aphrodite seemed to avoid the forest as much as possible except for battle practices. Although it wasn't really surprising to me that the goddess of love and beauty didn't want to spend her free time fighting monsters. Wouldn't want to break a nail, of course.

She sniffed and dropped her shoulders. "I don't know. I had this vision and it was, like, calling me into the forest." Here she had to take a pause, biting her quivering lip to hold off more tears from leaking out. "My mom thinks I'm at the mall in the next county with some of my Sightless friends."

No one said anything more. I knew Zeus, Poseidon, Apollo, and I shared the same thought: How could Aphrodite have been so careless and gullible? We were in a time of war, but here she was, falling into dangerous traps and running around on her own without a walkie-talkie, thus breaking pretty much all of our emergency protocols. I wished I could say that I felt more sympathy for her, but I really didn't.

Sighing, the five of us stepped out from under the trees and walked through the meadow, the only break in the dense trees for miles. When we reached the other side, Apollo carefully reached into a large hollow in one of the pine trees, pulling out the first-aid kit as Aphrodite plopped down in the long grass. Apollo then retrieved some old hand wipes from the red bag and handed them to the pale love goddess so she could wipe the smudged dirt and a few drops of golden blood off her face. After all, she couldn't exactly show or tell her parents what she had been doing in the forbidden forest.

Meanwhile, Poseidon and Zeus had stepped off to the side and were talking in low voices, probably discussing what to do next. Zeus pulled his black walkie-talkie off his belt loop and I guessed that he was radioing all of the other gods to inform them of what had just happened. I knew that Hermes, the messenger god, would then run and tell everyone else who still needed to hear the details, specifically the various groups of nymphs and satyrs in the forest.

With another sigh, I watched Apollo get up slowly and start to head toward Zeus and Poseidon. I was just thinking about joining the guys when Aphrodite whispered to me shakily, "How do you do this?"

I glanced at her in confusion. "Do what?"

"*This*. Fighting monsters, being a goddess . . . everything. I'm terrible at this and I just can't take it. I can't even believe I fell for Hades's stupid vision trick," she whimpered, shaking her blonde head, on the verge of tears again. "I should've known."

I shook my head quickly, knowing that if Aphrodite started to think so negatively, she would give up on saving the world right there, and we needed all the help we could get. Mental health was just as important as physical health.

"No, you're great at being a goddess. Do you know how many couples you've set up at school? Like, everyone. I'm not even kidding," I assured her, taking her cold and clammy hands in mine.

"Oh, come on, how is love going to help save the world?" Aphrodite complained, looking up at me with sorrowful, watery eyes.

I rolled my own eyes, slightly annoyed. All right, I had to admit that love wasn't the handiest or most useful weapon, but it was a kind of weapon nonetheless.

"Maybe love isn't as important or as useful as fighting monsters, but it is so much more powerful. You know that. Love causes people to do unthinkable things in the spur of a moment, for better or for worse, but most of all, it gives people *hope*. And hope is sometimes the only thing that keeps people going," I told her seriously, thinking in the back of my mind about what Alec had said and desperately hoping that Aphrodite would listen to what I was trying to say. Love was her specialty, after all.

Aphrodite's eyes started to light up, regaining their familiar shine, and I knew that I had reached her. "Alec told you he loves you, didn't he?" she accused me, a knowing smile stretching across her face.

Okay, so maybe I hadn't reached her as well as I thought.

Because Alec's feelings were *so* not the point of my whole love speech. I frowned instantly. Besides, Aphrodite could dream all she wanted, but Alec and I were never going to be together. In our hectic world, there was absolutely no way. The virgin goddess of wisdom and war with a hero? Nope. How many times had I said this before? Did I forget to mention that love was also one of the biggest distractions ever? And the very last thing I needed at the moment was a distraction from doing my job, no matter how Alec and I might have felt about each other. For as long as she wanted, Aphrodite could keep telling me I was in denial, but I vowed never to budge.

"I knew it!" she exclaimed loudly. When out of curiosity Zeus, Poseidon, and Apollo glanced back at us, I quickly shushed her. But upon seeing my dark expression, Aphrodite questioned, "Do you know what your fatal flaw is? Because I do."

I shot her an annoyed glare with my stone-cold gray eyes and protested, "Of course I do. I'm the freaking goddess of wisdom and—"

"Well, then let me remind you." Aphrodite smirked somewhat evilly as she interrupted me and I groaned, thinking that I really did not need a lecture right then, especially not one from her. I stood up to join the rest of the Monster Watch, but she wrapped her fingers around my wrist and dug her long fingernails into my skin, preventing me from leaving her side.

"Let go, Aphrodite."

"Oh, please. You know that your infinite wisdom and skill won't fix everything, yet you pretend like they will and you *throw* yourself into this Greek life, into being a goddess, just because something comes up that you don't want to deal with. Like the fact that Alec is *totally* and *completely* in love with you." She finished without even taking a breath and then sighed, looking at me like I was pathetic.

Ouch. She hit that one right on the nail. I was starting to regret coming over to cheer her up.

But, apparently, Aphrodite wasn't finished yet, because she also added, "You know it's true. You didn't have to come all the way back from the Knowing base camp in Kentucky to save me. You could have easily gone to the nearest pay phone and called Zeus to tell him the whole story. He obviously knows the forest well enough to have been able to figure out your message. But no, you had to leave Alec behind." She took a short pause, letting my guilt settle in, then continued, "Trust me, I know it's sometimes easier to deal with guys when they're on the other side of the country, the world, or even the Underworld, but that doesn't mean it's the *best* way to deal with them."

I couldn't help but admit her advice was good; she really knew the ins and outs of relationships. But then again, I wasn't *that* heartless and her short-sighted little idea wasn't the only reason I had ditched Alec at his place of birth. Glaring at her, I explained in a raised voice, "You don't think I know that? I left Alec there because I knew he could handle it and this was his chance to prove it. He's a hero now, Aphrodite. I carried out the ceremony." Aphrodite raised her eyebrows; that was news to her.

Still not done with my own lecture, however, I stood up again and crossed my arms. "For the record, fatal flaws aren't always blinding. Mine isn't, but yours could be," I warned her, fatigued, but with a ruthless edge to my voice. "You like to think that everyone can and should fall in love, even when you don't know half the truth about someone. Can't you see? I'm supposed to be the rational one here! Love may be powerful, but it's also a distraction that could end up killing us all. So please, use your powers wisely and you can just forget about Alec and me." Fuming quietly, I turned on my heel to walk away from Aphrodite who now looked more than slightly offended, though I couldn't say I really cared.

"Something wrong?" Apollo inquired nervously.

"Let's just go," I muttered to the boys and together we started the long walk east back to Main Street. Hopefully, I still had all afternoon to avoid going to my house to face the wrath of my father.

Zeus, Poseidon, and Apollo placed their weapons back in the hollow logs by the edge of the trees while I picked up my backpack from where I had dropped it earlier. As Aphrodite bid us farewell and headed off to her house, the three guys and I—the Monster Watch—just strode out of the dense forest and crossed the street toward the Fire Pit, not even bothering to check for cars. We opened the creaking door and, immediately, I smiled at the familiar warmth of the small restaurant and the wonderful smell of food while sounds of friendly chatter and the clanging of dishes filled my ears.

The four of us sat down in the back of the room at our usual booth and I glanced around at the rest of the tables to see that none of the other gods were there. I turned back to face the boys just as Zeus and Poseidon's—Zach and Luke's—human mother walked up, her thin eyebrows arched in surprise at seeing me.

"Ashley! You're back early," Martha exclaimed. "Didn't get kicked out of camp, I hope?"

Ashley? Oh, right, that's me, I reminded myself, shocked at how slow my reaction time was. The past few days had obviously taken a bigger toll on me than I originally thought.

Quickly recovering from my mental clumsiness, I returned her smile and replied shortly, "It's a long story. But I'm happy to be home again."

Their mom only nodded and retreated into the kitchen to make us some fresh lemonade and sandwiches. I couldn't help but notice that the other parents having lunch in the Fire Pit kept checking us out. Within five minutes, I knew that for better or for worse the entire town would be alerted that I was home early.

"So," Zach started in English, but quietly so no one could overhear. "How was the Knowing camp?" The three guys leaned in toward me, eager to hear every word about our new-found Sighted allies.

I just shrugged and told them, "Don't get too excited. They're almost completely corrupt."

When the boys raised their eyebrows in unison, waiting for me to continue, I realized I would have to start from the very beginning. Apparently, Alec had never told them everything he had confessed to me.

"Well, it turns out that no one in the Knowing base camp had had a vision from the gods or the Oracle in decades. They worshipped the gods less and less over time and now they very rarely even leave the camp out of fear of monsters and possibly facing the new gods' wrath. Furthermore, in order to maintain control and eliminate outside influence, they purposely haven't kept in touch with the other, smaller Knowing camps. So when Alec had his vision about us, no one believed his story. His entire family was ridiculed. At the beginning of summer, their leader, Jason, actually forbade Alec from leaving the camp and he had to sneak out to come find us. Naturally, the Knowing people weren't happy when Alec showed up with an outsider, but they imprisoned me and whipped him as punishment before I could even get out a word," I finished angrily.

"Are you serious? What did you do then?" Zach asked, his tone low and angry, while Luke and Connor—aka Apollo—cursed in Greek beside him.

I then summarized for them how I broke out from my imprisonment to stop the whipping and reveal my true identity. How the Knowing immediately apologized and acted like nothing was wrong, but later challenged my authority when a small group ambushed Alec after his hero ceremony. How Alec won the fight anyway. And lastly, I told them how Alec and I at least temporarily restored contact between Knowing camps and abolished the minimum age for warrior training in order to increase the size of our army. I mentioned only briefly the party the Knowing threw in my honor right before I had the vision of the dead Aphrodite, the vision that had led me back home.

When I finally finished outlining every minute of my past two days in Kentucky, I leaned back in my seat and took a deep breath while the rest of the Monster Watch collected their thoughts. "So Alec and the Knowing are meeting us in the forest in two weeks?" Luke clarified, and I nodded.

"Well, part of the Knowing. We'll be fighting a war on two fronts. Some of them have to stay at home and protect their camp. Since the day Alec and I showed up there, they've spotted way more monsters lurking around their territory than usual."

"That only leaves us about two weeks to defeat Hades and his army before school starts," Connor pointed out, running his fingers through his blond hair, but he stopped when he glanced toward the door. Josh, aka Hermes, had just walked in with Cole, a Sightless classmate who didn't know our true identities as gods, and they were heading our way.

Cole and Josh, who was covered in sweat from running to notify all the other gods about what had happened to Aphrodite, waved as they walked up to our booth. "Is Becca all right?" Josh asked us casually, but a slight tinge of concern was woven into his words.

I was opening my mouth to answer him when a confused Cole cut in, "What happened to Becca?"

"Nothing," we replied in unison and Cole gave us a dubious look with his soft, brown eyes. Sometimes I felt bad that Cole was one of the only kids in the entire town who was out of the loop, but I knew there was nothing I could do about it.

With a sigh, Cole sat down with Josh at our table even though we didn't invite them to. Since we couldn't exactly discuss battle plans with Cole right there, the conversation turned to regular human topics—school, TV shows, music, et cetera. Much less interesting in my opinion, not to mention unimportant.

About an hour later, the Monster Watch boys and I had finished our lemonades and grilled cheese sandwiches so we bid farewell to Josh and Cole then headed outside into the cool evening air. The four of us agreed that we had had enough of the woods for one day and slowly walked back to our houses instead, kicking little rocks along the way just to kill time because, for once, we seemed to have plenty of it.

A sudden loud thud interrupted the quietness of the empty road. I jerked my head up in the direction of the sound, the direction of my house, a sad-looking gray one that was sinking slightly on its ancient foundation. I didn't even have to walk inside and look at him to know my father was drunk. "You have got to be kidding me," I groaned, more to myself than any of the guys.

"Your dad?" Zach guessed and I nodded with an exasperated sigh.

"I may have seen or heard him on my way out of the airport . . . and possibly ditched him there," I explained sheepishly, and Connor and Zach erupted with laughter.

"Of course you did," Luke said with a smirk.

Another deafening crash came from inside the lit-up house and the boys exchanged indifferent glances before looking back to me. "Scary movies at our house later tonight," Zach added, gesturing to Luke and himself. "If you can manage to sneak out, you should come."

"I'll be there," I promised, eager to do something fun for once. Lately, all I had been thinking about was saving the world from Hades and his monster army. His mysterious motive for wanting to extend his rule outside of the Underworld kept me up at night more than I cared to admit to any of the Monster Watch.

I sighed and slowly made my way up the porch steps then waved to the boys as they disappeared into Zach and Luke's house, a dwelling slightly larger and much friendlier than mine. I slammed the screen door as I stepped over the threshold, letting my father know I was there. Sure enough, the grumbling monster of a man poked his head out from the lighted kitchen and his dark eyes grew even colder when they focused on me. I didn't say a word to him as I started up the stairs toward my room and he just stared at me, an almost empty beer bottle in his pale, shaking hand.

Suddenly, I heard the sound of shattering glass behind me and whirled around and grabbed my pocketknife, which I had hidden in my black leather combat boot in case a monster decided to venture out of the woods and barge into my house. You can never be too sure of these things in a time of war, after all, and since it would have looked awfully strange to my father if I had turned a small rock into a shining sword, my tiny pocketknife had to do.

But the good news was that the noise wasn't made by a mythical Greek monster and, to my relief, my father had turned away from me and retreated back into the kitchen. The only evidence that there had actually been a sound was the broken shards of brown glass from the beer bottle that lay at the base of the wall. At times like these, I wished I had the ability to read minds like Hera, to see what was going on in my father's messed-up head.

"I'm not cleaning that up," I told him defiantly, looking up from the drops of dark liquid staining the white tiled floor and tightened my grip on the black pocketknife even more. It had been a very long time since he had actually thrown something at me.

"You're grounded," he shouted up at me in a gravelly voice, and I smiled to myself. He really was too predictable.

I turned around and raced into my room, swiftly pulling my sleek laptop out of a drawer in the corner. For the next couple of hours, I looked away from the screen only to check my watch, wondering when my father would make some dinner. If I sneaked out too early, he would know. In the meantime, I quickly worked to catch up on my college homework since I had nothing better to do while I was stuck in the house. Plus, I'd never really minded the advanced summer classes because they were challenging and allowed me to stay behind in high school with the rest of the gods.

Finally, my father's angry call came and I ran downstairs. I scarfed down the macaroni as quickly as I could without throwing it back up then returned upstairs to my room. I paced the room for a few minutes until I was certain that my father wouldn't come to check on me; I was pretty sure that my mom was still cowering in the antique shop. Not waiting any longer, I simply picked up my old cell phone from my desk before opening the glass doors to my balcony from which I quietly climbed down to the soft grass. I smiled and took a deep breath, ready to let go of my worries for a while.

Connor jogged up behind me just as I left my yard. "Hey," he said with his usual mischievous smile. "I see that you managed to sneak out." I grinned back at him and together we walked up to the porch.

But strangely enough, the screen door opened for us and out stepped Zach and Luke's parents. Their dad was wearing a tuxedo while their mother wore a nice black evening gown, so I assumed they were going out somewhere very fancy, probably to the steak restaurant in the next county over. After catering to other people all day every day, they often preferred other people to cater to them for a meal. They never tired of the restaurant scene.

"Hi, Mom," Connor and I greeted our second mother in unison and she smiled along with her husband, a tall distinguished-looking man named Marshall whose short, dark hair was just starting to get a few gray hairs.

"Honestly, I'm not sure why we haven't adopted you yet," Marshall joked. "You and the twins are all as good as siblings."

"Oh, hush, honey," Martha said quickly to her husband, stealing a nervous glance at me. I'd always gotten the sense that she was holding out for the moment Zach and I professed love for one another. She didn't know that had already happened six years ago during an overnight trip into the forest, and it wasn't the soul-mate kind of love for which she hoped.

"Have fun, you two," she continued. "We will be back quite late so, Ashley, please make sure the boys don't destroy the house." I gave a short laugh then Connor and I bid the pair farewell as they climbed into their silver SUV.

As soon as Zach and Luke's parents disappeared down the road, Connor and I ran up the steps and burst into the open house. We then walked straight into the living room where Zach sat on his old, green couch with his strong arms around the small shoulders of none other than Becca. Both of them turned around to face us at the exact same moment and Zach said, as if we couldn't tell, "Hey, Becca's here too. I figured she could use some company after this morning's adventures."

Yeah, very good *company*, I thought, but held my tongue. Connor did not hold his, however.

"Does Alicia know that you're here?" Connor asked her pointedly, knowing that Alicia would be very angry with both Zach and Becca if she found out what was going on between the two of them.

"Does Alicia know that Ash is here?" Becca retorted, leaning into Zach even further just to bug Connor.

"I'm no threat to her and, besides, I'm over here practically all of the time anyway," I responded, rolling my eyes, and headed into the kitchen to grab myself a drink of water. When I returned to the living room, Zach was putting *Frankenstein* into the DVD player and Connor had taken a seat on the other side of Becca.

"So where's Luke?" Connor asked Zach.

"He's upstairs sulking because we're not watching an *Indiana Jones* movie. I thought about going up there and frying his computer just for fun, but I wouldn't want him to shake the house to ruins." Zach chuckled and Connor joined in as I collapsed into an ancient rocking chair I recognized from my mother's antique shop.

Becca groaned as she tied her long, blonde hair up in a loose bun. "Why do we have to watch a *scary* movie anyway? Can't we just watch the news again?"

I just laughed. "We fight real monsters for a living. I think we can all handle an old horror film about a fake one." Becca simply stuck out her lower lip in a pout and passed me a bowl of popcorn. I took a big handful before passing it along to Zach, and the TV screen lit up in black and white as the movie began.

———————

Luke had finally joined us downstairs and every one of us except Becca was laughing hysterically because a little girl had just fallen into a lake when my cell phone rang. "Hey, Alec," I said in Greek without even bothering to look at the caller ID. I had been expecting a check-in call from him all day. "Isn't it almost eleven there?" I questioned him, knowing he needed to rest and Becca smirked. She shot me a look with raised eyebrows that I read as something along the lines of *See, he loves you! I can't believe you won't do anything about it.* I didn't bother to respond to that.

"Yeah," Alec whispered into the phone, also in Greek. "Technically, I'm breaking the curfew rules, but who the hell cares? Anyway, I'm assuming that Aphrodite is okay?"

"Well, she almost got strangled to death by the Minotaur, but she's fine," I confirmed positively as if this sort of thing happened often. I heard Alec sigh in relief on the other end of the phone while Luke, Connor, Zach, and Becca watched me with great interest. "How did training go today?"

"Oh, it was so much fun," Alec muttered sarcastically. "The Warriors-in-training almost killed me three times today, but other than that it was just brilliant." I hoped he was exaggerating.

"And how are the archers and the other Warriors doing?" I asked him. After all, we couldn't exactly win a war with an unorganized bunch of wimps as our army.

"They're doing great, but I'm honestly bored. Compared to life in the Woods with you gods, base camp is even duller than I remembered. I've been itching to get my hands on a monster for days, but these stupid guards won't let me out of their sights, let alone the actual camp boundaries," Alec informed me with a sigh, his voice lowering as he went on to signal he was divulging secrets meant for only a god's ears. "In the meantime, I'm making sure Jason contacts the other Knowing camps of which he's aware and warns them they're about to be attacked by Hades's army. I still don't know how trustworthy he is, though. He claims he hasn't been able to reach the New York camp, but that's where he originally came from so I think the real problem is just animosity. No one seems to know much about his past there."

Suddenly, the line went quiet and I could hear muffled noises in the background. It sounded to me as if Alec had been caught.

"Alec, get to bed right now!" I heard the familiar voice of Jason yell angrily, confirming my suspicions. "Being a hero doesn't mean you get to ignore all the rules! Who are you calling right now anyway?"

"I have to go," Alec complained in annoyance, and I frowned at Jason's grumpy remark, not liking its tone of superiority at all. "I'll call you later. Bye,

Lady Athena," he finished loud enough so that Jason would be able to hear who he was talking to. Hopefully, Alec wouldn't get into too much trouble.

"Good luck and, as usual, try not to die. Keep me updated on the Jason situation," I told him in Greek, smiling to myself. Then I hung up the crappy flip phone, stuffing it into my pocket. "We're set," I notified the others and the four of them nodded in unison. When I grabbed another handful of popcorn, Zach started up the movie again.

Unfortunately, that was when the doorbell rang. Becca, who was still wrapped in Zach's arms, yawned and Connor groaned in annoyance that the movie was being interrupted yet again. After Luke made it clear he wasn't going to answer it, Zach just yelled loudly toward the door, "Who is it?"

"It's Cole," Cole's voice said from outside, and everyone in the room turned to glare at me, like his being there was my fault. They all knew he had a crush on me. Sure enough, Cole asked, "Is Ashley there?"

I shrugged and protested quietly, "*I* didn't invite him." Zach, Luke, Connor, and Becca only gave me dubious looks, none of them bothering to get up to let Cole in. Even though they too were his friends, they just wanted to finish watching the movie in peace. Such a simple act had been a rarity for us gods since the start of summer when Persephone had been reunited with us after many long years and Alec had first arrived in our forest.

"I'm not here," I whispered to the four gods pleadingly, sinking down in my seat and hoping Cole hadn't seen me yet. I already had to deal with Alec's romantic advances and in my opinion that was more than enough work.

"Ash is grounded," Luke shouted back at Cole who still stood outside in the dark. Technically, this part of the story was the truth, but then Luke added, "And our parents aren't here so we're kind of not allowed to let anyone in."

As if that had stopped the two rambunctious brothers before! I could remember many times when they had thrown wild parties without permission from their parents, some of which Cole had even been at. Jack would try to sneak in a few bottles of beer or wine every once in a while since he thought no high school party was complete without something illegal, but the Monster Watch would never allow it when I was in attendance. I had seen what that poison did to my father and didn't want anyone else to suffer the same terrible symptoms.

As Dionysus, the god of wine, Jack alone was able to handle the dizzying effects on a regular basis.

But knowing Luke only meant to throw salt on his wound of exclusion, Cole stopped asking questions. "Oh, okay," he said awkwardly after a moment of thought. "I guess I'll probably see you tomorrow." I heard the old floorboards of the porch creak a couple more times then everything went quiet so I knew he was gone. Finally, we could finish watching the movie . . . or so I thought. Because that was when a huge crash sounded from down the street followed by a male's terrified scream. We gods could never seem to catch a break.

Chapter 2

THIS WAR HAS ALREADY STARTED

The five of us only paused to exchange worried glances then simultaneously leaped off the comfortable couch and raced out the front door, heading down the empty street toward the direction of the scream. We were prepared to defend whoever was in trouble with only our pocketknives and godly strength. Down the road and cloaked in darkness one figure stood hunching over another. An old, wooden cane was lying on the pavement.

That meant it had to be Shane, or Hephaestus, lying in the middle of the street and yelling in pain. As the five of us slowed to a stop, we could see that the person standing over him was none other than Cole wearing an expression of fear and shock, his caramel-colored hair shining under the stars.

"What's going on?" Zach shouted, glaring at Cole accusingly.

But Cole didn't answer, his brown eyes just locked on me. Oops. "I thought you were grounded," he said, his voice tight.

"I am, technically. I just . . ." my voice trailed off guiltily.

"Escaped, snuck out, ran away—whatever you want to call it," Cole finished for me now frowning. "You were at Zach's house the whole time, weren't you?"

When I nodded slowly, not bothering to hide the truth anymore, Cole only turned away from me, a mixture of hurt and anger in his eyes. Before the start of that summer, if I had been in a situation like this, I would have had the desire to suddenly blurt out the whole truth, to get the secrets that had been weighing me down off of my chest and onto somebody else's for even a mere minute. My life as a god used to be an escape from my life as a human and I used to think bringing them together would make dealing with problems simpler. But not anymore. Things had changed. We were in a time of war now for one, though perhaps the most important thing was that our, the gods', attitudes had changed—if only a little—and Cole's had not. He was still that same Sightless boy from six years ago, the one who would rather pull pranks on a school bully and run away to hide than take a bigger risk. I realized now that he, as well as most Sightless humans, would never understand our experiences, our responsibilities, or our loyalties.

Meanwhile, gasping in agony, Shane explained, "I was walking home and one of those blasted harp—" He managed to stop midsentence right before he said "harpies" and his dark eyes glanced up at us in pure horror that he had almost given away our secret.

"What?" Cole asked in confusion. "When I got here, Shane was just lying on the street yelling in some weird language. Was it German? I don't know. I just came over here to try and help and that was when you all showed up."

The gods gave a collective sigh of relief that Cole hadn't seen anything important and, thankfully, I could see no golden blood anywhere on Shane, although his left leg was bent at an odd angle under his jeans. In a way, it was a good thing that his already crippled leg was the one that was now broken so at least he could still walk a little bit.

I was about to discreetly ask Shane what had happened to the harpy when I noticed a little pile of gray dust lying next to him. I had no idea how, but the short, seemingly unarmed Shane had managed to kill a huge flying bird with the torso of a woman.

Silently, I pointed the dust pile out to my fellow gods and they nodded in understanding. Shane saw what I was trying to ask as well and wordlessly picked up his cane. As soon as Cole looked away, Shane pressed a tiny red button on the cane which I was sure he had installed himself and a small knife covered in gold-green monster blood shot out from the end. We all gasped in surprise and Shane clicked the button again just before Cole turned around to see what was going on.

"I think my leg's broken," Shane complained as he tried to get up, but he failed miserably and fell back down on the damp pavement. His rough hands grasped his mangled left leg as he groaned in pain. I handed him his wooden cane, and Zach helped him off the ground.

"Um, you should probably go home now," I advised Cole awkwardly.

"Oh, of course. I wouldn't want to intrude on whatever the hell this is," Cole snarled, motioning to the rest of us. "Since you obviously don't want me here to help." Then he turned on his heel and stormed away toward his house a few streets south, disappearing into the night.

Becca raised her eyebrows at me in a silent question, but I just shrugged it off. At the moment, I didn't care what Cole said or did. A god life *always* comes before a human life.

"We need to take action," Zach announced in Greek and, sure enough, we were back to being our godly selves. His blue eyes flashing in anger, the king continued, "This is the second time today that Hades has directly threatened a fellow god. I'm done avoiding fights." Poseidon, Apollo, Aphrodite, Hephaestus, and I all nodded in agreement.

"Tomorrow, I'm sending Hermes to tell the other gods about what just happened and he'll also go down to the Underworld for one last try at peace. From now on, I want at least one patrol in the forest at all times during the day, and no god goes in there alone." Again, the five of us nodded and Zeus loudly clapped his hands together, ending the conversation right then and there. "That's it. Everyone go home. Be safe."

Aphrodite helped Hephaestus as they slowly headed in the direction Cole had gone toward their own houses while the Monster Watch—Zeus, Poseidon, Apollo, and I—turned around and walked back to our homes together. As I quietly climbed back up to my balcony and into my room to get ready for bed, I thought about all I would have to tell Alec the next morning and all there was still left to do to prepare for battle.

The next morning, I woke up breathing hard and feeling very grumpy; I had not slept well at all. Terrible images of my friends falling around me had haunted my dreams, ripping my heart to pieces. Automatically blaming Hades even though Hypnos was the Greek god who really controlled dreams, I angrily punched my fluffy white pillow before showering then dressed in jeans and a simple tank top. I grabbed my pocketknife, rock/sword, and walkie-talkie and raced downstairs, hoping to also grab a bite of breakfast before either of my parents came downstairs.

But as usual, I was unlucky. I was right about to open the door, a granola bar in hand, when my mother grabbed the back of my shirt, stopping me before I could get away. After all, I couldn't exactly punch or flip my own mother; I would have just gotten myself grounded yet again and then I would have been back to square one.

"Ashley, you have some explaining to do," my mother told me in a no-nonsense tone. I sighed and slowly turned around to face her as she continued, "Why on earth are you home almost two weeks early?"

Similar to Cole, she was both infuriatingly oblivious to the war and infuriatingly nosy as of late. I didn't have time to be interrogated. Moreover, I didn't have the patience. So I looked right into her big, brown eyes and lied just like I did to everyone but the gods and Alec. "The camp was cancelled. Didn't you hear about the flood?" I asked innocently.

My mother frowned and shook her head. I shrugged and turned around, ready to go meet the rest of the Monster Watch. "Wait," she whispered in a pleading voice. "Did you know your father was coming home?"

I raised my eyebrows, somewhat surprised that my father hadn't told her about the debacle at the airport, but I supposed he didn't want to worry her after his running away, seemingly never to return. Maybe my argumentative, alcoholic father and I really did have a better understanding of each other than I wanted to admit. "No," I replied to her simply, deciding that if my father chose to keep my actions at the airport a secret, I would too.

I watched my mother carefully to see how she would react. She just sighed, running her fingers through her curly brown hair, and suddenly she looked much older to me. I noticed that her pale skin was much more sunken in than it used to be and that she had lost some weight. Even though I knew nothing lasted forever, the fact that the people I loved were growing older seemed so strange to me. After all, the town itself hadn't grown and we, the Monster Watch, had been doing the same things in our free time ever since we were six years old. But I also recognized that I had never really paid much attention to what went on in town, outside of the Fire Pit.

I tilted my head to one side, wondering how I appeared in my mother's eyes. Was I still a little girl to her? Innocent and oblivious to what was going on around me? I hoped not, since I was really the exact opposite and had been for many years. Sometime or another, she would have to let go just like everyone does at some point. Just like I would have to.

"You can go now." She released me somberly, and I tore out of the house without saying another word, sprinting toward Main Street.

When I opened the creaking door to the Fire Pit, I saw that Connor, Zach, Luke, Alicia, and Haley were already waiting at the back table, slurping down lemonades even though it was around nine in the morning and still cool outside. "Hi," I greeted them as I sat down next to Haley and they flashed me small smiles. "What's the plan for today?"

"My patrol has first watch until around lunch and then yours takes over," Zach said and I nodded. After checking his watch, he glanced over to Alicia and Haley and asked, "Are you ready?"

"As ready as we'll ever be," Alicia muttered unhappily as she tied her reddish-brown hair up in a high ponytail. Haley only sighed in agreement while Connor smirked, silently mocking the two girls. "If anyone asks, Haley and I are at my house with Maddie," Alicia told us before picking up her own little walkie-talkie from the table.

Then Alicia, Haley, and Zach—or Hera, Hestia, and Zeus—scooted from the table and gave Luke, Connor, and me one last wave before they headed out. However, the three of us weren't alone for long because about two minutes later Josh and Cole walked through the swinging door. Automatically, Josh's brown eyes lit up and he started making his way toward our table.

But Cole just stopped and watched, his normally friendly eyes growing cold as they focused on me, obviously not happy that I had lied to him the night before and that we had sent him away when he was just trying to help Shane. While he stood like a statue in the middle of the doorway, I knew he was debating whether or not to sit with us. Sighing to myself, I figured I would make the decision for him since he was apparently slow at thinking on his feet.

I stood up and turned to the two boys, already tired of the drama that surrounded my normal human life. "I need to get my hands on a monster before I explode. Who's up for an early start?" I asked eagerly.

Luke grinned, his blue-green eyes lighting up as he nudged Connor in the side. "Sometimes I forget how feisty—and *annoying*—this chick is," Luke joked then continued only slightly more seriously, "but Patrol Three doesn't have watch until two so I have plenty of time to kill. Get it? *Kill.*"

Connor nodded his blond head in agreement with Luke, but Josh just sighed. "I should probably stay here and deliver some messages, not to mention babysit Cole," Josh said as he frowned, looking directly at me. I simply rolled my eyes at him then turned on my heel, and Connor and Luke followed me out of the restaurant. I didn't even make eye contact with Cole as I pushed past him. He was still standing dumbly in the doorway, a blank expression plastered on his face.

The three of us stopped just inside the forest to throw on our armor and then I pulled out my walkie-talkie. "This is Athena calling Patrol One. Poseidon, Apollo, and I are coming in right now. Need any help?"

A second later, Zeus's voice came over the device. "No, we're good for now, but have the guys show you the army at Pan's camp," he told me and I gave him a quick reply. Poseidon led the way as we trudged west toward the hideout by the river.

Strangely, we only ran into one monster on the way, which Apollo quickly killed with an arrow before it could even get close. But I didn't stop to think about the thousands of possible reasons for the missing monsters because I knew we were nearing our destination.

Sure enough, we rounded a familiar bend a few minutes later and climbed down the side of a small waterfall, touching down on the soft grass. What was formerly just a small deep swimming hole with Pan's rock and moss throne to the side was now the setting for a reasonably sized Greek army base camp.

Rectangular marquee tents—much like the ones at the Knowing camp—were set up in a tight circle beside Pan's throne, only these were smaller and green camouflage in color as opposed to blue, purple, or red. I even spotted the Oracle's tiny, old, battered tent among the mix, meaning she had come for protection just like the other nymphs and satyrs milling about. I had never before seen so many gathered in one place.

In the midst of all the chaos stood Pan, who was pulling at the curly, reddish-brown mop of hair on his head in anguish and gripping his own walkie-talkie very tightly, but his stance relaxed and his dark brown eyes immediately lit up when they focused on Poseidon, Apollo, and me. "Look who it is! I thought I heard a rumor you were back in town, Athena," Pan exclaimed in Greek and the nymphs and satyrs immediately parted and bowed to the three of us when they finally noticed us trying to get through.

I grinned and was about to say something when all four of our walkie-talkies crackled to life with Hermes's voice. "Hey, Hephaestus just got back from the doctor's office and his leg is broken pretty badly. Luckily, blood didn't seem to be a problem."

"All right," Zeus's voice answered. "Thanks for the update, Hermes. Keep up the good work, everyone."

Then Pan motioned to the three of us and we huddled around a large parchment map of the entire woods, which was spread out on a table under an open-sided green tent. There were tiny wooden figurines representing each of the gods as well as a few portraying the more well-known satyrs, nymphs, and monsters set up at different points. The figures representing Poseidon, Apollo, and I were currently stationed at the point on the map that signified Pan's camp while the ones representing Zeus, Hestia, and Hera were positioned at a point just east of the meadow.

"This map helps us keep track of every god or other being in the woods. This is where Patrol One was at their last check-in," Poseidon explained, pointing to the miniature Zeus, Hestia, and Hera.

"And all of the known entrances to the Underworld are labeled too," Apollo added, pointing to a red *X* to the left of the meadow which marked the huge boulder where we first saw Hades and Persephone.

"Nice. This will come in real handy for the battles," I said and Poseidon nodded. Then I took a glance at my watch. "Apollo and I have half an hour until we have to meet Artemis for our patrol watch so we need to start heading back now."

Poseidon started to collect his things as well. "I'll come too," he agreed and we waved good-bye to Pan and slowly made our way east back toward Main Street, keeping a close eye out for monsters.

The three of us were about a quarter of a mile from the street and hadn't seen a single monster when a distress call came over the walkie-talkies. "This is Hera. Athena, Poseidon, Apollo, if you're still in the woods Patrol One needs help. Hades has been sighted heading east toward Main Street. Repeat: Hades has been sighted."

"On it," Apollo said promptly into his walkie-talkie and together the three of us sprinted in the direction of the call. As we tore through the bushes and branches, I pulled out the rock from my pocket and squeezed it, instantly revealing the shining sword blade. Meanwhile, Apollo grabbed an arrow out of his leather quiver and readied it in his bow.

We had been running only a few more seconds when I heard Zeus yell, "Hades! Stop right there!" I knew then that we were very close and, sure enough, we quickly rounded one more bend in the winding trail and stopped dead, right before we crashed into Hestia, who happened to be holding a ball of fire mere inches from our faces.

"Where the hell did you come from?" Artemis called out in confusion to the three of us from about thirty yards away and, at once, three other pairs of eyes turned to lock on Poseidon, Apollo, and me.

Bodies stiff with tension, Zeus, Hera, and Hestia stood in a circle with Artemis. Artemis, who was facing west and away from the street toward us, had an arrow already placed in her bow. I guessed that she had heard the distress call and had come from the Fire Pit to cut Hades off before he could burst onto the street in the middle of the day when humans without the Sight would be wandering around in full force. Hera was directly in front of us and adjacent to Artemis, a ball of burning purple light levitating above her right hand which was held out in front of her. To our left, ready to strike out at any second, Zeus had a lightning bolt raised above his head and right in front of us was Hestia, who did not bother to turn around and still stood facing the center of the circle of gods with a ball of orange fire raging on her small palm.

But Artemis's question was quickly forgotten when the sound of a horse snorting redirected the gods' attention back to the center of the circle where all of their weapons were trained on one person: Hades. Quickly, I took my place on the circumference of the circle between Zeus and Hestia while Poseidon and Apollo went on Hestia's other side and the three of us joined in aiming our weapons at the lord of the Underworld.

"Hades, you're surrounded. Give it up," Zeus ordered once again, his muscles flexing as he tightened his grip on the white-hot lightning bolt.

Unsurprisingly, Hades didn't answer the king of the gods and instead just stared down at the angry Zeus from atop his huge, black horse. His dark hood blocked any light from reaching his snow-white face and, coupled with his black staff topped with a tiny crystal skull, I had to admit that Hades did look quite menacing. But none of us were afraid. It was seven against one, after all.

Silently, Hades turned his horse around, now facing Poseidon, who was studying the magnificent creature very closely. I knew that because horses were Poseidon's sacred animals, he was probably trying to politely convince the horse to buck Hades off.

"Don't even think about trying anything sneaky, Poseidon. I can feel you trying to talk to it," Hades growled, obviously realizing the same thing I had. "In case you hadn't noticed, this horse is under *my* control now."

And as soon as Hades said that, I knew exactly what he meant. Taking a closer look at the horse, I could now tell that it was, in fact, very dead. The big Friesian's nostrils were not moving or taking in any air nor was it even sweating, though I was quite sure that it had been swiftly galloping away from Patrol One for a couple of minutes before Artemis had cut it off. Not to mention the fact that the horse was floating about an inch off the ground.

Then Poseidon grumbled something I didn't catch and Hades smirked evilly, which made me despise him even more. I frowned, but took the stiff silence as a chance to speak my own mind. "Why do you even want to take over this realm anyway?" I asked Hades who only returned my frown.

"For the same reasons you all want to keep it," Hades replied simply. "Power. Comfort. Nothing else."

Having expected this answer, I retorted, "You know, there *is* a limit to how much power one person or god can control. That's partly why the ancient Greeks created so many gods to begin with. The Romans, however, figured out that lesson the hard way when their entire empire crumbled. I don't want to see that happen to the rest of the world too."

Zeus added, "If you're smart, you'll surrender and things can just go back to the way they were."

"It's far too late for that, brother," Hades answered him coldly, reaching down to pat his horse on the neck. "This war has already started."

With that, a huge crack sounded from the center of the circle and, at once, every single god who was there reacted by releasing his or her weapon. In one deafening bang, a lightning bolt, golden trident, burning spheres of fire and light, two arrows, and my sword all collided in midair at the spot where Hades and his dead horse had been not a moment before. However, the epic explosion of raw power sent us seven flying backward simultaneously.

Sheer pain spread throughout my body as my back slammed into a tree trunk, but I quickly shook off the aching sensation and focused on blinking to try to regain clear vision. It took a good twenty seconds, but I could finally start to see the other gods and that all of our weapons were in a cluttered pile at the center of the circle.

Miraculously, all of the weapons looked brand new except for the two arrows, lightning bolt, and spheres of fire and light, which had disintegrated in the explosion. The grass under the pile of weapons was now jet-black like the fronts of our shirts, but the other gods seemed otherwise unharmed. The pine trees in the 150-yard radius surrounding the seven of us, however, were not as lucky. The sides of the trees facing the explosion were charred and no longer had any branches. The one thing I still couldn't see was Hades on his horse.

"Damn him!" Zeus shouted angrily and suddenly chucked another lightning bolt through the thick treetops and into the dark sky, causing loud booms of thunder to fill our ears. When the thunder had finally subsided, Zeus put his head in his hands, perhaps trying to calm down. Sighing, I walked over to the clutter of weapons and picked up my sword, brushing off the blade before silently turning it back into a rock. I was already beginning to formulate a new plan.

"How do you think he managed to get away?" Hestia wondered aloud in exasperation while she twirled her long, light brown hair around her dainty fingers. She was still kneeling on the burnt grass, tilting her head sideways in deep thought.

Hera frowned and pointed to the spot on the black ground where the weapons had been. "That's how." The rest of us exchanged curious glances then walked over to see what Hera was looking at. A thin almost invisible crack in the earth ran straight through the patch of charred grass. Hence, it appeared Hades had retreated down to the Underworld for the time being.

"Move," Poseidon whispered to the rest of us, just barely loud enough to hear. Confusion wavered momentarily on all of the gods' faces and Hestia was about to ask for some sort of clarification when Poseidon yelled in a loud, desperate voice, "MOVE!"

In one split second, we jumped as far away from Poseidon as we possibly could and crouched for safety on the grass as the god of earthquakes slammed his golden trident on the thin crack in a last-ditch effort to break it back open.

I shut my eyes tightly as I felt the earth under my feet give a tremendous shake—the biggest earthquake I had ever experienced (and I had been through plenty of huge ones, mind you). When the shaking finally subsided, I slowly opened one eye, not sure what I might see. But what I saw definitely wasn't good.

The crack wasn't open. Poseidon stood alone on the small patch of black grass with his head down, his blue-green eyes glaring at the ground angrily, his black hair plastered to his forehead with sweat. Poseidon dropped his golden trident and I felt the earth give a tiny tremble again as he sank to his knees in defeat and slammed his fists against the ground in frustration, because if there was one person in the entire world who could have opened that crack, it was Poseidon.

It was absolutely silent for a moment as the reality of the war finally hit us. Reconciliation wasn't going to be simple and straightforward in any way like almost everything else hadn't been so far. This war was going to be a long, hard, traumatic struggle, as Hades appeared to have strengthened his powers by a huge margin over the last six years like the rest of us. Maybe the fact that so much death had already occurred in the Woods was enough to fuel him, to inspire a grand finale.

Even the birds were quiet, as if they too understood the gravity of what was going on in our beloved forest. Or perhaps they had just been killed by the powerful explosion.

After a long sigh, Zeus broke the thick ice frozen over our conversation and announced solemnly, his expression grim, "Well, it's the A Team's watch now, so anyone else who wants to leave can go." Apollo and Artemis walked over to my side and neither Zeus nor Poseidon moved a muscle.

"Sorry, Zeus, but Hestia and I are done for today," Hera said with a fatigued sigh and Zeus nodded in understanding.

"And we still have to clean off our shirts somehow," Hestia added darkly, trying in vain to brush off the black dust from the front of her lavender blouse. The two girls waved a forlorn good-bye then turned around and walked east toward Main Street.

When the two brunette goddesses had disappeared into the foliage, Zeus's blue eyes met my gray ones. "Poseidon and I will stay and patrol together for a while. Athena, if Alec calls . . ." His usually strong and powerful voice trailed off into silence and I could tell that he was still distracted by the fact that Hades had escaped his clutches yet again.

"I know what to do," I confirmed with a weak smile. Zeus then gave a short nod before he and Poseidon picked up their weapons again and set off deeper into the forest. Meanwhile, I spun around to face Artemis and Apollo. "Ready?" I asked softly and they responded in an echo. Together, the three of us slowly headed west and searched high and low for a monster of any kind to kill. I doubted that we would run into Hades again that day, but I honestly wasn't sure yet if that was good or bad . . .

Chapter 3

THE ABSOLUTE
WORST TIMES TO CALL

A rtemis, Apollo, and I had been patrolling the woods for about two hours so our watch was almost over. Luckily, I didn't have to do too much work for once since the twin archers shot almost every monster that came our way. That was a total of five, by the way. I won't bother recounting all of those details, because a lot of it consisted of Apollo cursing at everything, from the bushes that kept getting caught on his bright red sweatshirt to the monsters themselves. Though, I will say that Artemis and I got annoyed with his behavior after a while.

"Shut up, idiot! You're giving away our position!" Artemis hissed at him eventually. You might think Apollo would be used to navigating the thick undergrowth after spending nine years of our lives in that forest, but no, he was still just as clumsy as when he accidentally stepped on the skeleton the second day we went in.

Sure enough, I heard a low-pitched rustling of the bushes coming from the east and knew that the monsters had caught up with us. I exchanged curious glances with Artemis and Apollo, who had finally clamped his mouth shut and the three of us cocked our ears toward the sound, waiting for the monster to reveal itself. But as the rustling sounds grew closer and closer, I realized that it couldn't be just one monster. The creepy sound was coming from every direction now, and the silver mist seemed to be thickening suspiciously.

I tightened the grip on my sword as both Artemis and Apollo placed arrows in their wooden bows, ready to let them fly at a moment's notice. We were standing back-to-back-to-back, covering each other's blind spots because we still couldn't see the unknown number of creatures. I couldn't help but silently reprimand myself for not bringing my golden shield, as the extra leverage probably would have come in quite handy.

Suddenly, multiple dark figures came out of the shadows, moaning like zombies from one of the boys' video games. But there was another sound coupled with the moaning, a quieter sound that was definitely less noticeable, though I knew immediately it was the creaking of bones. I had heard the sound once or twice before.

So no, this was not our first encounter with a few of Hades's undead warriors—the "zombies" of our world—but we had never come across so many at once. There were about ten of them—skeletons with brittle old bones in disgusting shades of yellow and gray shrouded with the ripped remains of what looked like black, hooded cloaks. As they marched toward us, surrounding us, they growled menacingly and waved their swords made of sharp iron, slicing their way through the thick mist. And as if their appearances alone weren't enough to scare any child to death, the tips of their black iron blades were glowing like embers with a bright orange heat that would make skin boil on contact. Thin streams of smoke rose up from the blades into the cool air, making it quite obvious that the undead warriors were happily ready to burn, slice, and dice their poor victims all at the same time. What a way to die.

Frankly, Hades would have been stupid *not* to use the millions of souls down in the dark Underworld, though my side of the war would have been lucky if he hadn't.

"Athena, now!" Apollo yelled.

I heard a terrible cracking noise come from behind and knew the battle had begun. I didn't even look behind me to see what had happened because I was confident that either Apollo or Artemis had just sent an arrow straight through the skull of one of the undead. I wouldn't have had time to risk a glance, anyway. Instead, my courage unflagging, I just rushed head on at the skeleton a few yards in front of me, aiming for the rattling rib cage where its heart should have been.

I deflected a weak swing by the skeleton and managed to crush a few of its ribs before the inward-curving blade of my own Greek *kopis* sword punctured its rickety spine and the damned creature crumbled to a small pile of dust. I took a quick step back and its burning flat-iron sword narrowly missed my tight stomach as it fell down to the grass.

Relieved, I whirled around in preparation to face another attack, though it was hard to see through the thickening mist. I spotted Artemis furiously sending arrows in every direction at the creatures, but half of them did no harm at all and just went straight between the undead warriors' rickety bones. The only signs of her true capability of hitting her marks were the undeads' cloaks, which had even more rips and holes than before.

Off to my right was Apollo who had been forcefully knocked to the ground. He was angrily looking up with his normally cheerful hazel eyes into the shadowed face of an undead. His leather quiver full of arrows sat a few feet out of his reach in the long grass so, instead, he was smashing his wooden bow into the side of the single undead warrior standing above him. I raised my eyebrows, silently wondering how much more bone smashing that bow could withstand. It was of much more use to us in one piece and no matter how many times I'd told Apollo how important it was to have skills in more than one area of battle, such as hand-to-hand combat in case of times like these, I wasn't sure he'd ever taken my advice seriously enough.

I whirled around quickly, refocusing on the undead warrior that was now stumbling toward me, its sword pointing right at my chest. I deflected its weak attempt to stab me then blocked the next swing before kicking the skeleton in the pelvis. It fell backward onto the ground, though it wasn't yet reduced to ashes. When the skeleton got up with its bones seemingly guided back into their rightful places by the air, I easily avoided its next swing and used the opening to chop its skull right off.

Yet, as the skull rolled a couple of feet away and its jaw actually dropped off, the skeleton itself continued to run at me. Somehow not too surprised, I guessed that because an undead warrior didn't actually have a brain or eyes, its skull wasn't very important. Its spine, however, was obviously vital to its movement. Indeed, it was a blow to that area which had killed my first one.

"Go for the spines!" I shouted over my shoulder to Artemis and Apollo before readying myself for the next part of the fight: slash, parry, and repeat.

"Is that a cell phone I hear?" Artemis called out, breaking my concentration. This time I was forced to duck *Matrix* style to avoid the strike of an undead trying to sneak up on my left side.

But she was right. Now I heard the soft ringing too so I reached unconsciously for my back pocket. For the life of me, I wasn't sure how our cell phones still had service deep inside the forest, but especially now it seemed like more of an inconvenience than a utility. The outside world, particularly the Sightless part of it, wasn't supposed to be able to penetrate the forest's mysticism or, at the very least, I didn't want it to. Take that moment for instance: I was trying to fight off more than five undead warriors at once in order to stay alive and *someone* happened to choose that exact moment to call me. You can imagine my annoyance.

So what did I do, you ask? I answered it right in the midst of battle, of course. Was that a bit arrogant of me? Yeah, probably. But in my defense, it was an important call—the call that the other gods and I had been waiting for all morning to be exact.

"Hey, Alec," I gasped as I swung my sword at the headless undead warrior's midsection.

"Hey, Athena," came the reply. "What's up?"

I was about to answer him when the unthinkable happened. I took a step backward and tripped on a tree root, falling hard to the ground right as the headless undead warrior stabbed at me, the tip of the scorching iron blade catching the inside of my collar bone. I let out a yelp of pain as a burning sensation seared through my left shoulder. Knowing the undead would come back for more, I rolled out of the way just as the sharp sword jutted down and luckily stuck in the soil instead of my flesh.

"Are—are you okay?" Alec stammered in Greek into the phone, his voice suddenly sounding extremely worried.

"I'm fine," I said through gritted teeth, trying to ignore the pain and the golden blood seeping out from the wound in my shoulder. I squeezed my gray eyes shut for a moment and tried to pull myself together as I heard Apollo let out a similar cry from somewhere behind me.

"Do you want me to call back later? Or wait for you to call for backup?" Alec still sounded concerned.

"It's . . . fine," I breathed again and kicked the headless warrior to the ground as it unsuccessfully tried to pull its sword out of the firm soil. Before it even had a chance to try to get up again, I brought down my sword with one hand, slashing the brittle skeleton right across the spine. It crumbled to dust just in time for me to avoid tripping on its long, black cloak. "Only four left."

"Um, four left of what?" Alec asked curiously.

"Undead warriors," I answered with a deep breath as I twirled my sword around in my free hand, waiting for the next nightmarish creature to come at me.

"Wow. Are you sure you don't want me to call back later?" Alec clarified as I blocked the right swing of the next skeleton's black blade with a loud clang. Was that doubt in his voice now or still just worry?

I winced as my and the undead's swords collided, sending a shock wave of pain through my wounded left shoulder again. "No," I said firmly, readjusting my grip on the sword. "Keep talking." I needed to hear how he was doing and I needed him to know I was doing okay too. The pain only made me stronger, more determined.

Alec gave a forced chuckle and I knew he was still worried about me. "You may be the best multitasker ever, you know that? A very good-looking one, I might add."

For a fleeting moment, I wanted to scream at him, to tell him to forget about me, to forget about all the gods, and to stay wherever the hell he was. I was better off alone, I told myself, and so was he. We gods were better off dismissing the humans as unimportant and the forest was better off without a hero. His role in the war hadn't been truly confirmed so maybe, just maybe, he could still be pushed out of range of the wrath of the prophecy.

But the forest wasn't the only thing we were obligated to save. The Knowing still remained and after forcing them into a war, giving them yet another reason to reject us, a single young hero wouldn't be able to fix their corrupted beliefs on his own.

So I just held my tongue and redirected my aggravation into a jab at the musty rib cage of the skeleton and the bones shattered with an earsplitting crack. I knew I had hit the undead's weak spot when it crumbled to dust and I sneezed as the breeze blew its remains into my face.

"Anyway, training is going well," Alec's voice continued rather lightheartedly. "No one else at camp has attacked me yet."

Still pressing the phone to my ear with one hand, I forced a smile for his sake as I came to the aid of Artemis to help kill the last few undead warriors surrounding her. "You know, the Knowing are starting to call your generation the Forest Gods," Alec notified me.

"I wonder who gave them that idea," I muttered sarcastically through gritted teeth, flashing back to when he and I had jokingly decided to call our time here on earth the Not-So-Golden Age of the Forest Gods.

Within two minutes, the last three undead warriors had been killed and Alec had finished with his story. Artemis helped her brother up out of the mud and we quickly looked each other over, checking for wounds. Apollo had a deep gash on his leg, but Artemis looked fine for the most part. Still, I knew we had to get to the emergency supply kit and warn everyone at Pan's camp of trouble as fast as we could.

Moreover, I figured it was about time I did what Zeus had asked me to do and tell Alec my other reason for keeping him waiting on the phone.

"And when this so-called war goes down in the history books, Jason wants to call it the War of the Woods," Alec was saying, aware that I wasn't really paying attention. "I think it's kind of cheesy, but whatever. He still claims the New York Knowing are unreachable, by the way."

"Alec," I said seriously into the phone to get his attention, wincing slightly as I switched hands. How to refer to our generation of gods and its conflicts was definitely not at the top of my list at the moment.

"Yeah? What's wrong?"

"Hades almost went out onto Main Street about an hour ago . . . and you need to come home now." I bit my lip and tried to keep my voice from shaking. Even though I didn't want to, I was calling him right back into the prophecy's storm, *my* storm. Only knowing that he would brave this storm anyway kept the guilt from eroding my sanity.

"Bring as many sword fighters and archers as you think are necessary. Fast as you can. But leave most behind because the base camp will probably get attacked too."

"Of course," Alec breathed quietly, sensing my concern. "Anything to get out of this goddamn hellhole," he added lightly. If I hadn't been so preoccupied with thinking about him, I probably would have smiled. His obsession with the gods and need for peril were mysteries to me. While the Monster Watch's everlasting quest for danger stemmed from a yearning to use our powers freely and a decade's old exaggerated definition of fun, Alec's seemingly stemmed from us.

"You know I miss you, right? All of you crazy gods."

This time I really did smile, shaking my head in wonderment. "Yeah, I know. I still can't figure out why since we'll probably end up leading you to your death."

He laughed. "Oh, most definitely, but I live for danger in case you haven't noticed so I'm going to go get ready. Is that okay? I'll call you whenever I can," Alec promised me confidently. He hesitated not more than a second before trying to finish quietly, "I lo—"

"No, Alec," I warned him seriously, because neither of us needed his feelings for me to become a distraction. "Don't you dare say those three little words to me. I'm not allowing it. I'm not going to say them back."

As my mind whirled and my heart started to race, I heard him snort softly on the other end of the phone, which made it awfully hard to stay mad at him. He understood the gravity of my tone, but, in an effort to keep his spirits high, chose to completely ignore it. "Just try not to die," I told him, rolling my eyes and giving up on reasoning with him at the moment.

"I'll be there soon," Alec bid me farewell, still chuckling, and I hated how contagious his laugh was.

Next, I stuffed the old flip phone in my pocket and Apollo radioed the others before the three of us started to walk west toward the meadow where our emergency supplies were hidden. Artemis shot me a questioning look with her hazel eyes, but I just shrugged and shook my head, silently expressing my annoyance with Alec.

About an hour later, Artemis, Apollo, and I had cleaned and stitched up our wounds as nicely as we could in the middle of the forest so that the bandages weren't too noticeable under our clothing. We had already checked in at the army camp by Pan's hideout and safely made it back to the edge of the woods just barely avoiding Python, the small dragon originally from Delphi, when Patrol Three came in for its turn to watch. The three of us quickly hid our weapons and armor in the hollow logs and then turned to face each other, wincing in pain.

"Another shirt ruined. How in the world are we going to explain this to our parents?" Artemis asked no one in particular, gesturing to her ripped shirt. "My father already suspects me of coming in here. He says I've been hanging around with the Monster Watch too much."

I sighed and leaned against a tree for support. "That never used to be such a bad thing."

"No, just a little dangerous," Artemis qualified, meeting my gaze. "You used to come out of the woods looking like heroes, but now you come out looking fatigued. Even though people can't seem to place their fingers on it just yet, they're noticing it subconsciously."

"Is there a good explanation for any of this?" a distraught Apollo pointed out, rubbing a bit of his own golden blood between his thumb and forefinger.

"Not one we can use," I muttered forlornly. "But I'll figure something out."

Artemis nodded, showing her confidence in me. "Just don't try and fight this war on your own, Athena. I know you would."

I looked away from her and Apollo off into the mist. "Alec and the Knowing troops are on their way here. I won't be alone, but still you shouldn't be content. Honestly, I'm not sure their help will affect the outcome of the war either way." I heard Artemis kick a rock and sigh as she stepped out of the woods and into the sunlight. This time I didn't turn to watch her go.

———————————

I spent the rest of the afternoon alone in my room working on art history and physics homework for my online classes since I had nothing better to do and my shoulder still felt like it was on fire. I kept checking my watch and looking out my window as if Alec were going to show up on my balcony any second, even though I knew it would be at least two days until he appeared with more soldiers. I doubted that the Knowing could get fifteen plane tickets for the same flight to Washington on such short notice.

That night, I went to bed early after a short video chat with the rest of the Monster Watch and woke up equally early the next morning when the sound of Connor's guitar floated through my open window into my room. I knew no one else but him would be up yet so I grabbed my leather jacket and headed next door to Connor's quaint, cozy house, a one-story that was painted a pale yellow almost like lemonade. He forced me to play some violent video game based off of wars for a while, but I beat him every time. When he had had enough of losing, the two of us walked to Zach and Luke's house where we ate a small breakfast of cereal in their kitchen before moving to the old green couch to watch the news. Maybe that was an odd pastime for kids our age, but we gods liked to know what was going on in other parts of the world. To put it simply, watching the news helped Zach and Luke decide which people deserved a monsoon, hurricane, or gigantic earthquake in their area. They dealt out punishments only when they felt especially inclined, however. We were still fifteen-year-olds living in a tiny town in practically the middle of nowhere and, frankly, we weren't very concerned with what was happening elsewhere in the world even if it was our responsibility to pay attention. And although I, along with most of the other gods, knew better, I let our near-isolationism continue anyway.

Around eleven, the four of us decided to walk through the thick fog to the Fire Pit for lunch since none of the patrols were having a formal watch that morning. Zach was also ordering my A Team to take the entire day off, probably because Camille, or Artemis, had told him about my attitude and what I'd said at the end of the day. Moreover, we hadn't spent a full day out of the forest in sight of the townspeople in what seemed like ages.

We opened the creaking door to the restaurant and automatically walked to our booth in the back of the room, nodding at the townspeople socializing at the bar stools on our way. Becca and Camille joined us a few minutes later.

I heard the front door of the Fire Pit creak open again and Zach, Luke, and Connor, who happened to be facing the door, glanced at me with raised eyebrows, appearing a little uneasy. Therefore, I knew the next customer had to be Cole before I even turned around, slowly, in sync with Camille and Becca. Sure enough, there he was, standing in front of the door next to Josh, both of them sweaty and wearing running shorts. While Cole took his time to glare at me angrily, Josh looked back and forth between his best friend and the rest of us gods, trying to decide with whom he should sit.

Eventually, Josh followed Cole to a small, round table that was about as far away from our booth as they could manage. My expression emotionless, I turned back to face the others and met Becca's pleading blue eyes. "Why don't you just apologize to him?" she asked me, shaking her head, apparently mystified.

"Because I have nothing to be sorry about. Cole's the one overreacting and we can't let him in on our secret, so what's the point?" I fired back at her, biting my lip after realizing how insensitive I had sounded.

"Would you apologize to Alec?" Becca pointed out.

"Alec is *not* Cole. Besides, it depends on the situation. Apologizing to everyone for everything is just weak," I protested, crossing my arms. "If Cole really cared, he would be over here talking to me about it."

Camille only sighed and tied her curly blonde hair into a tight bun as she leaned back in her seat. "No, Cole just doesn't think you care about his feelings so he's not even bothering to try to talk to you. And you have to admit that you are kind of acting like you don't care," she tried to explain further without offending me. As my best friend, besides the boys of the Monster Watch, Camille knew she had a better chance of reaching me than Becca.

I shrugged and took a sip of lemonade before arguing, "I have a lot on my mind right now. Like the *war*, remember?" Becca smirked as if she wanted to add Alec to the list of things on my mind, but thankfully she didn't say anything.

Zach sat up a little straighter and his blue eyes met my gray ones. "Then maybe you should go tell him that. Not the war, of course, but definitely the other part," he advised me. I just sighed and turned back to look at Josh and Cole, still debating my options.

But my mind was made up for me when I was pushed off of the seat by the goddess of love, so I reluctantly weaved my way between the wooden tables toward Cole and Josh. When I reached the two of them, Josh glanced up at me knowingly. "Becca?" he guessed and I nodded. Cole, however, just seemed confused.

"Are you here to apologize?" Cole said harshly.

"No, not exactly," I started, and Cole's gaze hardened again. "I just wanted to say that I've had a lot on my mind recently, so . . ." My voice trailed off, unsure of what else to say as I glanced back at the other gods at the booth in the back of the room.

"Look," Cole began coldly, catching my attention again. "If you don't—"

But he was interrupted by the ringing of the cell phone coming from my pocket. Once again, I didn't even have to check the caller ID to know it was Alec; that boy really did pick the absolute worst times to call.

"I'm so sorry, but I have to take this," I told Cole sheepishly, my hands shaking involuntarily, and I risked a look back at the other table to see a scene that was almost exactly how I had expected it to be: an annoyed Camille rolling her hazel eyes, my temporarily defeated love counselor Becca with her pretty little head in her hands, and the three boys, along with Josh next to me, trying desperately to hold back laughter. It was safe to say that they all knew who was calling.

"What do you want *now*, Alec?" I asked in English and Cole shot me a curious glance. At least it wasn't a glare.

"Speaking English today, I see. Is someone listening to you?" Alec responded, also in English.

"Yes," I said, impatiently tapping my foot on the hardwood floor. Cole's look seemed to be getting colder and colder as the seconds ticked by.

"All right, I'll hurry. I forced Jason to give me a cell phone so I could call you and tell you that we're in Nebraska right now. We'll probably be in the Woods by late tomorrow night or early the next morning," Alec informed me.

"Okay. Any troubles so far?" I asked him.

"All three harpies showed up last night and tried to eat us for dinner, but no real injuries," Alec stated. "I brought Jan, the head nurse, along."

"I bet she's helpful. So is that all?"

"Hmm . . . can you give me a long-distance hug?" Alec asked me hopefully. I could almost hear that mischievous smile playing across his lips, the look that made all the teenaged girls swoon over him back at the Knowing camp.

"No, I'm not giving you a long-distance hug!" I hissed into the phone and heard him start to whimper, pretending to be offended. "Just don't die," was my annoyed three-word farewell.

"I'll try not to," Alec completed our little ritual and we hung up the phone at the same time. Then I stuffed the small, black flip phone away and looked back at Cole.

"Who's Alec?" he asked.

Josh quickly jumped in to answer him. "My cousin. He visited here a couple of weeks ago, remember? You know, a sort of handsome dude with dark hair and blue eyes . . ." Cole nodded, a flicker of jealousy flashing through his eyes, and Josh's voice dropped off as he realized that he could have left off the "sort of handsome" part.

"Why would Josh's cousin be talking to *you?*" Cole was still glaring at me and I silently hoped he would stop soon. I missed the mellow personality of the boy who played pranks during his free time, though I knew it was partly my fault that Josh wasn't as free to help him with that.

"Well, I tutor him in chemistry via webcam," I lied fluently, but Cole just gave me a dubious look. I can't say I blamed him for not believing me, even though I did happen to have a bachelor's degree in chemistry so it really was a plausible story.

"But it's summer," Cole said bluntly.

"The poor kid's in summer school," I explained as I shook my head solemnly and Josh quickly nodded in agreement. "And would you stop glaring at me like that? Most people consider it rude."

Cole frowned but didn't press the issue about Alec any more. "Fine," he muttered, crossing his arms. "It's just that if you didn't want to hang out, you should have come right out and said it in the first place."

I shook my head. "I do want to hang out, but like I said, there's been a lot of stuff going on—"

Cole interrupted me by abruptly slamming his fist down on the table in frustration. "See, that's the problem. It seems like everyone around here is suddenly 'busy' and in on some huge secret. Sure, ever since we were six and that reporter came up with the Monster Watch label, you and the guys have been tight-lipped. That's normal, I guess. But it's not just the Monster Watch anymore. You all are leaving me out of it." Cole's voice cracked with stress, forcing him to take a pause. "We used to be friends, Ash. *Good* friends, and I kind of wanted to be more."

I gulped, feeling very guilty as I glanced over at Josh who was still sitting awkwardly across from Cole and listening to the entire conversation. Josh's dark pupils moved upward, peeking out from under a stray piece of his brown hair, and he gave me a shrug, obviously as bewildered as I was in the tense moment.

So, instead, I just stood there like an idiot with my breath caught in my throat as I waited for Cole to say something else. "Well, are you going to say anything?" he asked hopefully, his brown eyes suddenly seeming much more kind and caring. After all, he did just confess that he had a crush on me.

"There's no secret, Cole," I lied again quietly, realizing I was in so deep that there was no going back. I then glanced back to the other table where Becca was leaning into Zach like she had been during the movie two nights before and figured it was much better to tell a little bit of the truth than to lie about everything, so I added, "Except for the fact that Zach might be cheating on Alicia with Becca. And we just didn't want to let you in that night because we were in the middle of a movie."

When Cole raised his eyebrows, I knew I had said the right thing. "Really?" he whispered slowly and I nodded. "Then I'm sorry I was being a jerk. Forgive me?" I nodded again, though I wasn't exactly sure why he was apologizing. *I* was the one lying to his face without a second thought, even if it was only to protect our secret.

I had bid Cole farewell and was turning around when Becca caught my eye again. Her arms were crossed defiantly and her eyebrows rose pointedly as she waited for me to add something else. "Oh, right. Do you want to come?" I asked the two boys hesitantly. Josh and Cole just exchanged grateful glances before nodding eagerly. "Thought you'd never ask," Josh said, grinning.

Chapter 4

DISTRACTIONS

T he next morning, the entire Olympian Council had a meeting near the edge of the forest to discuss the plans for the day. After a few minutes, we all went our separate ways to accomplish various tasks. To be specific, Connor, Camille, and I headed back to my house to hang out while all of the other gods (except for Haley and Shane, our smith) headed into the woods. The A Team had been given yet another morning off and we planned on going back into the forest later on.

Once inside my empty house, Camille, Connor, and I collapsed on the old lumpy couch in my living room and turned on the news, setting it on mute. I took my walkie-talkie off my belt loop and set it on the coffee table in front of us before turning the volume all the way up. This way, we could at least stay informed.

Currently, Hermes was hanging out back at the army base camp, helping Pan teach the younger nymphs and satyrs some more advanced defense skills than the ones they already knew. Somewhere near the meadow, Ares and Aphrodite had just taken out the Minotaur and an undead warrior with their signature moves—

Aphrodite using her beauty as a distraction, leaving room for Ares to suddenly attack from behind. Poseidon and Zeus also seemed unstoppable as they drenched the Python in seawater and then electrocuted it to death, killing it in record time. Meanwhile, Hera, Demeter, and Dionysus were using guerrilla warfare and ambush techniques against a small troop of undead warriors.

Feeling restless, I shifted in my seat for about the fifth time in five minutes. Artemis just snickered next to me and asked in Greek, "Is something bothering you?" Since neither of my parents was at home, it was safe to be our godly selves.

"Yes. I have a disease called *pinus ponderosa* deprivation," I answered her blandly, using scientific names just to sound even more intelligent than usual as I fixed my long, wavy hair into my signature ponytail.

When the blonde twins only exchanged confused glances and Apollo raised one eyebrow, I laughed. "Basically, it means I'm feeling deprived of our wonderful forest out there," I replied with a shrug. "But then again, I'm pretty sure I've already spread the disease to you guys so it doesn't really matter." They nodded in agreement, sharing an identical smirk.

"Want to go out back? I have an empty soda can begging to be shot at," I suggested after a few dull moments of idle silence. Apollo nodded eagerly and grabbed the black BB gun sitting by my back door. He ran out into the yard without another word as Artemis just rolled her eyes.

A few minutes later, Apollo and I were taking turns shooting at the can, sending it flying back a few more feet each time with a small pinging noise. Artemis was watching us from the porch as she munched on a red apple she had stolen from the fruit basket on my kitchen table, guessing as to which one of us would be able to hit the soda can the most times. But Artemis was probably the second smartest out of all the gods (at least intellectually) so she picked the goddess of wisdom, war, and skills and won the bet against herself. Apollo didn't seem to care about the loss, since he knew he could have beaten me in a shooting competition with a bow and a few arrows at any time or place.

After about an hour, Apollo and I had shot the poor aluminum can to smithereens, and it was now lying under the big tree where the Monster Watch used to meet to discuss the day's events in the week after we had first gone into the forest, back when we didn't have other ways of communicating and life was simpler. He and I joined Artemis in the antique rocking chairs on the porch to take a break and stared blankly out into the thick fog. The skies were cloudy and gray due to Zeus's involvement in the war, but there wasn't much besides houses to look at anyway.

We were still listening to the radio, but not much was happening in the mysterious forest. To be honest, I had a feeling that the so-called "battles" would be more like random skirmishes between one or two monsters and a god, at least until Alec arrived with the reinforcements. I kept checking my watch, waiting for his call to come, but it never did. Meanwhile, I was silently mulling over recent events in the forest when something suddenly occurred to me.

"Hey!" I exclaimed, bolting upright in my chair. Artemis and Apollo just looked at me with their hazel eyes, eagerly waiting for me to explain. It's safe to say they were used to me having these random moments of realization. In fact, the pieces of the puzzle were still putting themselves together in my brain when Apollo broke in impatiently, "Well, are you going to tell us or not?"

"The helm of invisibility," I whispered, lifting my chin. Because, really, it changed the whole freaking equation. Artemis and Apollo apparently agreed, since they both smacked their foreheads at the exact same time, as if they too should have thought of the helm earlier.

In a war against the Titans, a cyclops had given the original and most famous Olympian brothers tools to defeat their enemies—Zeus received the master bolt, Poseidon his golden trident, and Hades the helm of invisibility or darkness. Until now, we had ignored the helm. Hell, until earlier in the spring, we'd ignored Hades himself—our biggest failure in our duties as gods.

So, assuming that the Hades of our current generation had the helm, the rest of us were in an enormous amount of trouble. An invisible and undetectable Hades could be anywhere at any time, listening to anything we were saying or killing anyone with valuable information. With the helm, Hades was the ultimate spy. Forget all of our planned surprise attacks and secret weapons; we were back to square one.

"But how do we know for sure that he has the helm?" Artemis mused, tapping her chin, her brow furrowed just the slightest bit.

"That's exactly it. We don't know if he has the helm, but we have to assume he does, just in case. We don't want any more soldiers dying than necessary over this ludicrous argument," I replied and the twins nodded in understanding.

"But the thing I don't get is why Hades would have let us almost capture him in the forest a few days ago if he does, in fact, have the helm in his possession . . . unless he *wanted* us to see him for some reason," I continued aloud, though Artemis and Apollo just sat back and waited silently while I reasoned it out for myself. "But then again, there's no way of knowing for sure."

"Maybe Hades was out looking for the helm when we almost captured him," Apollo offered, running his fingers through his short, sandy blond hair in anguish.

Artemis frowned and shook her head. "It can't be that simple, can it? I mean, that's probably what Hades wants us to believe, if he actually has the helm."

"There's that 'if' again. Everything we do is going to revolve around this helm from now on, so we have to determine whether or not Hades actually has it. And fast," I added before the three of us lapsed into a short state of silence and deep thought as we tried to think of how to find the helm of invisibility.

"I've got it! The antique shop!" I exclaimed and Artemis and Apollo returned their attention to me.

"Of course," Apollo breathed, beginning to count off on his fingers. "That's where we found the other major weapons—the master bolt in its metal form, the trident, your shield, bows and arrows, a few swords. Where did your mom even find those things in the first place?"

But Apollo's question went unanswered when Artemis yelped, "What are we waiting for? Let's go!" And ignoring lunch, the three of us took off down the empty road, racing toward Main Street as if our lives depended on making it to the shop alive. While that might have been true, it wasn't something to dwell on. By the time we had reached the door of the antique shop, I had filled in all of the other gods via walkie-talkie and they were on high alert, wary of an invisible Hades.

I slowly opened the door, and the tiny bell rang as we stepped over the threshold. Surveying the room, I ordered in English, "You two search that side and I'll search this side." Camille and Connor just nodded and split up while I started to sort out the piles of old junk on the right side of the room. Ancient tables and chairs with intricate patterns carved into the legs made the room into one big maze, but I wasn't taking any chances by skipping over stuff. We had to find Hades's helm; the outcome of the war depended on it.

Just then, my mother walked out of the back storage room and her brown eyes lit up when she saw the three of us. She clasped her hands together and said enthusiastically, "Are you looking for something in particular?"

"Yes, actually," I told her, thinking that she might be able to help me for once. "A helmet. Probably bronze or iron and really old."

"Really, really, *really* old," Connor added, as if I hadn't been clear enough.

My mother immediately raised her eyebrows as if suddenly remembering something then pushed her way through the clutter toward her half-moon-shaped desk. The three of us waited patiently and exchanged curious glances while she rummaged through some old documents for a minute.

"Ah, yes, here it is," she rasped as she held a few papers up to the light so she could read them better. "A boy about your age came in here—a few months ago, according to my records—and bought it off me. Didn't give me much money for it, but oh well. I didn't recognize him so I thought he might be from a neighboring town. Pine Grove, maybe?"

"Yeah, maybe." I gulped, already knowing the answer to my own question, and tried to keep my voice from shaking with worry when I asked, "Mom, what did he look like?"

"Oh, dear me," she exclaimed, covering her mouth with one frail hand. "I hope you don't go around trying to make friends with him. He was a bad sort, you know, looked a bit Goth to me. Handsome, but Goth. Not that I'm against Goth people . . . it's just hard to describe."

I know exactly what you mean, I thought to myself with a sigh.

Realizing she was getting a bit off-topic, my mother put her hands on her hips and looked directly at me as she said, "Please, sweetie, just stay away from him. I'll find you another helmet exactly like that one and you can use it for whatever crazy games you want to play."

But there is no other helmet like that one, I thought angrily as I gritted my teeth and turned around, sending worried glances to my friends across the room.

I waved my mother a quick good-bye and wove through the antiques toward the door, Camille and Connor following close behind.

As soon as we were outside and out of anyone else's earshot, I whipped out my walkie-talkie. "This is Athena calling in an emergency situation," I rapidly spoke in Greek, the urgency in my voice unmistakable. "Hades has the helm. Repeat: Hades has the helm."

At once, the walkie-talkie erupted with the voices of almost all of the other gods. "What? Wait, when? What the hell? How? Why?"

I only sighed in defeat, rubbing my forehead as Artemis took the time to explain what we now knew. But even once she had finished speaking, none of the gods had calmed down. They were even more wound up now that they knew the details and rightly so. After all, this meant that Hades could have seen or heard anything we had done or spoken of in the past months and might know about our usual routes, fighting styles, and most importantly, the arrival of Alec and the troops. This also meant that Hades already had the helm in his possession when we had surrounded him in the forest that day, so he'd definitely wanted us to see him there. We just had to figure out why.

"Athena, can I meet you and your team in your room? I want to discuss some things and I've been throwing around so much lightning my hands are killing me," Zeus asked.

"Of course, Father Zeus," I answered promptly. "But if it's not too much trouble, climb up to my balcony. My human father should be home any minute and I don't want him getting suspicious."

About half an hour later, the rest of my team and I were holed up in my room, waiting for Zeus to arrive. Just as Apollo was about to ask what time it was for the twenty-third time in the last forty minutes, I heard a muffled noise come from outside. I immediately opened the glass doors to my balcony to see a frowning Zeus, his golden hair messy and dark with sweat and rainwater, his hands rough and covered in golden blood. Breathing heavily, he lowered himself into the leather seat at my desk and I quickly rushed over, yanking out a drawer to reveal a pile of various medical supplies.

"You keep all of this in your room?" Apollo wondered aloud as he grabbed some heavy-duty bandages and alcohol to clean Zeus's wounds.

I shrugged. "It's not like anyone else in this house ever needs bandages."

Just then, I heard the sputtering of an old car engine outside, so I knew my human father was home. Ignoring his arrival for the time being, I reluctantly turned back to watch Zeus wince in pain as Apollo wrapped up his hands.

When Zeus's eyes finally looked up to meet mine, he whispered solemnly, "This is crazy. Everyone out there is paranoid about Hades and, for once in my life, I don't know how to calm them down. I mean, he could be in this room right now for all we know."

Artemis just nodded in agreement, tying her hair in a bun before she started wandering about the room, waving her arms this way and that to make sure there wasn't an invisible person hiding behind the furniture. "I don't think Hades is here, but you're right; if we're going to win this war, we all need to be a little bit paranoid about Hades in order to keep our plans a secret," Artemis proclaimed. "We just can't become so paranoid that we all start turning on each other."

Zeus opened his mouth to say something else, but was interrupted by the loud ringing of my house phone. The four of us quickly fell into silence, wondering who could possibly be calling and trying to listen for the start of a conversation. You see, in a town as small as the Woods, people often made unannounced house calls, not telephone calls. For a fraction of a second, I wondered if my cousin Katie was calling, but I couldn't think of a good reason why she would. Frowning, I was about to open my bedroom door and race downstairs to answer the phone, but I stayed in the room when I heard my human father pick up the line. He kept his voice strangely low, however, so I couldn't hear what he was saying.

No longer seeming fazed, Zeus asked us three, "How are your own injuries?"

Apollo leaned over to inspect the gash on his leg and I quickly slid the sleeve of my purple T-shirt over my left shoulder, revealing my bra strap and the bandages he had put on for me yesterday. I carefully ripped back a small piece of the gauze so I could see the damage and was relieved to find that the wound was almost healed already. There was a bit of dried golden blood on the skin surrounding the dark brown puncture, which was now almost nothing but a scar, but other than that, I was fine.

"Looks good," I told Zeus. "I expect the scar to be completely gone by tomorrow or the day after." Most likely, a stab wound like mine would have taken weeks, maybe even months, to completely heal on a normal human and then there would probably always be a scar left as a reminder of the pain. But being reincarnations of the gods, we had found out early on that as well as being stronger than regular people, our wounds healed five times as fast and our skin always appeared unscathed afterward. Such natural gifts were proving to come in quite handy for this war.

Next, I looked at Apollo and Artemis for their own reports and, luckily, they were healing as well as I was. Suddenly, a gruff yell sounded from the kitchen below, "Ashley, get down here right now!" I groaned, giving the others in the room a quick look that meant *I'll be back in a minute.* Then I slammed my white bedroom door behind me as I reluctantly headed down the stairs to face my father.

Strangely enough, he didn't look mad or drunk as usual. He was simply leaning against the doorframe, running his fingers through his thinning light brown hair when I walked into the room. His dark eyes, which were narrowed like a hawk's, peered down at me suspiciously. "Have you been hanging out with Cole lately?"

Though taken aback at first, I quickly regained my composure and decided to give a diplomatic answer, just to be safe. "Not any more than the Monster Watch or anyone else. Why are you asking?"

My father frowned and stroked the sorry excuse for a beard that was on the tip of his chin. "Cole called to ask you out on a date. He'll pick you up at seven tonight to take you out for dinner," he told me slowly, and my jaw dropped to the floor.

Outraged, I glared at him and shouted, "You said yes for me? You didn't even ask me about it! What the hell is your problem?" I yanked at my ponytail in anger, suddenly wishing that I had never come downstairs and that I had ignored Cole instead of making up with him like Becca had suggested. But cursing under my breath in Aphrodite's name wasn't going to help the situation.

My father sighed. "Calm down, I'm not *that* stupid. I know you didn't want to go," he hissed and my jaw dropped for a second time, wondering again why he had said yes for me. I was starting to think even less of him than I had before, but then he elaborated, "You're going to do this to cheer up your mother. So please, act like a *normal* teenage girl for once. These past couple of weeks I swear she's had about five heart attacks from worrying too much about you in the forest."

I took a deep breath, finally understanding him and his reasoning, although I still wasn't happy about it. My father was using me to use Cole, just to try to repair my relationship with my mother and his formerly contented marriage with her, which I sometimes thought shouldn't have happened to begin with (but then again, I wouldn't be alive without them). Talk about complicated relationships.

Growling, I shot my father one last glare for good measure before I raced back upstairs and into my room where I was met with three shocked expressions. "Did I just hear what I think I heard?" Artemis asked me in Greek, her eyebrows raised and feet dangling off the side of my bed. My only response was an angry nod before I started to pace around my room in circles to try to calm myself down.

"What am I supposed to do? I don't have time for this! We have a war to win. Oh no, Alec's going to be so mad when he hears about this," I huffed in Greek, barely even taking a breath. I rubbed my forehead to try to stop my head from pounding, but to no avail. That was when I saw the movement of Zeus's head from out of the corner of my eye and turned to face him expectantly. But rather than showing any signs of bewilderment, Zeus just pulled out his own black walkie-talkie and muttered three words into it as calmly as possible: "Get me Aphrodite."

———————————

About an hour later, we helped Aphrodite climb up to my balcony and into my room where we filled her in on my father's plans. While Apollo, Artemis, Zeus, and I were still slightly horrified, Aphrodite just sat back on my bed and smirked to herself as she absentmindedly braided her gorgeous golden hair. The very first thing she said was, "Let's find you something to wear."

For a moment, I felt like punching her. "How do you expect me to go out for a nice dinner when an invisible Hades is running around town?" Aphrodite sighed, her blue eyes settling calmly on mine. "I didn't say this was going to be fun. Knowing you, I bet you'll be worrying about Hades the entire night, but it's better than making Cole mad and suspicious all over again," she pointed out and I groaned. She stole a glance at the black alarm clock on my nightstand then continued, "We have three hours to get you ready. That should be enough time."

My jaw dropped for the third time that day (which was quite an unusual occurrence, mind you). "Three hours? I can get ready in twenty minutes. That leaves plenty of time for me to make a quick run into the forest. Artemis, are you coming?" I said defiantly, and the goddess of the hunt smirked wickedly. Meanwhile, Aphrodite just shook her head in wonder and guessed, "You've never been on a real date before, have you?" My only response was another glare in her direction.

––––––––––––

A few minutes later, Aphrodite had forced Apollo and Zeus to go away while the three of us goddesses had some "quality girl talk" (whatever the hell that meant). I took a short shower then the two blondes tried to help me pick out an appropriate outfit. As a goddess, I was good-looking enough so that I didn't even need makeup, despite Aphrodite's repeated efforts to get me to wear a little mascara.

The three of us automatically assumed that Cole was taking me to a fancy restaurant in the next town over where most teens around here went for their dates. Aphrodite tried to force me into a dress, but, luckily, I convinced her that it would seem like I was trying too hard to impress Cole. Eventually, we all agreed on a cute navy blue blazer over a tight-fitting striped top with a deep V-neck. I also traded my ripped skinny jeans for black ones and my combat boots for ballet flats, since Aphrodite adamantly refused to let me out of the house wearing anything I would wear to fight in the forest.

Before I knew it, the time on the clock read 6:30 and Aphrodite and Artemis were just leaving me to wait for Cole. Alone again, I sat on the edge of my bed impatiently tapping my feet on the blue carpet as I mindlessly glanced at the hundreds of books on the tall bookshelves that lined the perimeter of my room. The seconds were ticking by way too slowly and, already, I just wanted the date to be over with.

Unexpectedly, the walkie-talkie on my nightstand crackled to life and Pan's voice blasted through the small speaker. "This is Pan calling in an emergency situation. I mean, it's not really an emergency *now*, it's just sad—no, horrible." Pan's voice continued to rant on and I wished he would get to the point before Cole picked me up. Finally, he said, "We have our first casualty of the war, a fellow satyr named Berry. There will be a vigil tonight. Just thought you should know. Over."

I hadn't known Berry very well compared to some of the other satyrs; his presence at Pan's hideout parties was often placid. But with his death, the war became even more real. For the first time that summer, I was thinking in depth about how many people were going to die because of my fellow gods and me. Was power really worth the fight? Maybe not, but I thought going to a vigil was definitely worth missing my date with Cole.

"I'm not going on the date, Aphrodite," I whispered through the walkie-talkie.

"No, you're still going," Aphrodite hissed back in determination. "We'll just tell everyone that you send your condolences and that you wish you could be there."

"She's right," came Zeus's tired voice. "Right now, you have a more important obligation. You just take care of Cole. Good luck."

"Thanks," I said glumly, knowing that I would, in fact, need a bit of luck to avoid thinking about all of the mythical distractions in order to survive the date.

A few minutes later, I heard a car pull up outside and my feet started to move involuntarily toward the door while my mind was still whirling. I remember getting into the black SUV and Cole greeting me, but the long ride to the restaurant was filled with stiff silence. I realized too late that Alec still hadn't called and even though I had my cell phone in my pocket in case of a true emergency, I couldn't call him now so I simply cursed myself during the rest of the ride as I stared out of the window.

Cole let the valet service park the car then a nice waiter brought us to a cramped corner of the room where a table set for two stood, empty but daunting. Half of my brain was rapidly working out strategies to use if Hades or a monster happened to attack during dinner while the other half was trying to come up with good topics for conversation with someone Sightless. I knew the hardest part of the date would be trying to focus on Cole and to forget what was going on in the forest.

"You look nice. I mean, you always look nice, but you look especially nice now," Cole whispered, obviously noticing my outfit. It was like the awkward moment of the first date in every romantic movie, except my life wasn't meant to be a romance. I barely even took notice of Cole in his buttoned-down shirt and black slacks, squirming nervously in his seat across from me; my mind was still on the wild hero with blue eyes.

Involuntarily, I found myself thinking of what Alec would have said in that same awkward moment. Probably something impulsive, such as, "You look better in battle armor." And while most girls would have been offended by a concise comment like that, I would have smiled because that was exactly what I thought too.

Forcing the thought of Alec out of my mind, I gave Cole a tight smile and then we ordered our food. If you really must know, I had chicken carbonara and it was delicious. There's not much else to say; I wasn't planning to burden you with the details of our insignificant conversations. Besides, it's Aphrodite's job to hand out free dating advice, not mine. And this is my book, not hers.

I will tell you, however, that the dinner could not have gone by any slower for me. I kept nervously fingering the belt loop on my hip, the one where I usually kept my walkie-talkie. It was the first time in many days that I didn't have my walkie-talkie on me and I felt guilty and naked without it. It's safe to say that I would not have had the upper hand if a battle had suddenly broken out during the meal.

Every flicker of the lights, every draft of cold air blowing, and every shadow moving around me set my teeth on edge as if the lord of the Underworld might pop out to kidnap me at any second. I gripped my chair tightly and told myself that Hades wasn't watching me, that everything was okay, but deep down inside I knew that everything was *not* going to be okay.

Blackness seeped into the edges of my vision, like a shadow trying to pull me into a state of unconsciousness. But I was able to resist its temptation. This time, the airflow that tickled the back of my neck and sent shivers down my spine wasn't frigid but warm—his breath, I discerned. How long had he been there?

Preparing myself for the worst, I closed my eyes tightly and didn't bother to open them again. Heart rate rising, I could feel his thin, pasty lips press seductively against my left ear as he taunted in Greek, "How does it feel to know you've lost?"

"I wouldn't know," I hissed back, sliding my chair directly into his side. The invisible god stumbled and fell and Cole jerked his head up, startled by the sound. The waiter walking by our table tripped then scurried off in embarrassment, as if nothing had happened. He didn't notice that he'd dropped an empty wine glass or that the glass had seemingly stopped in midair about five inches off the ground before being noiselessly set down.

"What was that?" Cole asked.

"The waiter must have dropped something." But instead of watching Cole or the waiter, my eyes were locked on the front door, waiting expectantly for it to open without being pushed by a visible being. As confident as I could be that Hades had actually left the premises, I looked back to Cole.

Finally, my quiet wishes and prayers were answered when, at that moment, my phone rang. Cole looked up at me in confusion and I just shrugged, pretending it was no big deal. I then desperately yanked the cell phone out of my pocket and pressed it close to my ear. I knew that if Cole found out Alec was the one calling me, he would have gotten mad again so I just pretended the young hero was someone different.

"Hello, *Father*," I hissed in English, hoping Alec would catch on quickly. "What do you want? I'm on a date with Cole, remember?"

There was static on the line for a moment until Alec's voice answered. Unsurprisingly, he sounded extremely hurt and angry. "What? Your father forced you to go on a date with Cole?!"

"Yes," I answered impatiently, "and I'm not happy about it either." Seeing Cole's confused expression, I added randomly, "No, you'll just have to talk to Mom later."

"What? Oh, never mind," Alec said bitterly and I could tell he was still angry. "Anyway—"

"Look, *Father*, I don't have time to talk with you right now. You just need to know that *he* has the *helm*," I interrupted. In front of me, Cole gazed blankly at his plate and twirled his fork in circles, not even seeming to try to understand me any longer.

"He? Helm? What helm?" Alec sounded baffled for a brief moment before he regained his composure. "Oh, you mean the helm of invisibility. Wait—Hades has it? When did this happen?"

"A few months ago. We just figured it out," I hissed back at him and slammed my fork on the table, angered by the mere thought of the lord of the dead. "So he might know where you're coming from and when you might get here. I have to go now, but good luck and don't die."

I hung up the crappy flip phone and stuffed it in my pocket before Alec could say another word. Hopefully he would forgive me for ever going out to dinner with Cole.

The rest of the date seemed to pass quicker, mostly because we just had to wait for the check. Cole offered to pay and even *I* found that kind of sweet. In just over an hour, I was back on my front porch. Cole awkwardly bid me farewell and I knew that he wanted to kiss me, but, thankfully, my dad was watching so he didn't.

With that, I raced into the house, not even bothering to stop and talk to my father about my date, and he just raised his bushy eyebrows suggestively at me. I gave him one last glare for the day, and he chuckled softly in spite of himself before I burst up the staircase and into my empty room to get myself ready for bed.

I came out of the bathroom a few minutes later and was about to crawl under the covers when I noticed shadows moving behind the turquoise curtains of my balcony doors. I quickly grabbed my pocketknife and yanked open the door, ready for some monsters to come at me, but was only met with the curious expressions of the rest of the Olympian Council. All eleven of them.

"What are you doing here?" I hissed in Greek at the crowded group of gods on my tiny balcony even though I knew very well that they just wanted to know how the date went. News travels fast in small towns, after all, and especially news about me.

Aphrodite, Artemis, Demeter, and Hestia rolled their eyes at me in unison. "How was the date?" Zeus asked, slipping one arm around my shoulders protectively and Hera narrowed her dark brown eyes to slits. I ignored her and rested my head on Zeus's shoulder.

"Well, Alec called and I told him about the helm," I started, my voice trailing off a bit. Sensing my hesitancy, Zeus raised his eyebrows expectantly.

"And?" Apollo coaxed aloud.

"And Hades showed up just to breathe down my neck and tell me we're going to lose this war," I admitted in a rush. Nothing traumatic had actually happened so I didn't want the other gods to dwell on it.

"Are you kidding me?" Zeus hissed, his voice low and angry. He probably would've yelled and summoned a full-blown thunderstorm had he not known my father was downstairs. "I swear I'm going to send that piece of shit down to Tartarus myself. Tomorrow."

The other gods muttered their own impassioned choice words while I just shook my head, doubting the likelihood of that scenario. "We'll see," I said, eager to change the topic. "But how was the vigil?"

Poseidon sighed as he ran his fingers through his jet-black hair. "Sad. There was a lot of crying and whatnot, but the nymphs and satyrs seemed glad we were there."

"We buried Berry next to Alec's dad," Ares, the god of war, added quietly, actually showing a feeling other than anger for once in his life.

I nodded solemnly, but after a rather short moment of silence for Berry, I extricated myself from Zeus's arms and ordered grumpily, "If that's all, I would like to get to bed and forget this date ever happened. So, I hate to be rude, but you should leave now."

A couple of the other gods chuckled and groaned in disappointment, but they jumped off my balcony without complaints, one after another. When I finally had some peace and quiet, I locked my doors for the night. Then I walked straight to my bed and tucked myself in, desperately hoping that an invisible Hades wasn't hiding somewhere in the dark corners of my room, patiently waiting for the right moment to kill me.

It was quite a creepy thought, actually.

Chapter 5

THE ORACLE AND I EXPLAIN

here are you, Hades?

WThat was the question begging to be answered. My head was pounding with a thousand thoughts and theories at once, the world seeming to spin faster and faster around me . . .

Hades had the helm of invisibility. He had the helm and I should have seen it coming. At that exact moment, he could have been in a million places, even in my dark and lonely room, but he was only in one. I tried to tell myself that Hades wouldn't be in my room, waiting to kill me, that it was illogical. Today he'd approached me alone for the first time and there had to be a reason for that, yet he never tried to harm me—only rubbing it in my face that he was one step ahead of me, that he didn't have a human persona to maintain. Furthermore, why would he be there in my room when he could be stalking around in the forest, listening to the troops' conversations to gain even the slightest knowledge of our battle plans?

The troops. That thought alone sent me bolting upright in my bed to face the alarm clock and check the time. 12:05 a.m. *Alec and the Knowing should be here by now,* I thought to myself. But they obviously weren't. Before I had gone to bed, I put my walkie-talkie volume on the loudest setting possible so, just in case something happened, the sound of the announcement would wake me up. I had not foreseen that I would be getting so little sleep in the first place.

Rubbing my forehead in anguish, I rolled out of bed. The first thing I did was grab my walkie-talkie and pocketknife from the nightstand as well as the rock/sword that I had apparently knocked to the floor in my restless sleep. Holding onto them tightly, I opened my balcony doors and took a quick glance at Zeus and Poseidon's house, silently hoping one of them would be awake to talk to (preferably Zeus). But I was disappointed to find it dark and cold. I knew that Artemis, being the goddess of the moon and stars, would probably be up and about at her house, though her company wasn't what I was truly looking for. I just wanted the second opinion of someone who had known the forest for as long as I had, someone more likely to run into battle right now than wait for morning to come and Hades to make the first move. I wasn't stupid enough to sneak into the forest alone.

Sighing, I climbed up to my roof where I sat on the rough surface to stare out at the night sky alone, wishing Alec was there like he used to be. For hours on end, I glared at the twinkling stars that shined through the silent night air as if nothing was wrong, as if there were no wars going on. It was a peaceful sky, but only because Zeus was sleeping and I wondered if Hades was too . . . .

"This is Pan calling in a happy situation. Wake up. Repeat: wake up," Pan's gravelly voice floated its way to my brain and I opened my eyes abruptly, only slightly surprised to find that I had fallen asleep on the roof. I blinked my eyes against the dim light of the morning sun shining through the thick cloud cover and knew that it had to be very early, since everything was covered with a fine layer of dew. Reluctantly, I sat up with a groan and rubbed my eyes.

"Happy situation, people. Wake up!" Pan demanded in Greek yet again and still it received no response via walkie-talkie. I just frowned, wondering what in the world a "happy situation" was. We had no protocol for happiness, only emergencies.

"WAKE UP, I tell you! Alec is here with the troops." I almost fell off the roof, knowing that last bit had probably woken everyone else up too. Finally.

Sure enough, Zeus ordered right away, "Everyone meet at my house in thirty minutes. Pan, we'll be at the camp soon."

I wasted no time in sliding down to my balcony and leaping into my bedroom to change out of my pajamas. I carefully slipped on my black leather jacket as I glanced at the clock, which read 5:30 a.m. Even though I knew I didn't have to rush, I didn't even bother to change the old bandage on my wounded shoulder. Zeus was right next door, after all.

A few minutes later, the other gods (except for Hephaestus, whose broken leg was still healing) and I were just inside the forest, pulling all of our armor and weapons out of the hollow logs. We took our time to make sure that every leather strap was tight and that each bronze breastplate, backplate, bracer, and greave was on correctly, because we all knew the real battles would most likely start within the next few days. I decided to use my small spear to fight with and grabbed my shield as well, although I had not often used it before. But today was different so we also took all of the extra weapons with us, realizing we would need some more for the troops.

Another half hour later, we were tearing west through the forest. Low-hanging branches slapped our faces and our ankles rolled every time we took a misstep over a tree root, but we didn't care. We sprinted like cheetahs down the steep hill by the small waterfall toward our army's base camp. As we burst breathlessly onto the scene, every single person, nymph, and satyr knelt on the grass in unison out of respect for us. Except for Pan, who just stood under a tent by the table with the map of the woods, his brown eyes shining as he grinned at us like an idiot.

I had to take deep breaths to slow my heartbeat as my eyes rested on the dark-haired boy in the center of the circle of camouflaged tents, the boy who was gripping the hilt of his sword as if his life depended on it. "Lord Zeus, I have brought you twelve sword fighters and two archers, plus a healer. More troops are on the way and they will be here soon," Alec said loudly and formally in Greek as he stood up, his blue eyes meeting Zeus's.

Our king just grinned, pulling Alec into one of those man-hugs as the rest of the Knowing warriors stood up behind Alec—the ones who were conscious, anyway. Some of the Knowing had been so blown away at meeting their gods and at how good-looking we all were that they had passed out cold (pathetic, I know). Perhaps our auras alone, probably much stronger and heavier than the air to which they were accustomed, were powerful enough to knock them out.

And I couldn't help but wonder what monsters they had been fighting, since all of them had scars and bandages of some sort on their fit bodies. Looking more closely, I even recognized a few faces among the Warriors, like Nicholas, the muscular brute with a Hydra tattoo on his chest, Jan, the middle-aged healer, and Hannah, the freckled young archer with sleek black hair whose little brother, Ben, must have been with the other group of Knowing members.

"Good to see you, Alec. Or should I say *hero*, yes? Well done, well done. What weapons have you managed to bring?" Zeus exclaimed a little too enthusiastically for me to take him seriously. He even gave Alec a pat on the back.

"Only a few swords, sir. Excuse my language, but airport security can be a real bitch," Alec responded, and everyone in the small clearing laughed.

"Certainly. It's quite alright," Zeus assured Alec then turned to face the rest of the gods and me. "Set the extra weapons by the table over there and we'll have Hephaestus make some more, if needed." We nodded and did as we were told then returned to greet Alec as the crowd of Knowing members, nymphs, and satyrs disbanded.

Laughing and joking around together, Apollo, Poseidon, Hermes, Dionysus, and even the angry Ares each gave Alec a man-hug similar to Zeus's. Then an eager Aphrodite interrupted the guys and pounced on Alec, planting a kiss right on his cheek and pressing her body into his. Such provocative gestures were normal to Aphrodite, since everyone—males *and* females—wanted her. I had honestly never seen someone able to resist her for very long so you can imagine my panic when Alec blushed but did not look my way. I just swallowed down a pang of jealousy and nervously fingered the rock/sword in my pocket, waiting for Alec to reach me, the fear that he was still mad at me growing stronger and stronger inside my chest.

Alec then moved on to talk to Hera, Demeter, Artemis, and Hestia, but he still had yet to meet my gaze. Frustrated with both Alec for ignoring me and myself for going on the date with Cole, I walked over to the mahogany table with the map and stood there glaring at it. Out of the corner of my eye, I noticed that the Oracle was having a heated argument with Nicholas, whom she had never even met before, and I silently wondered what it was about. Shrugging it off and anxiously tapping my fingers on the table to no particular rhythm, I studied the map and tried to ignore all the shouting that was going on.

Suddenly, a soft whisper drifted to my ears from out of the chaos behind me, one hopeful word, one name, that sent shivers down my spine: "Athena." I knew then that he was not as mad as I had feared.

I whipped around to face Alec but smacked right into him, not realizing that he was standing so close to me. Slightly embarrassed, my breath caught in my throat as I looked up from his chest to meet his eyes. "Hi," I said stupidly.

"Hi," Alec replied with a grin, his eyebrows arched. "What, no hug? After all of this? I'm not dead, you know. I did what you asked." He opened his arms for me, but I was determined to keep a safe distance so our relationship wouldn't get too close, or rather, so it wouldn't cross into physicality. I was stronger without him.

I smiled up at him before I accused, "It seems you've forgotten your first lesson." Alec smirked in remembrance and we finished in unison, "Don't mess with Athena."

After a moment of peaceful silence, Alec sighed and scratched his head before asking quietly, "How's . . . life?"

I knew the question was really about Cole so I just shook my head and got straight to the point. "Alec, I already told you, I didn't even want to go on that date with Cole. So just shut up and get over it."

Alec grinned in relief, but then his eyes narrowed again when he caught sight of the white bandage peeking out from under my leather jacket. "Oh my gods, I did this to you," he whispered, inferring that it was, indeed, the wound I had received while he was on the phone with me.

I quickly shook my head as he reached for my wounded shoulder. "Alec," I said to him, but he was still staring at my bandage with a mildly horrified expression. I gave him a soft slap on the cheek to get his attention then started again, "Alec, it wasn't your fault. I would've been fine if I hadn't tripped on that dang tree root. See? Like I've said before, we gods heal fast." I ripped off the remaining pieces of the bandage to show him that there was barely even a scar left, that there was nothing for him to be sorry about. I was just a little sore.

Immediately, Alec raised his eyebrows, a smile creeping back onto his handsome face. "Who knew the goddess of wisdom and war was such a klutz?" Nothing could bring him down in this moment, not even the terrible war. He was about to say something else to me (another attempt at a joke, I was certain) when he was interrupted by a call from the center of camp.

"The Oracle of Delphi is requesting an audience with the Olympian Council, plus Alec," Hermes shouted and the entire camp went quiet. Alec and I exchanged curious glances then reluctantly followed Hermes and the rest of the gods into the largest enclosed tent to talk with the secretive Oracle.

When we opened the flap, the Oracle was at the other end of the long tent facing us, her thick black braid cascading elegantly over her shoulder. With her bright green eyes locked on the thirteen of us, she started to weave her way through the many cots that the majority of soldiers would be sleeping on that night. "We need to discuss some things," the Oracle stated blandly, smoothing out her purple robes.

"So I figured," Zeus said hotly, his muscles bulging under his gray T-shirt as he crossed his arms. "What do you want?"

"Don't you want to know what happens when you die?" she asked, getting to the point so quickly that we were taken by surprise.

"Wait," I said, throwing my hands up in the air and avoiding her gaze. "We need to make sure that Hades isn't hiding here somewhere and listening in." The others nodded in agreement, eager for the chance to calm our growing paranoia, at least temporarily. Then we all karate-chopped and kicked at the air in the tent for the next few minutes until we were sure that an invisible Hades wasn't with us.

When everyone had settled down and taken a seat on a cot, Zeus looked back to the Oracle and slowly ran his fingers through his dark blond hair, already deep in thought. "All right, you have our attention. Now, what do you mean? I thought we just go to the Underworld like everyone else."

"Yeah, we know we aren't immortal," Poseidon added from beside Zeus.

The Oracle tilted her head sideways, as if trying to figure out how to best explain it to us. "Well, have you ever thought about what being a reincarnation truly means? I was just talking to a couple of the Knowing about it. Nicholas, actually," she started and I finally understood why she had been having a yelling match with him earlier. "He came along specifically to deliver some information about past generations of the gods. Unfortunately, it seems that in each generation, all the gods went just as quickly as they came, so to speak."

I sighed, realizing exactly what she meant. "Wait," Aphrodite cut in, crossing her arms over her chest. "You just said 'all.' As in every single one of them?"

"We all die at the same time, don't we?" Ares whispered gruffly, picking up right where Aphrodite left off. When the Oracle didn't answer, Ares started to get angry. "Don't we?" he shouted at her with his fists clenched and a vein popping out on his forehead. "We all die at the same time and you never told us!"

The Oracle held up her hands to fend off Ares. "I wasn't certain until now!" she hissed back at him. "I grew up in this forest, in the dark, just like you did."

Aphrodite took hold of Ares and pulled him away from the Oracle, trying to calm him down by stroking his chest and whispering in his ear. Then Hera spoke up as she slowly tied up her reddish-brown hair in a ponytail, "But why? Even though we're all the same age, we weren't born on the same day. So why should we die at the same time?"

At first, the Oracle stayed quiet then glanced at me. "I think Athena can answer that one for you," she whispered, and all of the other gods and Alec turned to face me, confusion in their eyes.

Still avoiding eye contact with the prophet, I pushed myself off the small green cot I had been sitting on. "You're partly correct, Hera," I started and the queen of the gods just frowned at me ungratefully. "But even though we weren't physically born at the same time, we were somehow *metaphorically* born at the same time. If I had to guess, I'd say our finding each other within twenty-four hours was part of it."

"When I was little, I was always told stories of how the gods' souls emitted their powers and the souls just needed human hosts to thrive," Pan offered helpfully. "There's also a slightly different myth that says the gods' powers needed to latch on to human souls in order to be used."

"Okay," I began again, scratching my head. "It sounds like no matter what, the souls inside of us are what make us Greek gods. Therefore, we became gods long before we even knew it, when we were just babies; our powers grew stronger as we did. Maybe there was a moment back then when we were all in the same place—in the hospital or the Fire Pit or somewhere—and the previous generation of gods just happened to die and their souls, their powers, for whatever reason chose us to be their hosts. That scenario still implies we die simultaneously, however."

A couple of the gods groaned, placing their heads in their hands. I could tell they were feeling lost and defeated, but a few were still hopeful. "Say the myth that states a god's soul intertwines with a human one is actually correct. What happens to our human parts?" Apollo piped up. "If we die as gods, our human parts would still live on, right?"

The Oracle only gave a small cough and again motioned for me to explain. "Wrong," I answered Apollo solemnly, my mouth suddenly feeling dry. "As our blood started to change from red to gold when we were younger, it symbolized us discovering our powers and becoming true gods. In other words, we never had two parts—we just thought of it that way. Think of our 'human parts' as facades that crumbled as we grew older."

"So we only have one chance," Apollo confirmed as the tension built up in the tent and both the Oracle and I nodded. "How long have you known about this? And why didn't you tell us before?" Apollo asked me sadly. I felt like I had betrayed him and the rest of them, but I just clenched my jaw and tried not to let it show.

I shrugged. "I've been thinking about it a lot lately, though it all pretty much came together right now."

Zeus sighed and tried to get the others to calm down as they shifted nervously in their seats. "Everybody relax. This new information doesn't have to change anything. We can't let fear get to us and we will still fight as hard as we can.

We've survived this long so who's to say we won't survive until we're eighty? We have powers and it's all of us against one. The monsters are just a side dish, so to speak. Now, we need to focus on convincing Hades *not* to take over the world."

"And how are we going to do that, exactly?" Artemis wondered aloud with an exasperated sigh. "You have to admit the monsters are a pretty big side dish."

"Wait a minute," Alec interrupted, running his fingers through his dark hair. "You all aren't the only gods. There were tons of minor gods of rivers and seas and such. What about them?"

"You just said it yourself," I told him. "Those gods would be spiritually attached to whichever river or sea they control so they would probably be reborn near the same spot in every generation. I doubt we'll be able to get any help from them. They might even be far enough away that they aren't affected by the war at all and won't have dozens of monsters prowling around."

The Oracle nodded before adding, "And they will all die with you as well. That includes Pan and Persephone, but probably not me. The other nymphs and satyrs will also be spared, since they have no direct spiritual connection with any of the gods."

"Okay, back to the plan." Poseidon switched topics, eager to talk about something a bit lighter. "We need more soldiers to fight the monsters while we find Hades. The Knowing Warriors aren't going to be enough, especially since half the group is blinded by fear already, and we haven't even done anything."

Several of the gods nodded their heads in agreement, but Zeus was already on the same page I was. "The centaurs," we said simultaneously and exchanged a high five. The other gods' faces lit up immediately, their hope renewed.

"Huh? What centaurs?" Alec asked in confusion. "I lived here with Pan and Persephone by the river in these woods for weeks and I never saw a centaur."

I smirked at him. "Have you ever wondered what's on the other side of the river?"

"That's where the centaurs live," Alec realized as he stood up next to me. I nodded.

"This one catches on quick, doesn't he?" Hestia stopped combing her long, light brown hair with her fingers and motioned to Alec with a small smile. "I like him." A short chuckle passed through the gods, and Alec blushed.

"Then it's decided. The Monster Watch will travel to the big meadow tomorrow to get the centaurs to help us," Zeus proclaimed, and Apollo, Poseidon, and I nodded. "Now we have to figure out how to convince Hades that being ruler of the Underworld already comes with enough power to satisfy him. Who can we get to do that, assuming we can actually find Hades?"

After we all thought quietly for a second, I cleared my throat and mused, "We need someone with whom Hades can relate. Someone who has a little bit of power but realizes that it's more than enough."

Suddenly, a growl sounded from the corner of the tent behind us and we all spun around to face the origin of the noise. Demeter stood scowling and glaring at the rest of us, her brown eyes peeking out from under a stray piece of blonde hair. When she clenched her fists, a few leaves of poison oak sprouted from the soil under her dirty, yellow Converse sneakers and I wondered if it was intentional or by accident. She snarled menacingly, "Have you all forgotten about my daughter? Persephone is still trapped down in the Underworld with Hades and we've done absolutely nothing about it since Alec went down there to confront him a few weeks ago."

It was eerily silent for a moment as we glanced nervously at each other, waiting for someone else to speak up. Finally, Alec stated, "Persephone's smart. I think she'll be okay on her own until we solve our problem with Hades, and besides, Hades loves her too much to even think about hurting her."

Demeter growled again, her eyes flashing. "I understand that you know her pretty well, Alec, but you don't quite understand. Every night, I hear her voice screaming in my head. Every night, she prays to me, begging to be saved from his wrath. Every single night. So if none of you want to help, I'll go rescue Persephone by myself."

As Demeter turned on her heel and stalked out of the tent, her long hair flowing out behind her, Alec gulped nervously and looked to Zeus, who appeared equally baffled. "She'll get over it sooner or later." He waved her off, but I wasn't so sure he was right. Leaving that problem for another time, however, Zeus continued, "It's past lunchtime so I'm going to head back to the Fire Pit. I think we'll stay off the battlefield for the rest of the day. That way we can reorganize ourselves and the Knowing can get settled in."

Everyone else in the tent nodded and left the Oracle alone. Deciding I could use some fresh lemonade, I bid Alec farewell for the time being and followed the rest of the gods back east toward Main Street. We took our time, pausing a couple of times to kill a few monsters and arrived at the edge of the trees about an hour later. Then the Monster Watch, along with Josh, headed to the Fire Pit for lunch while the other gods walked southwest toward their respective houses.

A few minutes later, the four guys and I sat down at our booth in the back of the room and waited while Zach and Luke's mother brought us some fresh lemonade and grilled cheese sandwiches. I didn't ask him, but I assumed Josh was there with us because he was waiting for Cole. Sure enough, the caramel-haired boy walked up to the table halfway into our meal.

He sat down next to me with a nervous smile, and I had to hold back a groan as Zach, Luke, and Connor exchanged uncomfortable glances. They understood as well as I did that my parents had no idea how much trouble they had caused me when they set me up on that date. I knew that, all too soon, Cole would ask me out on another date and then I would have to leave a battle or something like that just to keep my promise to him. Needless to say, that was a promise worth breaking.

"Hey, Cole," Josh greeted his friend and smiled. "What have you been up to?"

Quickly, I shoved the last piece of sandwich into my mouth and said, "Excuse me, but my college homework is begging to be finished." I left the table before Cole could even get in a word, and the other boys just snickered behind me.

When I got home, relieved to find that neither of my parents was there, I ran straight up to my room and started my physics and art history homework. After I had finished working, I decided that I would save my energy and not run around town trying to find the rest of the Monster Watch so I just sat on the couch to watch the news instead. Around five o'clock, my father came home looking as drunk as usual. Without even acknowledging him, I retreated back into my room until dinner. The fact that my father and I had reached an understanding about my mother still didn't mean I would tolerate his grumpy alcoholic presence.

Much later, I climbed onto my roof and sat down, hugging my knees, to watch the stars, but instead, I ended up scanning the black treetops of the forest for signs of trouble. My mind continued to whirl as I thought about the conversation with the Oracle earlier that day. I knew that even if we did win the war and manage to survive, our problems with Hades would not be solved unless his desires were completely satisfied. I sighed, running through a list of people in my brain who might be able to capture the attention of Hades, but came up with nothing.

Just then, I noticed Zach open his own balcony door across the grass lawn, light pouring out from his room and into the dark night. He saw me lying alone on my roof and waved and I waved back, permitting him to come over. I was humbly reminded of a time when he did that more often, when he felt too cocky, excited, or invincible to even think about sleep, rather than feeling nervous or stressed. I missed that time. I missed not having to think about battle plans, and I missed not feeling guilty about what only I knew would come out of this goddamn war, about what I'd known for years.

Zeus pulled me from the shadow of my flashback when, not two minutes later, he solemnly sat next to me and rested his handsome head in his rough hands. Just that one simple gesture caused the sky to darken and the clouds to build up above us. He was silent for a long time, but eventually he lifted his head to speak. "The townsfolk should be worried. They should be preparing to protect themselves, but they have no idea Hades is about to take over. They have no idea about any of this," he whispered slowly, and I was only somewhat surprised to see his philosophical side coming out of hiding. "And if they knew, I suppose they would wish that they didn't. So . . . we're stuck."

I nodded glumly, not quite sure how to respond, and followed his gaze to our right to see scattered lights from quiet houses glowing in the blackness of the evening. I was certain that Zeus and I were sharing the same thought: We gods were here to stay and protect our beloved home, but for how much longer? How long could we possibly keep such a big secret from the tight-knit families in our tiny town? To be honest, what worried me the most about the prophecy was that it foretold a war, but no end to it.

"Is something bothering you?" Zeus asked in Greek, glancing back at me.

I shrugged and responded truthfully, "Pretty much everything. But that's normal for me."

"You're such a control freak," he laughed. "You don't have to carry the burden of knowledge alone, you know. We're all in this war together, and it's not the end of the world. Yet."

At once, a muffled noise sounded from down below and both Zeus and I froze. I gripped the rock/sword, which was still in my jeans pocket from this morning, and a wave of worry washed over me. "Who's there?" we said loudly in unison, hoping the sound hadn't been made by Hades himself.

"I am," Alec's pained voice reached our ears as he struggled to pull himself onto the roof. I gasped when I realized that one arm was dripping with red blood and that he wasn't even wearing armor.

"You're such an idiot!" I exclaimed breathlessly as I rushed to his side and helped him carefully sit down. "What were you thinking, coming here without armor during a war? I guess I must have trained you pretty damn well, since you actually managed to survive. Did you do everything I taught you? Was your stance okay? You didn't let yourself get distracted, did you?"

Alec just smiled weakly at me, not even bothering to answer my barrage of questions, and I grunted in annoyance. Leaving him with the bewildered Zeus for a moment, I raced back into my room and returned with my full supply of bandages.

I then knelt down next to Alec with an exasperated sigh, inspecting his entire body as a tiny pool of dark blood collected on the rough, black surface of the roof. "It was an undead warrior," Alec croaked out the answer to the question I was about to ask, sheepishly picking at the soles of his worn-out sneakers. I wordlessly raised my eyebrows and pulled out a damp rag to wipe a bit of blood off his cheek, but then Alec said softly, "I think the wounds from my whipping are bleeding again. My armor was irritating them."

I turned Alec's back toward me to see his blood just starting to seep through his dark gray T-shirt. Somberly, I helped him lift it over his head, revealing a lot of smeared blood and, rather shockingly, a black owl imprinted on his skin, its wingspan stretching all the way between his shoulder blades. The detailed feathers, coupled with the way Alec's back muscles moved, made the owl seem even more real.

"You got a new tattoo," I observed dryly, certain he had gotten it in honor of me. Other people would see it as a simple tribute to his patron goddess, but *I* knew it was there because he also had feelings for me, unfortunately for both of us.

Alec only nodded silently as I started to gently wipe off the blood from his skin. As I did this, I also noticed that his wild, dark hair had grown a bit longer and as a result was now able to cover his other tattoo, the small black sword imprinted on the back of his neck which signified his membership in the Knowing Warriors. I sighed again, tracing the tiny circle with my index finger and thinking about how Alec could never go back to live with the Knowing and truly be a part of them; he had changed far too much since he first arrived in the Woods.

"I wanted to cover up my Warrior identification with a different tattoo, but I figured I was in too much trouble already," Alec explained, reading my exact thoughts. Another bout of whipping would not have been good for my little hero.

"How many monsters did you run into on your way here?" Zeus asked Alec, finally breaking his silence as he stroked his chin in thought.

"More than you want to hear about," Alec muttered, wincing again as I dabbed at one of the reopened scars on his back. "But I'm perfectly fine. Anyway, I was wondering if I could tag along with you to go talk to the centaurs tomorrow."

Zeus just laughed again and shot me a look that read, *This guy is crazier than you!* and I joined in.

"Sorry, but there's a reason I said that only the Monster Watch could come; we're familiar faces," he told Alec with a short chuckle before beginning the backstory, telling it like he would a funny story. "We were seven, didn't even know we were gods yet, and we were exploring the other side of the river for the first time. We ran into a group of centaurs late in the day and they would have killed us, but Ashley convinced them that we were valuable assets. Centaurs definitely aren't the friendliest of creatures, and we've only seen a couple since that day, but I guess it's finally time to join forces . . . if they agree to it, of course."

Although he frowned, Alec nodded in understanding and yawned as the three of us stared off into the night sky. A shadow at the corner of my eye caught my attention and I turned to watch the figure shaped like a human walk down the street toward us. "If that's Cole, kill me," I hissed, furrowing my brow slightly.

Both boys smirked, and as Alec moved his hand over mine for just a split second, I felt my heart start to race involuntarily before the warmth slipped away again. "This guy is just like that one harpy—or Hades, actually. Reappearing at the worst times, haunting you like a ghost," Alec complained bitterly, and I rolled my eyes. What a wonderful thought.

"We should just go somewhere else before he gets up here," Zeus grumbled.

"You're the king," Alec agreed all too eagerly and obediently as he started to get up. "Back to the army camp?"

Zeus nodded in agreement and the three of us carefully climbed to the ground after I returned the extra, unused bandages to my room. While we stopped briefly at the edge of the forest to put on our bronze armor, I checked behind me one last time for that shadowy person. Sure enough, Cole stood patiently at my front door, probably waiting for me to answer, but I just peeled my gaze away and followed the guys deeper into the woods without saying another word.

We slowly made our way single file through the misty forest, careful to be as quiet as possible so we had a better chance of avoiding any monsters. For once, the woods actually seemed calm and peaceful, like they used to be before the war. However, the three of us were about halfway to the camp when we heard a rustle in the thick bushes directly in front of us. Simultaneously, Zeus's hand crackled with bright electricity and Alec and I squeezed our small rocks, causing the shiny sword blades to pop out.

Zeus, who was currently in the rear, stepped in front of Alec. "If that's a monster, let us handle it. You've taken down enough of them for one night," he whispered to Alec then rambled on, giving himself a pep talk. "And if that's an entire *troop* of monsters, no matter how many, just prepare to be blinded by a flurry of lightning flashes because we are *not* going to run. Yep. That's all there is to it."

Although I didn't argue, Alec opened his mouth to protest. He thought better of it, however, as a dark red spot on his arm bandage started to grow bigger in size. I heard him hold back a gasp of pain and he tried to quickly cover it up with a bored yawn. I had to stop myself from rolling my eyes.

The anxious Zeus was just about to chuck his lightning bolt into the bush when out flew a toddler, clutching a miniature bow and arrow with his tiny hands. Flapping almost as rapidly as a hummingbird's, his little white wings poked out of his long Grecian tunic. With a small huff, he blew a golden curl out of his baby face and looked directly at me with his big, blue eyes. I supposed he could have taken any form, but I thought this deceitful, stereotypical, infant like one suited his trickery and immaturity quite well. As if to confirm my observation, while aiming his mischievous grin straight at me, he said brightly, in a deep voice that *so* didn't match his appearance, "Why, fancy meeting you here, Athena!"

As you can probably infer, this was not the first time I had met Eros (who is more commonly known by his Roman name, Cupid). No, the first time we ran into each other happened six years earlier, a couple of weeks after we had all found out that we were gods . . . .

Apollo, Zeus, Poseidon, and I had been playing a round of reverse hide-and-seek, and I was searching high and low for the god of the skies. I was walking near the meadow when Eros suddenly appeared out of nowhere, aiming a magic arrow straight at my heart. My eyebrows shot up in surprise and, just as Eros let the arrow fly, I dove into a nearby bush for cover. Even back then, I knew that all hell would break loose if the goddess of wisdom fell in love. As Plato once said, "Love is a serious mental disease."

Letting out a sigh of relief and ignoring the leaves that were now tangled in my hair, I bravely faced my attacker. "One of my favorite pastimes: messing with fellow gods!" Eros exclaimed as he loaded another arrow into his bow. "Love triangles can be so much fun!"

I glared at him menacingly. "Lucky for me, I'm not an easy target," I told him.

He smiled and his other arrow whizzed by my head. "That's okay. I love a challenge," he said and the chase was on. I sprinted through the trees, diving right and left as the arrows kept coming. Every couple of seconds, I would stop to catch my breath behind a tree or in the bushes as thorns scraped my skin, but Eros was quite persistent at continuing our twisted game.

This went on for a couple long minutes, until I accidentally tripped on a tree root and fell hard to my knees. Wishing I had my shield with me, I whipped my head around and held up one arm desperately, as if it would somehow stop his arrow from hitting me. I squeezed my eyes shut, but nothing happened because just then a voice from behind me shouted, "Eros, stop!"

I slowly opened one eye to see the Oracle standing next to me, glaring up at Eros with her bright green eyes. Then her body began to shake violently and mist started to build up into silver clouds around her. I had seen this spectacle once before and knew that she was about to tell a prophecy. She began:

"In six years' time will come one god's prime,

And he will be tired of being under fire.

He will fight for what he thinks is his right,

But it could tear apart the balance that's fair,

And the duty will fall upon you all

In order to save the world."

I was certain that she would stop there, like she had the first time, but no; my jaw dropped as the Oracle kept speaking. This was the part of the prophecy no one else had heard before:

"Still you must listen, for the goddess of wisdom

Will no longer be free of that blasted curse called love.

Her beloved hero is great, but he is only bait

For the man who will decide this mighty one's tragic fate."

Eros simply raised his eyebrows at me as the mist around the Oracle started to clear and then he flew away without another word. We had reached an understanding at that point; if he interfered with my love life in any way, Eros would disrupt the prophecy and possibly cause the end of the world—a risk not even he was willing to take. I never saw him again after that first day and had no desire to seek him out.

Until now, six years later, when we were fulfilling the prophecy.

Back when Alec had first arrived in the forest, he mentioned that the Oracle told him he would be needed to help us save the world. The other gods were confused because as far as they knew, he wasn't part of the prophecy. Still, I knew better, and even though I had originally contemplated sending him off on his own to be killed and thus to prevent the war, some tiny part of my conscience (which, perhaps, had even been influenced by the Fates or the Oracle herself) had gotten the better of me, to my dismay. I was trying as hard as I could just to be good friends with Alec to prevent whoever's "tragic fate" was coming and to keep Athena's loveless legacy alive. After all, it was still anyone's guess as to what would happen if one of the virgin goddesses broke a rule, since it had obviously never happened before. My pessimistic prediction was that our entire generation of gods would die or at least be stripped of our godliness somehow. In the absolute worst-case scenario, we would die and a new generation of gods would not be born at all.

Yet even considering all of the consequences, Alec still wanted something more from me and, deep inside, I knew—though I really hated to admit it to myself—there was an uncontrollable part of me that liked him a little more than a friend as well. But it didn't matter. I wouldn't let him change me.

Now Eros glanced over at Alec, a knowing smirk on the god's face. "I don't need to shoot this one. He is already truly, deeply in love. With *you*, Athena," Eros stated firmly as he turned back around in midair to face me. "You have chosen well, unsurprisingly." With one last smirk, the never-aging toddler flitted up into the treetops and out of view. I didn't have the chance to point out to him that I really hadn't had a choice in the matter at all.

"What on earth was that about?" Zeus wondered aloud, exchanging confused glances with a blushing Alec.

"Nothing," I lied, quickly deciding that if the Oracle hadn't told them about the last part of the prophecy, they didn't need to know. Plus, I had been keeping the big secret for six years already, so why stop now? They didn't need yet another thing to worry about, anyway. Even though the Oracle's prophecy wasn't clear about whose fate would actually be deadly, I was already 98 percent sure. Many years earlier, I had chosen not to reveal my theories to anyone, not even to these pages, for the certainty that my speculations were, indeed, correct would have caused even more chaos than there already was at that point. I will readily admit, however, that sometimes, carrying the great burden of knowledge alone really sucked, even if I knew it was for the best.

"Let's keep going."

Chapter 6

THE CENTAURS

When Alec, Zeus, and I reached the army camp about fifteen minutes after running into Eros, not many people were still awake, but it was past ten o'clock, after all. The few satyrs and nymphs that were milling about gave us short nods as we passed by, though they didn't say anything. Unbothered, Zeus and I slowly walked Alec into one of the large tents that was filled with cots and carefully set him down on an empty one in the corner. I did a quick scan of Alec's bandages to make sure they were clean enough for the night before turning back around to face Zeus.

Zeus yawned, stretching out his arms. "I don't know about you, but I'm way too tired to walk all the way back home. We probably wouldn't get there until almost midnight, anyway," he said, hinting at the fact that he wanted to spend the night at the camp. I nodded in agreement and he continued, "I'm going to talk to Pan real quick. I think I saw him around here somewhere . . ."

With that, Zeus excused himself and quietly walked outside, careful not to disturb any of the other sleeping soldiers. I sighed and looked back down at Alec, who was trying to hide the pain he was in with the phoniest smile I had ever seen on his handsome face. I rolled my eyes at him and murmured, "You should get some rest."

"Fine. But you're staying here for the night, right?" he clarified, his voice hopeful.

I elected not to answer his rhetorical question as my mind abruptly flashed back to Eros and the whole prophecy. It was silent in the tent for a moment as I chewed on my lip thoughtfully, running my fingers through my long, dark hair. Alec narrowed his eyes, wondering what I was thinking about, and stealthily slid his hand over mine in an effort to comfort me somehow, but I moved mine away from his and back into my lap, nervously avoiding his enchanting gaze. I knew now that trying to fight the prophecy was useless, but I also knew what terrible things the future held, and it would have been cruel to give Alec false hope of any kind. As so many Greek heroes of old proved, the Fates must always get their way.

"Back when you were down in Hades . . . you shouldn't have declared war, Alec," I whispered solemnly, closing my eyes and lowering my head.

Taking offense at my comment, Alec tensed up immediately. He frowned, tightening his grip on the edge of the cot, and argued fiercely, "Maybe you should have tried harder to stop me. Given me a sign or something like that."

I just sighed. "I should have done a lot of things. But it's too late now."

At this, Alec backed off a bit. He narrowed his eyes, studying me a little closer than before, though I only frowned at my shoes in silence. He probably sensed that I was angrier with myself than with him, and I hoped he knew that would always be the case.

Alec just gulped, scratching his head a bit guiltily. "Do you think that was the only reason the Oracle sent me the vision that led me here? To start the war?"

I bit my lip, wishing yet again that I could tell him about the second part of the prophecy. But all I could do was shake my head and tell him honestly, "I don't think what you were meant to do matters as much as what you make of the whole situation. Look at it this way: You became a hero and befriended the gods. Not much compares with that."

I must have said the right thing because the young hero smiled weakly and nudged me in the side with his elbow. I, however, simply stood up, ready to go to bed on my own cot, though his sigh, a mixture of happiness and longing, stopped me in my tracks.

As if from an outside perspective, I heard the sound of my own voice cut through the sound of snoring soldiers and ask, "Alec, why do you love me?" Even though I was pretty sure I already knew the reason, part of me must have wanted to hear it straight from him.

Alec took a deep breath and his blue eyes met my gray ones uncertainly, knowing full well that love is mostly irrational and, therefore, my question was kind of pointless. His fake smile had long since vanished, and he was no longer trying to hide the pain his arm was causing. When he still didn't say anything, I just sighed. "You know I could never give you everything you would want," I told him seriously, taking a seat on the dark green cot next to him.

"Maybe not, but you've given me everything I've ever needed. And that's all that matters," he argued, shaking his head. He watched silently as I put my head in my hands, and continued in a softer tone, "You really don't see it, do you?"

I glanced at him quizzically. "Alec," I began, but was interrupted.

"Athena, listen. Before I came to the Woods, I was just a rebel, too smart for my own good and hating everything about my life. But when I met you and the rest of the gods, I suddenly had something to live for, and life was actually pretty fun—you know, our endless rounds of reverse hide-and-seek, watching the stars from up on your roof, and even fighting monsters. Plus, I like a girl who will hit back," Alec stated, the corners of his mouth turning slightly upward. "So, I'm not going to let you sit here and feel sorry for me, yourself, or for anybody else because there's no place I would rather be."

I lay down on my own cot. "I just . . . I just wish the war could have been prevented somehow. If only we could have had more time to figure out what this is between the two of us."

Alec put his hand on my shoulder for a minute then told me brightly, "I promise we're going to win this war, Athena. But we're going to need to get some sleep first."

I smiled weakly, my mind still on the prophecy, then bid Alec goodnight. I fell asleep almost immediately on the cot between his and Zeus's, still wearing all of my armor. Strangely enough, I slept better on that old, worn-out cot in the army camp than I had in a long time on my own bed at home. Needless to say, Hades did not enter my dreams that night.

The next morning, Zeus shook me awake and I bolted upright. "What happened?" I demanded, immediately expecting the worst.

Zeus rolled his eyes. "Poseidon and Apollo just arrived. We're going to leave in a few minutes to find the centaurs," he explained as we walked out of the tent together. Since it was always pretty dark under the thick cover of trees, I had to check my watch to pinpoint the exact time, which was ten in the morning—much later than I usually woke up. Most of the nymphs, satyrs, and Knowing Warriors were already up and about, wandering around the small camp and trying to figure out their orders for the day.

Zeus and I met Poseidon, Apollo, Pan, and Alec by the giant map of the woods. They too were already dressed in their battle armor and looked ready to go. "Morning, sleepyhead," Apollo greeted me, holding out a wooden bowl full of berries. I smiled and grabbed some, realizing that the berries might be the only food I was going to get all day.

"So, what is everyone else doing while the Monster Watch is with the centaurs?" I asked no one in particular, glancing at all the little figurines of gods and mythical creatures set up at various points on the map.

"One of the other satyrs went out on a scouting trip early this morning and spotted a huge troop of undead warriors by the meadow," Pan said, pointing to a miniature undead warrior that was standing on the tiny oval meadow drawn on the map. "Alec, Ares, and Hera are going to take some of our own over there to face them a little later."

"We'll plan the rest of the day by ear," Zeus added. "Is everyone ready to go?"

Poseidon and Apollo nodded, grabbed their weapons, then followed Zeus out toward the edge of the busy camp. "I'll be right there," I shouted after them before turning to face Alec.

"What's wrong?" Alec asked me cautiously, crossing his arms.

"Nothing, really. I just want to make sure you're still prepared for anything that might happen and that you'll keep your hero vows, no matter what," I said, looking him in the eye.

Alec nodded and whispered, "Athena, I've already told you that I would give my life for you and the rest of the gods any day."

I sighed. "I know that, and thank you. But what I'm worried about is whether you would still sacrifice *others*, no matter who or how many it may be. And not just to protect the gods, but to protect the entire world before anything else, before me."

Alec gulped, glancing around the camp at the people around him that he might lose or have to sacrifice in the war. Even though he wasn't close friends with many of them and probably hated quite a few of them, it was still the hardest question to answer. I knew that possibly being considered a murderer was not on Alec's original agenda when he first met the rest of the gods and me, but I hoped he understood the gravity of what he was agreeing to.

When he finally spoke, he answered me boldly, "I made those promises when I became a hero, and I intend to keep them. I'll be honest in saying I'm slightly offended that you felt like you had to ask."

I smirked at his courage but apologized—something I didn't do very often. I suppose I cared about him a little too much, and although I knew that was very dangerous, I was never one to let fear rule my life, as you can probably tell.

"Sorry, I just had to make sure," I said, glancing down at the grass awkwardly.

We were then interrupted by Zeus's anxious call. "Athena, hurry up!" I turned my head to see him beckoning to me, twirling around a small, bright lightning bolt in his hand impatiently. A white-hot spark suddenly jumped toward the wooden recurve bow Apollo was holding and Apollo had to quickly jerk it away to keep it from being set on fire. Zeus and Poseidon just laughed at him.

"You should probably go before Zeus accidentally electrocutes someone," Alec whispered with a sigh, reluctantly bidding me farewell. "Good luck."

Noticing his forlorn look, I decided to give him one last piece of advice. "Before I go, Alec, I want you to remember something for me," I told him, and he nodded slowly. "No matter what happens, it's *always* better to die a hero than a monster. So please, don't ever let your feelings, this war, or anything else turn you into a monster. The world has plenty of those already."

Me included, I wanted to add, but didn't.

Alec smirked in an effort to lighten the mood. "How long have you been waiting to use that line? Those are pretty wise words coming from someone so young."

"I haven't felt young in many years and you know it," I reminded him, rolling my eyes. He laughed and I gave him a soft punch on the shoulder before I grabbed my silver shield and spear from under the mahogany table. "Don't die while I'm gone, all right?"

"I'll try not to," Alec promised, and then I ran to catch up with the rest of the Monster Watch without looking back.

Poseidon, Zeus, Apollo, and I stopped at the edge of the river, glancing to the right and left, looking for a good place to cross. No one in the forest had ever bothered to build a bridge since everyone was usually able to hop across on the rocks. However, due to the recent storms that Zeus had caused during the war, the water level was much higher than usual and there was no way to cross the river without the danger of slipping on a wet rock and possibly cracking our heads open.

Seemingly unfazed, Poseidon stepped out in front of us and the water slapped at his feet as he took a deep breath. Exhaling, he slammed the butt end of his golden trident onto one of the gray river stones in front of him and the water immediately parted, leaving a rocky but dry path in between the two walls of murky liquid. As soon as we stepped onto the muddy riverbank on the other side, the water splashed down behind us in a huge wave then settled slightly, continuing to flow as if nothing had disturbed it.

With a sigh, I took one last glance behind me at the camouflaged camp across the river. Alec waved at us, and then we quietly disappeared into the trees, heading northwest. I couldn't help but worry that that might be the last time I would ever see my little hero.

Let's just say it was lucky that I had a photographic memory, since it came with knowing everything. If I had let any of the bickering boys lead the way, we probably would have ended up right back where we started. However, it had been eight years since we had crossed the river and found the centaurs and even though I knew exactly where we were heading, we were still taking a while because so many new trees and mazes of foliage had grown over our old paths.

"Are you sure we're going the right way?" Apollo asked me as he lazily plucked at the tight string on his bow.

"Yes," I responded with an aggravated sigh, pushing a large branch out of my way. "This is the fifth time you've asked me that question!"

With a mischievous smile, Poseidon bounded up beside me and whispered into my ear so the others couldn't hear him taunt, "I think the *real* question is whether or not you're sure that you don't love Alec."

I whipped my head around, shooting Poseidon a quick glare with my stone cold eyes. Forcefully, I slammed my round shield with a golden picture of the head of Medusa into Poseidon's armored chest, knocking him backward into Apollo and Zeus before the lord of the sea could even begin to comprehend what was happening. "Shut up," I growled with a smirk, seeing that I had successfully wiped the wicked, arrogant grin off Poseidon's face for the time being.

But Poseidon just rolled his sea-colored eyes and continued to speak, this time so everyone could hear, "So, I've been thinking—" He never got to finish his sentence, however, because just then, the whole sleeve of his blue sweatshirt got caught on a bush full of thorns. "Ow!" he exclaimed loudly and followed up with a long string of curse words.

"Are you *trying* to attract all of the monsters within hearing range?" Zeus hissed quietly, glancing around for any sign of a mythical creature. But Poseidon didn't answer, for he was busy struggling to pick out each tiny thorn from his sleeve.

"I think we're okay. Hopefully all the monsters are at the battle by the small meadow," Apollo said. "Let's just keep going."

"Wait," I whispered, holding up one hand as I studied the bush a little more closely. Noticing the way that the thorns spiraled out from the thick center in a distinct pattern, I grinned. "This is it." Then I used my metal spear to hack at the branches, trying to clear a path for us that was free of the prickly thorns. Poseidon joined in with his shiny trident and within a few seconds, a little bit of sunlight was shining through large holes in the shrubbery.

The four of us squinted as we stepped out of the darkness under the trees and into the light of an early afternoon in centaur territory, though it was still quite cloudy. I grinned again as the brilliant purples, blues, reds, and yellows of thousands of wildflowers filled my vision, and I began to wonder why the Monster Watch had never thought to come back to the secret meadow earlier. Although our own meadow was nice, it was mostly long grass with a few scattered groups of daisies, more like a field than a garden.

I was just beginning to think that there was a major gap in the centaurs' lookout patrols when a group of five half-men, half-horses burst out into the open from across the meadow, galloping straight toward us with bows and arrows at the ready. Simultaneously, the other gods and I dropped our weapons and threw our hands into the air; we knew exactly how hostile and trigger-happy centaurs could be.

"We come in peace!" Zeus shouted loudly, assuring the centaurs that we were not their enemies. Really, they should have been able to tell who we were by the famous weapons we had been holding, if not by sensing our auras of power.

Thankfully, the centaurs slowed to a stop in front of us and did not shoot, though they did not actually lower their weapons. "Who are you and what is your reason for being here?" asked a palomino centaur with blond hair and blue eyes. I decided that he looked about thirty years old and guessed that he was the leader of the little group. But before Zeus could respond, another centaur cut in with an exasperated sigh, "I knew you four were trouble."

Surprised, the Monster Watch turned to face the speaker, a centaur with fur as dark as night and eyes as bright as the sun. I instantly recognized him as one of the centaurs we had met on our first trip to the meadow, although his pale face looked much more weathered now. The palomino centaur shot him a quizzical glance then looked back to us for an explanation.

"I am Lord Zeus," Zeus proclaimed then pointed to the rest of us in turn. "This is Lord Poseidon, Lord Apollo, and Lady Athena. We have come to you to seek assistance in the war, which I am assuming you already know about."

The palomino centaur bowed his blond head out of respect and the other four centaurs followed suit. "I offer my deepest apologies. We did not realize," he said. "I will gladly offer you any amount of help you may need, though I do not know much about this so-called war you speak of. It does, however, explain the nasty weather and the extra trouble we've been having with monsters these past couple of weeks. A few of our own have been lost, unfortunately. Call me Sunny, by the way."

"Of course, Sunny," Zeus began as we picked our weapons up off the ground. "It appears that Lord Hades is trying to take over the world, as if the Underworld isn't enough for him anymore. He is offended by our having ignored him for many years. We thought we would be able to convince him otherwise, but he is impossible to find with his helm of invisibility on and it seems as if he sends out more and more troops of undead warriors every hour. It will only be so long before they begin to raid the town or something else along those lines."

Sunny frowned. "Yes, Lord Zeus, this does sound like a crisis situation. May I inquire why you did not seek us out earlier? We could have helped to slow down the progression of this war."

I held back a snort as my eyes flicked back to the black-furred centaur. "Well, the centaurs have not been very . . . friendly, shall we say, toward us in the past. Plus, we were busy dealing with the Knowing," Zeus explained, also looking pointedly at the big centaur from our first adventure in the big meadow.

"Ah, the Knowing. Many rumors of such societies have been told throughout the ages between groups of centaurs, but I am intrigued to find out that at least some of them are true," Sunny stated diplomatically, though I could tell that he did not really care at all about the Knowing. He just kept glancing curiously back and forth between us and the black-furred centaur, probably feeling threatened by his lack of knowledge. "And by the looks on your faces, I'm assuming that you have met Anton before?"

Poseidon frowned, dusting off his golden trident, and said dryly, "If you mean did he try to kill us when we were only seven years old, then yes, we have met Anton."

Sunny gasped and glared at Anton. "What were you thinking, trying to kill the gods? You are crazier than I thought you were, old man!"

"I am not much older than you," Anton growled menacingly at Sunny, his yellow eyes flashing as he stomped a large hoof on the ground. "Plus, we did not know that they were gods and, back then, neither did they."

Sunny's mouth set in a hard line as he chose to ignore Anton's rude tone, determined to keep on topic and to appear in control of the situation. He cleared his throat and asked, stroking the short goatee on his chin, "So where is your camp? And when should we bring more soldiers?"

"Do you know where Pan's hideout is?" Zeus responded, and Sunny nodded thoughtfully. "Well, that's where most of the army is camped. Send a third of your centaurs there by nightfall. You can stay here at your camp to lead the rest of your troops into battles on this side of the river. If we need more help, we'll send Hermes to let you know."

Sunny nodded again and bowed his head one last time. "It was an honor to meet you, my gods."

"Likewise. And thanks for not trying to kill us again," Apollo replied, taking another cautious glance at Anton, who still looked angrily at Sunny.

The Monster Watch quickly waved good-bye to the group of centaurs then we crawled back through the bush full of thorns to start our treacherous return trek to the army base camp. Even though retracing our steps was much easier, the walk was still almost two hours long. No monsters had bothered us so far and I was trying to figure out whether that was a good thing or bad. I knew the fact that we hadn't run into any monsters could very well mean that our troops were greatly outnumbered at the battle by our own meadow.

When we finally reached the river, Poseidon parted the waters again and we raced to the army camp on the other side. I couldn't help but notice that there were almost no Knowing Warriors, nymphs, or satyrs around the camp, meaning that they were all fighting or injured. Beginning to worry, the three boys and I ran over to the map of the forest to move our pieces back to the army camp and to check on the position of the troops, since we hadn't heard anything over our walkie-talkies in a long time.

According to the map (and assuming it was up-to-date), Hera, Ares, and half of our troops were still battling a group of undead warriors near the small meadow, and someone had even made a new figurine to represent Alec, which was stationed at the same spot. That group had also been joined by Demeter and Aphrodite. Meanwhile, Artemis, Pan, Dionysus, and a few of Artemis's huntress nymphs were busy battling the Hydra, a ferocious monster with multiple heads, farther down the river and south of the army camp. The map had Hephaestus stationed in the town, hopefully making more weapons, and in theory Hestia was right here at the camp.

Sure enough, Hestia walked out of one of the large tents a minute later and smiled. "Hey, you're back!" she exclaimed in that soft voice of hers. "How did it go with the centaurs?"

"Fine," Zeus replied with a sigh. "A third of them are being sent over here later tonight. What have you been up to?"

Hestia combed her fingers through her long, light brown hair. "Oh, not much," she answered, gesturing to the tent she had just come out of. "I've been helping out in the infirmary. Luckily, there haven't been too many serious injuries or deaths, but I should probably be heading home soon."

"Same here," Apollo agreed with a yawn. "I'll walk with you." With that, they collected their things and strode out of camp together, heading east toward Main Street while Zeus, Poseidon, and I watched them slowly disappear into the trees.

Not five minutes later, Artemis called in over the walkie-talkie to inform everyone listening that she and Dionysus had killed the Hydra and were heading back to their houses while Pan and the huntress nymphs were coming back to the camp. Soon after, Hera, Ares, Demeter, Alec, and Aphrodite also agreed to retreat for the night, since their battle had pretty much reached a stalemate, for better or for worse.

"Are you two ready to go home?" Zeus asked, and Poseidon and I shrugged, not caring one way or the other. "All right then, let's go," Zeus continued, deciding for us. "I'm starved."

A few minutes later, we were on our way home, keeping as quiet as we possibly could to avoid running into any sort of monsters. We had walked well over seven miles that day and our feet were screaming in pain. We had only been walking for fifteen minutes when my shoelace caught on a bush, as if demanding I stop for just a few moments, and I just barely avoided falling on my face.

"I'll catch up with you guys," I groaned, waving at Zeus and Poseidon to carry on without me. They nodded quietly and disappeared into the bushes. Sighing, I stood back up after retying my shoelace and was about to start running after the two boys when I heard a high-pitched evil laugh coming from somewhere off to my left. Without the slightest hesitation, I raced to where I thought the sound was coming from, ignoring the low-hanging branches that slapped my face and the pain of my tired feet. I was so focused that I didn't even bother to call Zeus and Poseidon for help.

I burst into a small clearing just in time to see none other than Alec dive into a bush and out of the range of a giant, green snake tail that was aiming to knock him down. My eyes slowly followed the tip of the snake tail all the way up to the point where the opalescent scales faded away into the pale-skinned torso of Echidna, the half-nymph, half-serpent "Mother of all Monsters." Her long, dark hair flowed elegantly over her shoulders as she spun her head around and her beady, black eyes settled on me. "What do we have here?" she hissed under her breath.

Hearing Echidna's comment, Alec chose that moment to poke his head out of the bush, his dark hair now covered in dead leaves and cobwebs. "Hey, Athena, what's up?"

"Not much. How are you doing?" I responded, trying to appear equally calm. We did, in fact, have a slight advantage over Echidna, since her long, heavy tail made it difficult to maneuver around the dense trees and brush, and by the look on his face, I was certain Alec realized that as well. After all, every capable fighter knows that sometimes an environment itself can be used as a dangerous weapon.

Alec smirked, twirling his sword around in one hand but still keeping his bright blue eyes on me, and replied, "I'm okay. You know, just fighting a monster."

Only a few feet away, Echidna looked momentarily confused as she glanced back and forth between Alec and me, wondering why we were almost completely ignoring a frightful creature like her. The frown on her face told me that she was quite offended, but then she shook her pretty little head, refocusing on trying to kill us quickly and efficiently. I had to bite back a laugh when the beautiful monster lunged at Alec. She had twisted her tail around a tree without even realizing it and was forced to pause her attack to extricate herself. Alec easily rolled out of the way, not even bothering to try to strike back yet.

I smiled as I nonchalantly leaned back against the rough bark of a tree trunk to watch the scene play out in front of me, waiting for my turn to take a whack at the beast. Meanwhile, Echidna lunged at Alec again and, again, Alec jumped out of the way. Glaring with rage, Echidna then swung her fifteen-feet-long tail in the opposite direction, hoping to catch Alec off guard and knock him down. Unfortunately for the monster, Alec, still smirking, just leaped over her tail as if it were a jump rope, which only enraged Echidna even further.

With a cry of anger and frustration, Echidna whirled around, this time slithering swiftly after me, and I had to jump over her gigantic tail like Alec to get out of her way. I heard the monster let out a hiss from behind me and instinctively somersaulted forward so that she couldn't squeeze me to death in the thick coil of her tail. I stood up quickly and gave Alec a high five, ready for more. Our little game of teasing Echidna continued for another couple of minutes until she opened her mouth to call for help from other monsters.

"On three?" Alec suggested, deciding it was about time that we stopped toying around with her, and I nodded wordlessly. "One, two, three!" And we took off toward the monster, Alec to the left and me to the right. Before Echidna even had time to think about which way to turn, Alec had launched himself into the air and was flying over her serpent half, a confident gleam in his eyes. Echidna only let out a bloodcurdling wail as the sharp, inward-curving blade of Alec's *kopis* sword sliced cleanly through the end of her tail.

The monster continued to try to trap Alec in her strong tail, but now off-balance, Echidna had to lean against a decomposing log to keep herself from falling forward, leaving a gaping hole in her defense. The half-nymph, half-serpent spun her head around to get a better look at the damage and started to whimper as her golden-green monster blood gushed out of the open wound. Finally choosing to put Echidna out of her misery, I took a deep breath before hurling my spear at her and, with a sickening thud, it sank deep into her heart, just below her brassiere made of leaves and grass. A thin stream of blood had just started to trail down her flat stomach when Echidna, as well as the severed piece of her tail that lay a few paces away, crumbled to dust.

Letting out a small sigh of relief, I walked over to the log and retrieved my short spear, wiping off Echidna's sticky blood on the lush, green grass. "Nice job," I told Alec with a nod of approval.

"You too," he replied, walking over to join me.

Suddenly, we heard a rustle in the bushes from behind us, and both Alec and I whirled around to face the sound, weapons raised and at the ready once again. But it was lucky that I didn't release my spear right away, because it was just Zeus and Poseidon. "Is everything all right?" Zeus asked, panting. "We heard a scream."

Alec chuckled as his sword abruptly changed back into its rock form and he stuffed it into his pocket. "Yeah, you heard the scream of Echidna. We're all good now."

"Well, that's a relief," Poseidon huffed, "but it means we just ran all the way back here for no reason!"

Alec grinned, adrenalized. "You're always welcome to hunt down some more monsters. I know I'd be down for more."

I couldn't tell if that was supposed to be a joke or not, so I turned to face him, taking the chance to study the young hero more closely. Overall, Alec looked good—well, no worse than he did the night before. I could see no new major wounds on his body, although he was still wearing all of his armor so it was hard to be sure. Nevertheless, I sighed and out of concern told him quietly, "Alec, don't follow me home tonight, okay?" He needed to take a break from being so imperiously brave, from being so much like us gods.

Alec just stared at me, slightly confused. "Why not? Is Cole going to be there?" he growled in a low voice.

"No, of course not," I answered quickly, readjusting my ponytail that had been messed up in the fight with Echidna. "It's just that you need to get some rest and I don't want you walking all the way back to camp from my house alone after what happened last night. We need you to be strong enough to help lead the battles."

Alec sighed, running his fingers through his dark hair in deep thought. Then he took a step closer to me and with one eyebrow arched, he whispered suggestively, "What if I can't fall asleep?"

I smirked. "You're smart; I'm sure you'll think of something. Now, you're less than fifteen minutes away from camp. Do you think it's at all possible for you to make it back *without* running into a monster?" Alec laughed, and it was difficult not to join in. "I'm serious. This path you're on is reckless," I said as I looked into his deep blue eyes, suddenly not sure which path I was really talking about—the physical or metaphorical one.

Alec must have caught on to what I was thinking, though, because he whispered back mysteriously, "So is yours." Without another word, he waved good-bye and sprinted off toward the army camp hidden in the trees.

Once we'd gotten word over our walkie-talkies that Alec had, in fact, arrived safely at the camp, Zeus, Poseidon, and I changed our course, now heading southwest for our own houses because it was almost dinnertime. Just over half an hour later, we had reached the edge of the forest. Carefully, the two brothers and I took all of our armor off and hid the pieces in trees so no one would find them. As soon as we stepped outside of the forest, we were abruptly forced back into the reality of our human lives when the headlights of my father's old pickup truck, which was driving toward us, lit up the darkness, illuminating our faces.

"Do you want to come over to our house for a while?" Zach offered in a low voice, in English.

I just shrugged as my drunken father slammed the door of his truck and headed into the house without even giving the three of us a second glance; he was too busy trying to walk in a straight line. I silently thanked the Fates that my idiot father hadn't gotten in an accident while driving intoxicated, but all of a sudden, I realized he probably had a lot of practice and it had never even crossed my mind before. I made a mental note to confront him about that later when he was at least slightly more stable.

"Hey, what if we just stayed in the forest?" I wondered aloud, wishfully staring off into the distance.

Luke glanced at me with a confused look on his face, his brow furrowed. "What do you mean? We can't just leave our families."

"No, I mean during the war. You know as well as I do that Hades will probably be carrying out some surprise attacks at night in the near future and we should be there to support the troops, especially since the other gods wouldn't be able to. They still have to sneak out into the woods and lie to their parents, remember?" I explained slowly, getting more and more excited about the idea by the second. "It's also a good way to smuggle better food to the troops, so they won't have to eat berries and deer all the time."

"I see where you're coming from," Zach started, running his fingers through his dirty blond hair. "But what do you suppose we're going to tell our parents? And do you think they will actually let us go? Even if they don't really show it, they aren't very happy that we go into the forest all the time. Especially your mom."

"Easy," I replied with a shrug. "We'll go camping. It's not really a lie. We'd be staying in tents anyway and my dad will probably let me go without a second thought, drunk or not. He always has. I just won't tell my mom."

Zach sighed. "All right, but tell us if your dad says yes or no and then we'll ask our parents."

I nodded and the three of us were about to walk across the street when a voice called out to us from farther down the dark, quiet road. "Hey, stop! Ashley, is that you?" came the befuddled voice of Cole. I only exchanged irked glances with Zach and Luke, knowing the fact that Cole had sought me out this late in the day could not mean good things. Plus, after an entire day of negotiating with centaurs and running around the forest, none of us were really in the mood to converse politely with him.

"I swear," Luke began in a low voice, shaking his head, "if a monster doesn't kill Cole by the end of this war for being just plain nosy and annoying, I will." Zach and I just laughed, ready to get our conversation with Cole over with.

Chapter 7

HE KNOWS

S o, um, where have you been all day?" Cole asked me, ruffling his caramel-colored hair nervously.

His question alone made me want to walk away from him right then. First of all, we had just walked out of the forest so wasn't it obvious where I had been? And second of all, Cole had absolutely no reason to know exactly where I was at every second of the day. I belonged to no one.

"Well, we were in the forest. Where else would we be?" Luke shot back at him harshly, his blue eyes flashing, and like Zach, I held back a snicker.

Cole cleared his throat awkwardly, sensing the tension between all of us. He sighed and started, "All day? Oh, right, I guess I should've known . . ." His voice trailed off, and he nervously stuffed his hands into the pockets of his gray sweatpants before he continued, "I just wanted to see what's been going on, I guess."

"Cole, get to the point," I said softly. "We don't have all night." As if to prove my point, a loud crash sounded from inside my dimly lighted house, followed by angry voices yelling. Cole glanced worriedly between Zach and Luke so I knew there was something he didn't want to say in front of them. Unfortunately for Cole, I wasn't in the mood to stick around after the brothers left. Rapidly tiring of his presence, I told him bluntly, "If there's nothing else, we'll be leaving now."

"I—I just wanted to see if you wanted to do something with me tomorrow," Cole finally sputtered, and Luke, Zach, and I raised our eyebrows. "And I had something . . . but never mind. I left it at home."

I frowned, wondering what Cole could possibly want to give me and why. Plus, he had just lied right to our faces; I could tell that whatever he wanted to give me was in his left pocket, which he kept fingering unconsciously. I suspected that it was some kind of jewelry or other keepsake. Gross.

"We're going camping tomorrow," I said flatly, crossing my arms. "For a few days actually, just as an end of summer celebration." Zach and Luke quickly nodded in agreement.

"In the forest?" Cole exclaimed, his brown eyes widening. "Have you guys ever camped in there before? Isn't it going to be dangerous?"

Unable to control themselves, Zach and Luke burst out laughing. After all, danger was no stranger to us; we had faced that wily beast every day since the first time we had gone into the woods. In fact, you could say that we were close friends.

"Dude, that's kind of the point," Luke snapped. "Learn to live a little."

"Okay . . ." Cole scratched his head then glanced back at me. "Well, I guess I'll go now. Ash, can you meet me in front of the Fire Pit tomorrow?"

"Sure," I answered him and nodded slowly, noticing Zach and Luke exchange mischievous glances. I knew that they would beg their mother to listen in on the conversation the next morning, since they weren't going to be there. Realizing it was best for him to leave now, Cole waved good-bye as he headed east down the dark road, his footsteps echoing off the pavement, while the two brothers walked with me across the street toward our own houses.

"When did Cole get so annoying?" I muttered, more to myself than to Zach and Luke.

"When we found out we were gods," Luke replied with a snort.

Zach sighed. "Don't be so hard on him, Ash." Both Luke and I quickly looked to him for further explanation, mild shock on our faces. I raised one eyebrow at Zach and he continued, "Cole has some guts, asking you out. You can be quite intimidating, you know—sometimes even menacing. But then again, we all are. We can't blame the kid for being curious when we leave him out of the group so often." He then lovingly patted my shoulder and disappeared with Luke into their cozy house, leaving me to quietly ponder what he had said as I stepped onto my creaking front porch.

As soon as I walked through my front door, my mother was in my face and annoying me, as usual. But this time she wore a smirk that somehow did not suit her pale face and it made me wonder what she could have possibly been up to. I hadn't seen her appear so excited in years, and it was strange seeing her this way. Smoothing out her blue apron covered with flour, she said smugly, "I heard that you've been spending time with Cole lately."

I groaned, covering my face with my hands because I knew exactly what she was thinking—that I was going to end up marrying Cole. In a town as small as the Woods, it was assumed that each child would settle down right where he or she grew up and marry a classmate or someone else from one of the neighboring towns. Much more often than not, people really did marry their high school sweethearts. Unsurprisingly, parents would sometimes gossip about who they thought would end up together, like Zach and Alicia, even though they were well known as an on-again, off-again couple. But boy, people would be really surprised when the beautiful, conceited Becca ended up marrying the crippled, humble Shane. Gods have to follow the myths, after all.

"Come on, sweetie, give me the details," my mom encouraged, a hopeful look in her brown eyes. Perhaps she was happy because I was actually acting like a normal teenage girl for once, like the daughter she had always wanted.

"Mom, there's nothing going on between Cole and me," I informed her as I tried to take a step past her, but she blocked my way, her thin eyebrows arched. I held my tongue as I shot a glare toward my father, who was leaning on the kitchen counter with a beer bottle in his hand. Going on a date just to make my mom happy had more consequences than he thought.

My mother sighed, giving me one last disapproving look as I pushed my way past her and headed up the old staircase. Within a few seconds after I had left the room, my parents resumed their shouting match. Rubbing my forehead to try to get rid of a headache, I walked slowly down the empty hallway toward my bedroom door and tried to ignore the loud creaking of the floorboards under my feet.

Wait a minute, I thought to myself suddenly, looking down at my black army boots. I had lived in that house my entire life and had been sneaking around enough to know every inch of the creaking floor. So unless it was a new development, the small area of the floor I was standing on should not have been creaking—and I was 99.99% sure that it wasn't a new development.

I cannot believe this is happening.

Acting purely on instinct, I dropped to the floor just as a flower vase flew out of nowhere, aiming straight for where my head had been not a second earlier.

Damn him.

The glass shattered into hundreds of tiny pieces at it crashed against the white wall behind me, and the water and colorful flowers fell softly to the carpet as I rolled forward, sliding the pocketknife out of my pocket. I was vaguely aware of the fact that my parents were still yelling at each other and, with any luck, hadn't heard the commotion. With a low grunt, I swiftly hurled the knife at my bedroom door, which had mysteriously swung open on its own. The shiny blade shouldn't have been large enough to kill him, but just in case, I'd aimed low so it stuck about halfway down the door with a loud thunk. The knife had just barely scraped by the target, but I smirked when I saw what I was really looking for: a few drops of golden blood sinking into the navy blue carpet.

I stood up and pressed my back against the smooth, cool wall next to my bedroom door, waiting for the perfect moment to barge in without getting myself injured or even killed. I did realize that my walkie-talkie was still attached to my hip, but even if I had called the other gods for help, I knew they probably wouldn't get there in time; I was on my own.

"In case you don't already know, I should inform you that in the unfortunate event of one of our deaths, the situation is going to be quite tricky. 'All for one and one for all,' to quote *The Three Musketeers*," I mused in Greek, just barely loud enough for him to hear. After all, I couldn't be sure of how long I had until either of my parents came stomping upstairs.

The response started with a quiet yet devilish snicker. "Of course I know about that, so I wasn't trying to *kill* you—merely injure you seriously. I'm offended that you question the extent of my knowledge, Lady Athena," the gravelly voice floated its way to my ears and I rolled my eyes.

"Well, you're obviously stupid enough to trespass into the house of a war goddess," I retorted, reaching back into my pocket to pull out my rock. It was lucky that I hadn't left it at the army camp like I had originally planned, since we still needed more weapons for our soldiers. Trying to decide on the best way to use it to my advantage, I quietly rolled the small, gray stone around in the palm of my hand.

Then the creepy voice came again, jeering at me, "So far, I almost knocked you out with a vase and you gave me a measly scratch on my side. Plus, I'm invisible at the moment. Now, great goddess of wisdom and war, who do you think is *really* in control here? It's not a trick question." I simply raised my eyebrows; this moment of cockiness was exactly what I was waiting for.

In seconds flat, I jumped into the seemingly empty room before abruptly chucking the rock toward the other side, and my efforts were rewarded with the loud clank of the rock hitting metal—the metal of Hades's one and only helmet of invisibility. Without waiting another moment, I lunged in the direction where the sound had come from, where the rock had fallen to the floor, and tackled the invisible body before he could get away. For once, I was lucky that my room was small enough so that it was relatively hard to move around comfortably.

Promptly, a bronze helmet appeared out of thin air, sliding off the head of the now visible Hades, his black hair drenched in cold sweat. The lord of the dead's dark eyes enlarged, but before he could try to fight back, I had him pinned to the floor with his arms over his head and one of my knees putting pressure on his most sensitive area. "Who's in control now?" I sneered at him menacingly.

Hades gulped as he struggled against my grasp, trying unsuccessfully to escape. "An entire troop of undead warriors could be here within a few minutes. They're just waiting for my call," he threatened meekly, forcing himself not to show his panic.

I only tightened my grip on his arms, ignoring his comment. "You came here for a reason, Lord Hades, and I doubt you stalk the other gods like this. What is it?"

Hades was silent for a moment as he studied my face. "I needed to tell all the gods something. And let's face it; Zeus would have just called you for advice anyway. In fact, you would make a much better ruler than your father. I don't know why you've never done anything about it," he whispered, and I could clearly see the hunger for power swirling around in his eyes. I couldn't believe he was actually trying to get me to betray my friends and come over to his side of the war, to overthrow Zeus. But I had mentioned to the other gods that we needed someone to talk to Hades with whom he could relate, and maybe *I* was that person . . . .

I cleared my throat. "Unlike you, I am satisfied with what I have. You should be too. Everyone has a place in this universe and yours happens to be in the Underworld, as the freaking ruler of all things. How many more people and other beings must be killed in battle for you to realize this? Millions of people around the world have a life way worse than yours."

Hades smirked, his pale face lighting up. "If everyone has a place in the world, where does Alec belong? In the forest with a large price on his head . . . or maybe in your heart? I often wonder which is safer."

My eyes instantly widened with shock at what he was saying, and he continued with an overconfident gleam in his eyes, "That's right, I know about the prophecy. The *entire* prophecy, actually. You see, that's the *real* reason I've been coming here, since the look on your face confirms that no one else knows about the last bit."

"How did you find out?"

"I've had the helm for months now, remember? And I've been using it to its *fullest* extent. You assume I've been watching the gods, and I have, a bit, especially when you and Zeus are together. He treats you so well compared to all the other divine ladies, and I thought I could learn from him how to treat Persephone. Obviously, it didn't work out as planned. But what did turn out in my favor was that, often while you all gallivanted to your hearts' content in the forest, I came into town to visit what I've missed. It's *so* wonderful people never lock their doors around here. Your journals really are great reads and very insightful too." He grinned with devilish pride at my horror.

"You can pretend you belong in this realm all you want, but you never will. Just like you'll never win this war. We gods and, yes, Alec, will make sure of it."

"If Alec even lives long enough to see the end of the war, you mean," Hades corrected pompously.

His pupils dilated as he winced and groaned softly when I chose that moment to put even more pressure on his delicate lower extremities. I glared at him and spat, "If you kill Alec, I *swear* that I will personally chop off both of your arms and let you live in pain for the rest of your pathetic life."

Seemingly unfazed, Hades only raised his bushy, black eyebrows and smirked again before he whispered hoarsely, "Alec's a hero. I'm sure he can handle the pain. After all, you trained him, right? You know as well as I do that you put too much of yourself into him. You trained him to fight exactly like you, to concentrate so hard that you almost lose yourself in the battle. Both of you will try to forget everything and everyone else in the moment just to be able to fight smarter, on better instincts and without a weakness. But unfortunately, no matter what you do, your so-called perfect little hero will always have one weakness that makes him beatable."

I squeezed my eyes shut for a moment, hoping that Hades wouldn't continue. I knew what was coming, and he really didn't need to say it. Moreover, I didn't *want* him to say it, to confirm yet again that fulfilling the tragic prophecy was inevitable, but of course, he did anyway:

"His weakness is *you*, sweetie. He's got a fatal flaw just like the rest of your heroes of old. Get ready for another Greek tragedy."

I bit my lip and glared at him, struggling to refrain from punching him in the face when he used my mother's horrid nickname for me. He knew exactly what to say and do to set me off—probably from spying on me for countless nights under the cloak of darkness—but I couldn't let him have the satisfaction. Instead, I settled for watching him squirm like a bug under my frigid gaze, leaving him in a panic as he wondered what in the world I was going to do next. A word of advice: sometimes silence speaks louder than words.

After a few seconds of this eerie quietness, Hades opened his mouth to say something, but was cut off when we heard the sound of soft footsteps coming toward us. "Ashley? What on earth happened to this vase?" my human mother exclaimed in a shrill voice, and her footsteps continued to get closer and closer as Hades managed to writhe his way out of my grasp. I knew that if she recognized him as the "Goth" boy who had bought the helmet from her antique shop, I would get in a huge load of trouble for being with him (especially alone in my room), but I also knew that I didn't have enough time to tie Hades up and hide him in the tiny closet. Even if I was forced to let him go, however, I had to get that invisibility helmet. Without it, Hades had almost no chance of winning the war.

I desperately lunged for the helm at the same time as Hades, but he had a slight head start and grabbed it before me, beginning to stand up. In a last-ditch effort, I karate chopped the back of his left knee, making it collapse, and he fell back down immediately, though the bronze helmet was still in his rough hands. I stretched as far as I could to try to touch it, to save it, but Hades slammed the bronze helm back onto his head and became invisible once again. I let out a small cry of frustration as my fingernails dug into his cheek and raked through the velvety skin, but then he was out of my reach. The door to my balcony was thrown open by the lord of the Underworld at almost the exact same moment my mother walked into the room to see me sprawled out on the carpet, defeated. Hades and the helm of invisibility, the scent of victory, were gone with the wind that now blew through my room.

At least I gave him some scars, I thought bitterly.

"What's going on, sweetie?" my mother asked me in a worried voice, glancing down at me quizzically with her brown eyes. "Get off of the floor this instant. And why is your knife stuck in the door? I knew I never should have given it to you . . ."

With my head in my hands, I groaned in annoyance, wishing she would leave me alone. The rest of the gods needed to be informed of what had happened, and Alec needed to know that Hades was out to get him. I just needed a break. My Greek life was finally starting to clash with my regular human one and I wanted some time alone to collect my thoughts.

I stood up slowly, not meeting her eyes. "Nothing happened, Mom," I told her quietly, switching back to English. "I accidentally dropped the vase when I was filling it with more water. I'll clean it up in a minute."

My mother frowned then wordlessly turned on her heel and left the room. Angrily, I walked over to my bed and picked up my pillow. I glared at it one last time before abruptly stuffing my face into it and letting out a frustrated scream. *I shouldn't have let Hades get away. This is my fault,* I kept telling myself as I threw down the pillow and stormed into my small bathroom.

But you didn't have a choice, another part of me argued as I turned on the water in my sink and started forcefully scrubbing under my nails with soap to try to rid myself of the dirty remnants of Hades's cheek skin. I had almost rubbed my skin completely raw before I realized what I was doing.

After I dried my hands with a soft towel, I yanked the walkie-talkie off the belt loop on my hip. "This is Athena calling in an emergency situation," I reported loudly in Greek, deciding it was about time that I informed everyone about what had happened. "Hades has been spotted in town. Repeat: Hades has been spotted in town. He knows what happens when we die and I think he's going back to the Underworld now, but, Alec, he's out to get you. Don't go anywhere alone."

Almost immediately, the walkie-talkie exploded with a dozen voices at the same time until one was finally able to be heard above the others. It was strangely calm but full of concern at the same time and I knew it had to be Alec. "Athena, please. Tell me what happened. Was he in your house?"

I frowned, deciding whether or not they should know the whole truth. "Yes," I answered vaguely after a moment of stiff silence. "My mother walked in and he got away clean."

"But are you okay?" Alec asked softly.

We lapsed into a short state of silence again as the others waited for my reply. "No," I said wrathfully, shaking my head. "Don't you see? I let him get away. And I could've stolen the helm, but I didn't. He got away. That's all there is to it."

I shut off the walkie-talkie and threw it onto my bed, not in the mood to talk to anyone anymore. Sighing, I bent down to pick up my rock/sword and pulled my knife out of the door before stuffing them into my pocket just in case someone or something else tried to attack me. Then I slowly made my way down the hallway to clean up the mess Hades had made, silently cursing myself.

———————————

As expected, the night was long and sleepless, my thoughts revolving around the war and Hades. Thankfully, the other gods and Alec had enough sense not to come over to try to talk to me; most likely, I would have snapped and just yelled at them to leave me alone. But with a new day came a slightly less pessimistic attitude, so I threw on my leather jacket, grabbed my weapons and walkie-talkie, and was out of the door in a matter of minutes. My parents weren't even awake yet.

I quietly shut the door behind me and started walking through the thick fog toward Main Street, where I had promised I would meet Cole. Sure enough, he was already waiting for me right outside the Fire Pit at one of the small, green tables set for two. But as much as I would have loved a cool glass of lemonade in the morning, I was not in the mood to spend a lot of time with Cole. After all, I had a war to fight and there were less than three weeks until school started.

"Am I late?" I asked, checking my watch.

"No, I'm just early," Cole replied as he stood up and pulled the chair out for me. I thanked him and sat down awkwardly, waiting for him to explain why he had invited me here. Instead, he just made small talk and asked, "So, the rest of the Monster Watch isn't awake yet?"

I shook my head. "Well, Connor probably is, but you asked me to meet you here, so . . ." My voice trailed off, expecting Cole to pick up on what I was saying and continue, but he didn't. (Are most Sightless boys this clueless?)

"Do you have trouble getting to the point or something? You did ask me to meet you here for a reason, right?" I asked him, one eyebrow arched.

"Oh, yeah," Cole mumbled with a soft chuckle, making me crack a smile involuntarily. "Well, if you're not in a hurry, I was wondering if you wanted to have breakfast with me."

I was then vaguely reminded of a time when we were on the same page in life, when we were better friends. I remembered when I had so badly wished he were a god, but I realized now that Cole never had the guts for the job; he'd really made his final choice six years earlier when he decided not to hide from the cops in the forest with Josh and the rest of the Monster Watch. Being a goddess had given me so much that I loved, like freedom and independence, but it took away an equal amount of childhood and simplicity. To me, a breakfast meeting with an old friend was now almost meaningless—just an act to cover up my many secrets.

I gulped, checking my watch again, and lied, "Actually, I have to go in a few minutes."

Cole nodded. "Thanks for meeting me here, Ashley. Oh, here's what I wanted to give you last night." He reached slowly into his pocket and pulled out a necklace—a simple, silver chain with a golden leaf. "For the queen of the forest," he said softly as he handed the piece of jewelry to me. With a small smile, I took it from him, refraining from pointing out that, rather regrettably, Hera was the real queen, not Athena. I then waved good-bye, and Cole watched me as I strode away without another word, still clutching the necklace in my hand.

I had just rounded the corner onto Maple Street, heading back to my house when a flash of movement at the edge of the forest caught my eye. I turned around slowly, half expecting to see Hades. Instead, my eyes rested on Alec, who was leaning against a tree trunk with his arms crossed, his dark hair somehow tousled perfectly by the strong winds. (Not to mention the fact that he wasn't wearing armor. What an idiot.) His piercing blue eyes locked onto me, mixtures of emotions swirling around in them like storm clouds, but he also wore a frown, a clear sign that he was not the least bit amused by my actions the previous night.

Yes, I knew this was not the lost, confused boy who had first shown up in the Woods hesitant to look a god in the eye; this was a true hero, not afraid to die the most painful death or stand up to the most powerful gods. He had absorbed everything we gods had ever told him and more—our attitude, our way of life, et cetera. Even his appearance made him seem more like a god— perhaps *too* much like a god—as he had obviously learned how to use stature to his advantage and had gained quite a bit of muscle mass during our long, strenuous battle practices in the middle of the night. And by showing up here on the street, in daylight, he just proved that he was no longer afraid of being seen for who he was, of being challenged by people either much stronger or much more human than him, which might have been the most dangerous thing about him.

Therefore, I simply stared at him, patiently waiting for him to make the first move. Taking a few bold steps toward me, he cleared his throat and said quietly yet firmly in Greek, "You must enjoy scaring people. Because I can't think of any other reason why you would break protocol and shut off your walkie-talkie in the middle of an emergency."

I shrugged. "I needed to think," I said bluntly, also in Greek.

"We all know better than to disrupt your thoughts, Athena, but we still worry about you." Alec paused, taking a deep breath before admitting, "I guess . . . well, I would've liked to hear something from you before you went to bed. Just to make sure you were okay."

I sighed glumly, finally breaking eye contact and glancing down the empty road into the silvery mist, the wind whipping my long hair around wildly. "It wasn't your fault that Hades got away," Alec continued, and my frown deepened. "I know you so I know that you would have done everything in your power to try to stop him. Please, don't beat yourself up about this."

We lapsed into silence and Alec took another few steps toward me, now standing mere inches away. "But I could've ended this war, Alec, or at least gotten us a whole lot closer," I whispered to him bitterly, biting down on my lower lip. I couldn't help but worry that I'd already fallen and that I was bringing my friends down with me.

"It is what it is," he argued, shaking his head. "Hades and I started this war, not you. We just have to hope he knows that he would be stupid to ignore the goddess of wisdom's warnings."

I just closed my eyes, letting this thought sink in for a moment as Alec calmly reached toward me to tuck a stray piece of hair behind my ear. I could have sworn that his touch sent sparks shooting through me, and I tried not to shudder as a whole slew of different emotions—both good and bad—washed over me all at once. "Are you okay now?" he asked softly, carefully lifting my chin to his level.

I opened my eyes immediately, my heart racing like a cheetah. "I won't be okay if you kiss me. I swear I'll punch you in the face," I warned him seriously, ignoring his question.

"That's my girl." Alec smiled fondly before he leaned in even closer, cupping my face in his warm hands and told me, "But unfortunately for you, I don't care too much about being punched."

"Alec!" I hissed at him nervously, placing a hand on his chest so he couldn't get any closer than he already was. However, he glanced down at my hand with one eyebrow raised suggestively so I quickly removed it, my face burning with embarrassment. I gave him a soft slap on the cheek before ordering hoarsely, "Pull yourself together."

"That was one hard punch," Alec joked.

I glared at him, feeling the bright pink color finally start to fade from my cheeks. "Whatever. Now, are you going to tell me why you aren't wearing your armor? And did you come all the way here alone again? We've had this conversation before . . . ."

Alec sighed and explained, "Well, thanks to your cryptic message last night, Pan was freaking out and made me sleep in my armor with five Knowing Warriors surrounding me at all times. When I decided I needed to talk to you about it this morning, they followed me here, but I sent them back to the camp a few minutes ago. My armor is hidden in a log at the moment, since I was tired of wearing it." He paused and lazily gestured to the lush, green forest behind him. Then he patted a round lump in his pocket and said, "But don't worry. I have my sword right here. I haven't run into any monsters today, though."

I rolled my eyes. "I hope you're not expecting to be lucky all day. Because you'll be severely disappointed."

Alec gave me a small smirk, but then his face fell when he caught sight of the sparkling necklace still in my hand. He reached for it in what seemed like slow motion and I willingly dropped it in his hand, not wanting to hide anything more from him. Alec just narrowed his eyes as he fingered the golden leaf, trying his best not to show any emotion, though I knew he was upset. "Cole gave this to you?"

I nodded quickly and explained, "I was going to throw it away as soon as I got home. I swear." As soon as I said that, however, I regretted it. What Alec thought about Cole should have been no concern of mine and throwing away a gift out of frustration was a childish thing to do.

"I believe you," Alec stated glumly, running his fingers through his hair, "but how long do you have to keep pretending for him? I know you were doing this for your mom, but I don't see the point anymore." He sighed, looking into my eyes sadly.

"I know. I never wanted it to be like this with Cole. I was going to talk to Zeus and Aphrodite about it today, actually. When Hades showed up last night, he said some things that make me think he's been spying on me for a while, so I'm probably just putting Cole in danger," I said, and he nodded in understanding as he passed the necklace back to me.

Distracted, I paused for a minute and glanced down the road toward my quiet house. The thick fog was finally starting to clear, though it was still very cloudy and I could see that my gray home was sitting empty, with no cars left in the short driveway. Remembering what I had originally been on my way to do, I lightened the mood and asked, "Hey, want to come help me collect some food for the troops?" Alec nodded again eagerly and the two of us silently jogged up the street together.

Alas, that decision would prove to be a big mistake.

Chapter 8

FIRE AWAY

Alec and I bounded up the porch steps together and threw open the screen door, racing inside my house without a second thought. We passed by the living room and turned the sharp corner into the kitchen, but then in complete shock, I stopped dead in my tracks and Alec almost smacked right into me. Our jaws immediately dropped to the floor. *Oops*, I thought helplessly as I gulped and exchanged horrified glances with the wide-eyed Alec. At that moment, I would have rather come face-to-face with an undead warrior. Or five.

"Well, aren't you going to say hello?" my father asked gruffly, raising his bushy eyebrows at Alec and me.

To be fair, Alec still had a white bandage loosely wrapped around his left forearm from two nights earlier (not to mention the various other scars we shared), so we probably looked pretty suspicious. Therefore, my father took his time studying Alec very closely as he took a long sip of beer from the near-empty bottle. That's right; if you thought lemonade in the morning was weird, try beer—no, wait. Whatever you do, *don't* try beer.

"Oh, hi, Dad. I didn't expect to see you here. We're just going to go now." I started backing out of the room slowly, but Alec was frozen in place, still staring blankly at the beer bottle in my father's hand. When I forcefully elbowed him in the gut, Alec mumbled some profanities under his breath before following my lead, turning around to race out of the front door just as quickly as we had come in.

"Wait," my father ordered firmly. I just sighed, exchanging worried glances with Alec as he and I reluctantly backed up into the kitchen again. "Ashley, do you want to tell me who this is?" With his free hand, my grumpy dad gestured to Alec, who then looked at me, unsure of what to do next.

"No, not particularly," I responded truthfully, crossing my arms over my chest. My dad sighed. Not at all surprised by my defiance, Alec lowered his head and hid a smirk.

"So where's your car? It wasn't in the driveway," I changed the subject suddenly, wondering what my father was still doing at the house. He did have a job, after all.

"My car is in the shop. Now, let's try this again. Tell me who this boy is or you're grounded for the rest of summer."

Well, that gave me absolutely no choice at all.

"This is Alec," I started slowly, and my father looked at me expectantly, waiting for further explanation. To be honest, I had never brought anyone home with me besides the boys of the Monster Watch and occasionally one of the goddesses, thus, I had never been questioned by my father for anything like this, for anything so nonchalantly meaningful.

When I looked back to Alec, my breath caught in my throat and I froze, at a loss for words for the first time in ages. He knew as well as I did that we couldn't tell my father the lie about him being Josh's cousin, because like any polite parent, my dad would mention it to Josh's parents the next time he saw them and then I would be in a load of trouble. Plus, my dad worked in the neighboring town and probably knew almost everyone so I couldn't exactly say that Alec lived there either; he would see straight through that lie.

Gulping, I glanced at Alec and his blue eyes locked with my gray ones as a single thought passed between us. Alec raised one eyebrow in a silent question and I nodded, squeezing my eyes shut as I prepared myself for my father's reaction to what was coming. I knew my father was smart enough not to tell my mother about Alec, but that didn't mean his reaction would be any less erratic. The fact that he was drinking at the moment would probably make his bad response even worse. Nevertheless, Alec knew what he had to do.

"I live in the forest, sir."

To my surprise, my father didn't yell and didn't even look confused. He simply raised his eyebrows again and carefully set the beer bottle back on the counter. "In the forest?" he clarified, his voice gruff yet strangely quiet, his brow furrowed. Alec and I nodded simultaneously, waiting to see what my father would say next. "For how long?"

"He's only been here since the start of summer, Dad," I cut in, knowing what he was thinking. In the eyes of the public, there were still around forty unsolved missing person cases of people who had gone into the woods before the Monster Watch, even though we gods knew that they were really killed by monsters.

"No one else lives in the forest or has ever lived there. Alec and I don't know what happened to all of those people, and no one else does either," I lied, fingering the belt loop on my hip which held my walkie-talkie.

My father's frown deepened as he became lost in thought. The slight twitch of his crooked nose, which had been broken in a bar fight long ago, was a clear sign of how hard his brain was working to try to digest the information. "May I ask why you live there?" he asked curiously—almost sorrowfully—looking back at Alec.

"I ran away, sir," Alec answered curtly, running his fingers through his dark hair and wiping a drop of nervous sweat threatening to slide down his forehead.

"I should've guessed," my father sighed. "But running away from home because life sucks is a pretty stup—" He stopped midsentence, realization hitting him abruptly, like a knife in the chest, as he glanced back at me and held my gaze. After all, I ran away from my human home every day, even if I did return most nights. And my father knew better than to call me stupid.

"Something wrong, Dad?" I asked with a supercilious smirk. My father narrowed his eyes at me, and I felt Alec shift over so that he was standing closer to me, as if he felt like he was protecting me somehow. My father must have noticed this as well because he quietly raised his eyebrows at Alec, but the young hero just shrugged it off nonchalantly. Both of them knew I didn't really need to be sheltered.

Then my dad did something I never would have expected from him: he laughed. He actually *laughed*. "I think I like this kid," he chuckled to himself, shaking his head, and I exchanged confused glances with Alec, who threw his hands up into the air at a loss for words. I didn't even understand what was going on, but I suddenly found myself cracking up along with the two of them because the situation was so absurd. I had known my whole life that my father really wasn't the monster I always portrayed him as inside my head; he was just a grumpy alcoholic in need of a good laugh to cheer him up. But I never thought that I would actually see his softer side come out, especially not when his only daughter showed up with a random troublemaker who claimed to live in the mysterious forest. A bit of advice: people aren't always what they seem.

This peculiar, relaxing state of laughter lasted another minute or two before we all finally calmed down a bit. "So why are you two here?" my father eventually asked. He chortled, "It's obvious that you didn't come just to talk to me."

"The rest of the Monster Watch and I are going camping in the woods. I was getting some food," I told him seriously.

"And I suppose Alec is tagging along since he lives in that terrible place?" my father questioned, stroking his chin, and I nodded. "Well, don't let me stop you." He gestured to the cupboard after a slight pause, and I gave him a tight smile in return.

"Thanks, Dad," I said quietly. "I just need to get some other stuff first."

Without another word, Alec obediently followed me upstairs and into my empty room. The way he stuffed his hands into his pockets and glanced back over his shoulders multiple times told me there was something else he wanted to implore of me, and me alone. Sure enough, when we were out of my father's earshot, Alec leaned over and whispered cautiously, "What's his name?" Somehow, the young hero, like no one else I had ever met, understood the true gravity of such a simple question.

"Henry," I answered, surprised by how easily the name rolled off my tongue. Maybe it was because this was the first time there wasn't any contempt in my voice when I mentioned my old man. "His name is Henry."

I was just about to start looking for my black backpack when I caught sight of a pile of papers on my cluttered desk. It was then that I realized there was something important I needed to do before I left the house that day, since I was going to be so busy the last few weeks of summer and only the Fates knew when I might have another pause in the action like this. I knew it would come back to haunt me whether it was completed or not, but it had to be done nonetheless. Perhaps it should have even been done years earlier, just in case, by some slight chance, I happened to forget.

"Hey, I found the backpack," Alec informed me, pulling it out from under my bed.

"Cool, can you just throw some extra clothes in there for me? Thanks," I said to him absentmindedly as I sat down in the chair facing my messy desk and picked up a pen. I gulped as I twirled it around in my fingers, my heart racing. I had been subconsciously thinking about this exact moment so much that I knew precisely what to write and how.

Zach said there was always something slightly melancholy about me; there had been ever since I had heard the entire prophecy six years earlier. He once admitted with great relief, however, that it seemed to disappear from my face whenever we went into the forest, and I believed him, for I knew exactly what caused it. But now, due to Alec ceaselessly following the gods around and due to the war finally beginning, the forest alone, with its promise of freedom and power that fueled the gods, could no longer peel that melancholy off of me, off of my spirit. Only the true end of the war would allow me to shed the itchy skin that was my biggest secret, though writing was a good start.

"Did you just ask me to pick out clothes for you? Are you all right?" Alec's concerned voice came from behind, but I waved him off, starting to write furiously, my blue pen flying across the page. "Okay . . . well, don't blame me if I pick out the wrong outfit for you or something." I just ignored him and mumbled to myself as I continued to scrawl swiftly on the piece of paper.

Anyway, my wardrobe consisted mainly of jeans and a random collection of T-shirts, meaning he shouldn't have had too much trouble.

"Oh my gods! Is this a bra?" Alec exclaimed about a second later, and I whirled around in my seat to see him fling a white bra onto my bed like it was a snake or perhaps the most disgusting thing he had ever seen. You would have never guessed that he killed monsters almost every day, but then again, he probably wouldn't have minded the bra so much if he had been flinging it off of me instead.

I just rolled my eyes. "Yes. Now grow up and finish packing for me," I ordered, my voice harsher than I meant for it to sound as I turned around and started to write again. When I had finished a few minutes later, I stuffed the paper into the inside pocket of my leather jacket and leaped out of the chair, my mind still whirling around what I had written and my hands shaking from stress. Clenching and unclenching my fists to get the blood flowing normally again, I raced downstairs with Alec back into the kitchen, where my dad was still leaning on the counter and nursing his beer bottle.

"Back again?" my father mused lightly.

"You should really stop drinking," I muttered to him in a much more serious tone as I opened the wooden door to the cupboard and Alec started to help me grab some food from off of the shelves. Neither of us was really paying attention to what we were taking, but it didn't matter. We were trying to feed the troops just enough for them to stay strong; they didn't *need* a five-star meal, even though they probably deserved one. And if my father thought we were taking an awful lot of food for just the Monster Watch plus Alec, he didn't say anything about it.

I heard a soft clank and turned around to see my father set his bottle back on the granite countertop, his eyebrows raised. I had never actually told him to stop drinking before and I could see that he was slightly perturbed. "All right . . ." his voice trailed off, unsure of what to say next. After a silent moment of thought, he put his hand on my shoulder and forced me into the living room, where he could talk to me privately. I could tell I was in trouble now.

"Is *he* the reason you didn't want to go out with Cole?" my father asked me in a low voice, jerking his thumb over at Alec, who was still throwing food into the backpack.

I winced and wrinkled my nose at the strong stench of beer that bombarded me as soon as it escaped my father's mouth. Sighing, I admitted to him, "There were a lot of reasons, but yes, he was the main one."

I watched as my father nodded quietly and strode back into the kitchen. He tapped Alec on the shoulder, and the dark-haired boy quickly whirled around, his eyes wide. It looked to me like Alec was afraid my father was going to yell at him about taking too much food or something like that, but Alec was happily surprised when my father only muttered something into his ear. Then it was my turn to widen my eyes when the lanky drunk took his right hand and placed it on Alec's right shoulder, his left shoulder, and finally his head. It was a motion that resembled all too closely my naming the boy a true Greek hero.

"Dad!" I exclaimed, appalled and rather stunned. "Are you *knighting* him?" The only responses I received were a shrug from my father and a huge, goofy grin from Alec. I knew my parents had been obsessed with the medieval time period for a while because of all the junk in the antique shop, but my dad had just taken this fixation to a whole new level.

Deciding that it was best for Alec and I to leave before my father could embarrass me any further, I commanded, "Alec, let's go." Every minute's delay was another minute lost to the war and to Hades.

Alec shrugged and made his way toward the front door as I took one last glance into the kitchen, where my father had just tossed his beer bottle into the small, blue recycle bin. I fought back a proud smile, settling instead for a simple nod of approval. "Well, bye," I quietly bid him farewell, zipping up the backpack and flinging it over my shoulder, just as if I were heading off to a normal day at school.

"Alec, take care of my daughter!" my father shouted as Alec and I raced through the screen door. Not once did I look back. I wanted to let him have this moment to internally revel in his personal "calm before the storm."

"I will, sir!" Alec yelled over his shoulder enthusiastically, and together we raced down the road. Turning his head toward me, he winked and whispered lightly, "Now I'm your hero *and* your knight in shining armor. You, Athena, are one lucky girl. *Sir* Alec, first official hero of Mount Olympus of the twenty-first century and knight of the Woods—I think that has a nice ring to it, don't you?"

I just rolled my eyes and frowned ungratefully as we continued to jog, our feet loudly slapping the damp pavement. "*Unofficial* knight," I corrected him gravely, not in the mood for jokes. "My dad doesn't have the proper authority to make you a real one."

Noticing my tone, Alec lapsed into a state of tense silence as we crossed the tree line and were plunged into darkness because the weak daylight failed to penetrate the thick cover of leaves and branches. When we finally slowed to a walk near the part of the forest where our armor was hidden, he stopped me by placing a hand firmly on my shoulder. "Are you going to tell me what you wrote on that paper? Because, whatever it was, it put you in a terrible mood," he whispered, switching back to Greek.

Looking Alec straight in the eye, I sighed and said honestly, "I promise I'll tell you in a couple of days, but not right now. Just know that it has to do with the prophecy." He crossed his arms and gave me a very annoyed look, but I just rolled my eyes at him again. "Hey, I don't like this any more than you do."

Alec looked like he was about to say something else, but we were unexpectedly interrupted by a loud bang or an explosion from the east—most likely around Main Street—followed by the flapping of wings as a large flock of black birds hidden in the trees swiftly took to the skies for safety. Alec and I snapped our heads up as we pulled our rocks out of our pockets, completely alert once again and ready to attack.

"What the hell was that?" Alec wondered aloud, his brow furrowed. "Hades?"

"Maybe," I said in a low voice. "But it was definitely a distraction of some sort."

Another bang sounded, though this one was not nearly as loud as the first. When Alec gulped nervously, I continued darkly, gripping his arm to keep his attention focused on me, "Alec, I want you to run back to the army camp as fast as you can. If a battle breaks out, you're leading it. I'll send more gods to help once I find out what's going on."

He nodded and I whirled around, about to start running out of the forest when Alec grabbed my hand and pulled me back. "Wait. Just in case I die out there . . ." he whispered as he turned me around, and I didn't even have time to prepare myself before he pressed his soft lips against my cheek, making my heartbeat flutter nervously. My mind was suddenly reeling from the blow to my pride, so gentle but so rough at the same time. I was only thankful that he hadn't actually kissed me on the lips, which showed just how much respect he had for me, and I was desperately hoping that he wouldn't die out there, wouldn't leave me wanting more.

"Good luck," he added as he reluctantly let me go.

"And don't die," I replied under my breath, and he smirked as he started to back away from me. "Wait! Don't forget your armor!" I shouted just as he disappeared into the thick, green undergrowth, but then he was back a moment later, pulling his bronze chest-plate out of a hollow log and blushing as he fumbled with the leather straps. We exchanged a solemn high five and briefly interlocked our fingers before splitting up, Alec heading west and me heading east out of the woods.

As soon as I ran back into the open air and toward Main Street, I felt my heart drop to my stomach. I was not in view of any of the old shops yet, but thick, black smoke billowing up into the low cloud cover was clearly visible from over the tops of the trees. As I sprinted faster and faster, I could only cling to the hope that the fire wasn't in the Fire Pit or my mother's treasured antique shop next to it. For a second, I thought about radioing the other gods via walkie-talkie to tell them what was going on, but as I rounded the sharp corner onto Main Street, I saw that they were already there. Actually, the entire town was there to see the terrible spectacle since things like this didn't happen every day in the Woods. Or even every ten years, for that matter.

Dozens of people stood in a giant yet loose circle around a single burning car in the middle of the street. Dozens of people standing with their arms held out to shield their faces from the dark smoke and heat of the bright orange flames. There were dozens of people, but no one was doing anything to put out the fire that was eating up the mangled vehicle, the fire that could have quite easily spread to the homey shops behind it. They were all too busy shouting and pointing and taking pictures with their cell phones, apparently oblivious to the true danger at hand. I was probably biased, but sometimes I thought things were better in ancient times, without technology that affected people's judgment. In that moment, I was far too angry and confused to be thankful that none of the beloved shops were caught in the flames.

People continued to cry out in shock and anguish and my eyes were stinging with hot smoke. Curiosity overcame me, however, and as I rubbed my watering eyes with the cool sleeve of my leather jacket, I pushed my way toward the inner ring of the circle that was closest to the fire while waves of sickening heat and worry began to wash over me. For the first time, I was able to get a close look at the destroyed bunch of metal and, to my dismay, saw that it was a black SUV—the one that belonged to Cole's mother.

"Luke!" I tried desperately to shout above all of the other anxious voices, but I could not continue because a strong gust of wind blew a black cloud of smoke into my face, leaving me coughing and sputtering. Beginning to hyperventilate, I wildly looked around the crowd for the rest of the Monster Watch until I felt a hand firmly grab my left shoulder.

"It's going to be okay, Ash. The fire department is on the way," Zach whispered into my ear in English, and I whirled around to meet his worried expression as well as Connor's and Luke's. From the tiny beads of sweat sliding slowly down their faces and from their soaked shirts, I could tell that the three of them had been standing there quite a while. They had probably been inside the Fire Pit when the fire first started.

Tugging at my ponytail in anguish, I hissed at them, "We're in the middle of nowhere! It's going to be at least ten minutes before the firemen get here! Luke, you have to do something." With an exasperated sigh, Zach wiped his brow as he and Connor fanned themselves in a halfhearted effort to cool off although it wasn't really helping since we were only a few feet away from the flames. Luke, however, just rolled his sea-green eyes at me and crossed his tan arms over his chest, his expression unreadable.

"Athena," he started in a low voice in Greek. "You know as well as I do that it would look awfully strange if the fire hydrant over there conveniently exploded and the water just happened to fall right onto the burning car." Poseidon paused to gesture pointedly at the bright yellow hydrant in front of his human parents' restaurant, the only fire hydrant in our tiny town.

"Besides," Zeus cut in seriously, smoothing back his dark golden hair, "Hestia has it covered. She can't put *out* the flames, but she's keeping them confined."

Zeus pointed to the other side of the circle, and I could just barely make out Hestia's petite silhouette through the wispy smoke as she subtly clenched her fists and stretched her fingers out by her sides, the tips of the bright flames seeming to mimic her every move. Her long, light brown hair and short, purple dress flowed out behind her in the slight breeze, not bothering her at all and somehow making her appear as if she were at a photo shoot. The sight of Hestia silently concentrating on controlling the fire comforted me only a little bit, however.

"What about the people who were in the car?" I questioned, my gray eyes narrowed dubiously. "Are they okay?"

"Yeah, Cole's mom got out just in time," Apollo chipped in, motioning to the sorrowful woman sitting on the curb in front of the Fire Pit, her clothes charred and tears streaming down her face. She was surrounded by at least five sympathetic people who were trying to comfort her by handing her endless amounts of tissues and softly patting her back. But there was still one person missing from the whole mess, one person who should have been by her side no matter what.

"Has anyone seen Cole lately?" I asked in a hushed voice, already beginning to panic. My hope dissolved completely when I was met with only silence from the three boys.

"You don't think . . ." Apollo gulped, trailing off midsentence, but he didn't need to finish because we all understood what he was proposing. I had already known the fire would be a distraction from something happening at that exact moment in the forest, but I honestly never imagined that Hades would do anything as horrifyingly misguided as this. I took a deep breath, trying to prevent myself from losing my head over the fact that Cole, who had absolutely nothing to do with the war, was now a helpless prisoner in a world he didn't understand. I was beginning to think that the rest of the gods and I had made a big mistake in underestimating the lord of the Underworld.

Zeus quickly grabbed his black walkie-talkie off his belt loop and muttered in Greek, "This is Zeus, calling in an emergency situation. Repeat: emergency situation. Cole has possibly been kidnapped by Hades." Immediately, there was a small surge toward the woods on the other side of the street, made by the other gods hidden amongst the crowd. For a moment, Hestia lost control of the flames and they roared and cackled, stretching up like arms to embrace the darkening sky.

"Wait," I said into my own radio, and the gods all stopped dead in their tracks, the hot flames starting to die down again as Hestia regained her composure. "We can't all go in there; it will look suspicious." A low grumble of reluctant agreement floated through the crowd and faded away.

However, another wave of worry passed through the gods when the walkie-talkies burst to life, but this time the speaker wasn't in the vicinity of the burning car. "This is Pan. Your emergency has been acknowledged, but we have one of our own. Alec and the troops are greatly outnumbered at the small meadow, and the centaurs are outnumbered in their territory as well. The rest of the Knowing troops are almost here, but they've run into a blockade near the north edge of the forest. Over."

I exchanged worried glances with the rest of the Monster Watch and was sure that the other gods were doing the same. The day just kept getting worse and worse.

"Situation acknowledged. We'll be there as soon as we can," Poseidon solemnly muttered to Pan via his walkie-talkie while rubbing his forehead.

"Okay," Zeus continued quietly. "Hestia stays here to control the fire. Hermes and Hephaestus stay, too. When the firemen finish investigating, I want a full report of what caused this. I mean, it obviously wasn't a real crash. There aren't even any other cars around."

The rest of the Monster Watch and I made eye contact with Hermes, who was standing near Hestia and nodded obediently, just as the wailing sirens of the county fire truck made their way into earshot. I glanced north down Main Street, the only street that led directly out of the Woods, and squinted through the haze from the heat of the fire to see the bright red, flashing lights inching closer and closer.

"Everyone else goes into the forest. Stagger your entrances. Quickly, now. We don't have much time," Zeus ordered firmly, motioning in turn to each of the gods. "Hestia, give us some cover."

Hestia responded instantly by snapping her fingers, and the SUV exploded on cue, creating an expanding fireball accompanied by a loud bang. Tiny, sharp bits of debris were sent flying everywhere, and the boom temporarily made us deaf. I bit down hard on my lower lip as I felt flames lick at my now blistering skin. A few slivers of metal sliced painfully into my sides, but I simply sprinted faster into the trees with the rest of the Monster Watch, Demeter, Dionysus, Hera, Ares, Aphrodite, and Artemis while the public was distracted. There was no time to let pain bother us.

We paused only long enough to wipe the sweat off our brows and to carefully throw on our bronze armor over our newest areas of raw, opened skin. I slowly reached into the pocket of my leather jacket and was relieved to find that the important piece of paper was still safe and unburnt. When Zeus raised his eyebrows at me questioningly, I just shrugged and stuffed the letter back into my pocket. Within another minute, the ten of us had regained the ability to hear correctly and were racing west through the thorny bushes and branches of tall pine trees slapping and stinging our faces. All the while, our armor scratched our sides, inflaming the new wounds from the explosion.

We trampled over bushes, branches, rocks, logs, and anything else in our path like a herd of stampeding elephants, not caring if any monsters heard us coming or if we kept to the narrow path. I heard the loud rolling of thunder from above us and looked to my left to see Zeus muttering darkly to himself. His normally sky blue eyes had turned a cloudy, stormy gray color like mine. I could sense that buckets of rain were about to spill down from the heavens and that the strong stench of death hung heavily in the air, a looming reminder of those who had already fallen and those who had yet to fall. Gulping, I peered ahead through the thick foliage, some of which had blood—golden and red—smeared across the large leaves and dripping into tiny pools in the soil. I couldn't help but think yet again that the woods had never before seemed so cold and dark.

But things can always get worse.

Part Two

WHEN THE
STORM WORSENS

Chapter 9

FOR OLYMPUS

I knew our group of gods was nearing the small meadow, as confirmed by the thinning trees, but the mounting clouds were so black and thick that, for once, it wasn't any lighter outside the cover of pine trees than it was under. The meadow wasn't in sight yet, though I could already hear the loud battle cries of monsters, nymphs, satyrs, and Knowing Warriors alike. Some were courageous shouts of rage while others were screams of pure terror that only sent shivers down my spine. I knew instantly that these were the terrible sounds of people dying, the sounds that no one but Ares really wanted to hear. And they were all dying for us, the gods and secret keepers. I still wasn't sure if this fight was really worth that permanent collateral damage; unless you're talking about monsters, you can't bring back the dead.

I took a deep breath, readying myself for the gory sights to come and focusing on opening up all of my senses so I could fight even better with the help of my instincts. As we came closer to the battlefield with every heavy step, my peripheral vision seemed to widen in range, and I was now even more aware of the other gods gasping for breath beside me. Still, the sounds of wind whistling through the trees and the bushes trembling in fear from our urgent movements did not drown out the demoralized prayers ringing ceaselessly through my mind.

Behind me, Aphrodite was whimpering softly, dreading what lay ahead of us. Even though she had actually been involved in a battle the day before, these massacres didn't get any easier to deal with—mentally or physically. Killing a couple monsters by yourself or with a friend is one thing, but facing five at once while watching your most devoted followers and people you don't even know helplessly die around you is completely different. Most people don't understand what post-traumatic stress disorder really feels like until they have actually been through a whole war or some other trauma; movies just can't capture the right atmosphere. And although I, along with the other gods, was able to ignore the stress for the duration of a fight and keep it from affecting most of my decisions, I could honestly say that I understood PTSD perfectly:

Paranoia? Definitely. Hades could have been anywhere at any time, after all.
Nightmares? Check.
Difficulty falling/staying asleep? Duh. I probably mentioned having this symptom too many times throughout these pages.
Vivid flashbacks? Well, this entire book is a flashback so . . . check.
Hopelessness? Check.
Feeling of detachment from others? Absolutely (except from the other gods and Alec, of course). Since the start of the war, polite social interaction with un-Knowing humans had been one of the very *last* things on my mind.

The list goes on, but you get the point. Probably the only reason we gods didn't suffer from more dramatic symptoms than these was that we always had each other for support.

"Poseidon and Hera, go to the river to protect the army camp. With all the different battles going on, it's probably defenseless, and I doubt that Hades gives a damn about our injured soldiers," Zeus ordered grimly as we slowed to a stop on a hillside riddled with bushes and tangled tree roots. Poseidon and Hera exchanged solemn glances and nodded obediently before changing their course, now running west.

"I'll take Patrol Three to the north border of the forest," Ares offered helpfully, rubbing his fingers through the bright red plume on his bronze helmet.

"Fair enough," Zeus agreed, stroking his chin. "But go *around* the small meadow, not through it." Although Ares frowned at the fact that he would be avoiding another fight by taking the detour, surprisingly, he didn't argue. Ares simply motioned to Aphrodite and Dionysus, and the three of them bounded up the steep hill in perfect unison. Perhaps the god of war finally realized this was not the time to start fighting amongst ourselves again.

Next, Zeus turned to face Demeter, his stormy eyes meeting her determined brown ones. "Where would you like to go?" he asked her calmly, his voice flat and even, his body oddly still.

The goddess of the harvest and fertility closed her eyes thoughtfully and ran her fingers through her long, blonde hair as she took a minute to silently think over her options. "I'll catch up with Hera and Poseidon," she finally announced, raising her voice so she could be heard above the nearby screams.

"Okay—" Zeus began, but all of a sudden, Demeter took a few steps closer to him, her brown eyes burning with a mixture of frustration and desire. Before anyone could protest, she pulled his handsome head in toward hers and planted her lips on his, kissing him passionately and entangling her fingers in his hair. I hoped Zeus would have been smart enough to just push her away and wreck their meaningless attraction once and for all, but he only wrapped his arms around her waist and pressed his body into hers because, in the end, he couldn't resist the kiss. He never could. It was the thrilling type of kiss that would make one's insides squirm, that would feel so dirty yet so passionate at the same time. It was the type of kiss I would never have.

As I watched Demeter disappear into the undergrowth, I did nothing but frown in surprise, flashing back to the start of summer when Zeus's previous affair with Demeter had almost caused a different war. To be honest, I had thought she had long since moved on from her infatuation with Zeus, especially since she knew more drama really was the last thing we needed.

"So . . . I'm assuming that the rest of us are heading to the meadow?" Artemis spoke up, breaking the awkward silence as she readjusted the tight bun in her wavy hair. She had to pause again, however, in order to quickly load her bow and shoot down a screeching Stymphalian bird that had suddenly swooped down toward us from a high tree branch. Luckily, it disappeared in a puff of ash just before its bronze talons could reach out to latch onto her vulnerable throat. A bit of advice: always be prepared for the unexpected.

"That's correct," Zeus answered her, his face beginning to lose its bright pink color in response to the immediate danger of the giant, metallic bird. "I want you to take half of the archers to the east edge of the meadow and—" Zeus paused and turned to face Apollo, who was twirling around an arrow in his fingers absentmindedly before he continued, "Apollo, take the rest of the archers to the west edge, and hopefully we can set a trap." Then the blonde twins nodded grimly and stalked off in opposite directions, arrows already placed in each of their bows.

That left only Zeus and me.

"Ready, Father?" I asked him quietly, and he nodded. I followed him slowly up the hill, rolling my left shoulder in an effort to prevent my arm from tiring of holding for so long my heavy, round shield known as *aegis*. With every cautious step toward the bloody battlefield, I heard more and more voices echoing in my head—the voices of the soldiers praying desperately for my help. My frown only deepened as my headache began to worsen and, taking a glance at Zeus, I could tell he was having the same issue, though perhaps not quite as bad.

"I know what you're thinking," Zeus said suddenly, breaking our state of tense silence. I raised one eyebrow at him questioningly as we picked up the pace and he continued, "That getting involved with Demeter right now is a bad idea."

"It *is* a bad idea," I interjected as I brushed a stray piece of dark hair out of my face.

Zeus just sighed, scratching his head as he kicked his way through a thick bush. Trying to come up with a good explanation, he scrunched up his nose. "I know, but it's fine, really. Hera doesn't even know."

"The fact that Hera doesn't know about your affairs doesn't make the situation any better. Don't forget that she can read minds," I argued, rolling my eyes impatiently. "Plus, you were 'getting involved' with Aphrodite only a couple of days ago."

Zeus sighed again as we reached the top of the hill and looked like he was about to protest my logic, but I waved him off, signaling that I didn't want to talk about his troubled love life any more. Besides, the busy field below us had just captured our full attention. There was no order—only mayhem.

The normally bright green meadow was now dull and dismal, littered with the blood, bodies, and limbs of Knowing Warriors and covered in the gray dust or ashes of killed monsters, centaurs, nymphs, and satyrs. Right below where Zeus and I stood was a group of about twelve sword fighters and a few centaurs who were attempting to surround a giant troop of dark, hooded undead warriors. On the north side of the meadow, more troops of undead warriors filed out of the trees in seemingly endless lines. There was no sign of Artemis or Apollo yet and to say that we were greatly outnumbered was an understatement.

Then a random rock fell from the sky, and I looked up to see where it had come from, my mouth all of a sudden seeming very dry. Circling in the black thunderheads above the battlefield were three of Hades's most trusted servants, the Erinyes (aka Furies)—pale women with large, leathery wings who wore black robes and living snakes as belts and armbands. In the bony, paper-white hands of these psychotic Erinyes were large, heavy rocks not quite big enough to be called boulders, which they were trying to drop onto the poor, fragile soldiers fighting below.

When one Erinye ran out of rocks to throw, it quickly dove down toward the field, arms outstretched like the talons of an eagle going in for a kill. I gasped when the terrifying creature somehow mustered the strength to pick up Nicholas, the biggest Knowing Warrior out there, and began to fly higher and higher with the flailing, buff man still in her clutches. Sadly, there were no archers on the field yet and, therefore, no one could stop the flying monster. I could only hope that the Erinye wouldn't drop Nicholas, as he surely would have died on impact with the cold, hard ground or at the very least be seriously injured.

Zeus must have noticed the malicious Erinyes as well, because the next thing out of his mouth was, "I'm going to call Pegasus." I nodded grimly and instinctively plugged my ears as Zeus put two of his fingers to his lips and let out a piercing whistle. Seconds later, the gleaming white horse appeared out of nowhere, his wings outstretched as he gracefully glided down and landed on the hillside next to us, bravely ignoring the chaos going on around him. Mouth set straight in determination, Zeus launched himself onto the horse without a saddle or bridle then took off into the black sky, his strong fingers gripping the long mane of Pegasus for dear life. The rain had just started to fall.

I took a deep breath, closing my eyes as I readjusted my helmet and white-knuckled grip on my spear in silent preparation for my bold charge onto the field. I shook my arms again to keep the blood flowing as my mind whirled around a thousand different things at once, from my human parents to school to Hades. I vowed to myself that I would avenge the deaths of all of my nymph and satyr friends as well as the Knowing Warriors whom I did not even know very well. After all, a goddess should treat her people with just as much respect as they treat her.

Only a mere second later, my eyes were wide open and I was racing down the steep hill at top speed, pushing thoughts of anything besides the battle out of my mind for the time being. My heart began to pound, and I felt as if I couldn't get to flat ground fast enough. The terrified pleas for help from the soldiers that echoed loudly through my thoughts pushed me forward faster and faster. I was too focused on the battle ahead of me to worry about tripping and rolling down the rest of the slick slope. However, I was also very aware (and thankful) of the fact that the undead warriors weren't archers because I was definitely a clear target at the moment.

Finally, as if on some unspoken cue, Artemis ran straight out onto the field followed by five other determined archers. They planted their feet firmly in the long, knee-high, wet grass a few yards from the east edge of the trees, aiming their arrows at the undead warriors on the north edge across from me. Not a minute later, Apollo and five more archers appeared on the west side of the meadow, also aiming their weapons to the north. I had to squint my eyes against the blinding lightning flashing across the sky in order to watch twelve slim arrows soar gracefully through the air in perfect arcs. Within the blink of an eye, they had disappeared into the dense formation of undead warriors.

"This is Hermes calling to report on the fire," the messenger god's voice suddenly crackled through the speaker on my walkie-talkie, stopping me in my tracks. "The firemen said that the car fire was caused by a severed gas line. In other words, the fire was *not* an accident. Over."

"Roger that. Get down to Hades ASAP and give me a report when you get back," Zeus responded to Hermes. "But leave your walkie-talkie at the army camp. We don't want Hades accidentally getting hold of it, and you won't be in range all the way down there anyway." Once Hermes agreed with Zeus, the line went quiet again.

As the short conversation ended, however, I noticed that the arrows continued to pelt the undead warriors, but also that the persistent undead only advanced faster toward the sword fighters on my side of the meadow. The brainless soldiers were apparently following an invisible Hades's orders and somehow understood that it was too dangerous for the archers to try to kill them near our own living soldiers. Even though Artemis and Apollo were the best archers in the world, they had to compensate for the wind, flashing sky, heavy rain, and other distractions that could cause an arrow to stray from its planned course. Plus, the sword fighters were beginning to fall out of formation due to obvious fatigue and confusion. I knew something drastic had to be done before we lost any more ground.

"Zeus, Artemis, Apollo, I need you all to draw attention to the north side of the meadow so the sword fighters can take a few minutes to regroup. Got it?" I ordered through the walkie-talkie, slowly jogging over to meet the troops. In accordance with my exigent request, the lighting and thunder temporarily faded away.

No more than two minutes later, bright flashes were lighting up the sky again, one after another, followed by the continuous rolling of deafening thunder. At the exact same time, more arrows were released from the ground. I held my breath as one long, jagged lightning bolt reached down from the sky, striking the ground between the sword fighters and the advancing undead. As I felt the intense heat of the bright bolt radiate across the entire battlefield, I realized that if it had not been for the rain, the long meadow grass probably would have caught fire, creating a very different kind of divide. A couple sword fighters were blown backward when the lightning bolt touched down, and a few undead warriors standing in its target area had completely disintegrated.

I knew I had little time to reorganize the troops' formations, so I shouted at the top of my lungs, "RETREAT!" Straight away, the muscular sword fighters and the two centaurs turned and sprinted toward me, a mixture of surprise, fear, and determination in their eyes. Their prayers to me stopped momentarily, giving my brain a much needed second of rest. I rapidly gestured to the group, giving each of them specific directions, and they slowed to a stop, catching their breaths as they faithfully formed into two rigid rows of six behind me. Unfortunately, there were still two missing: Nicholas, who I was forced to consider lost for the time being, and Alec.

I gulped, reluctantly forcing myself to carry on without him. After all, he was a hero; he could protect himself and carry out his own missions. So I took a deep breath, triumphantly thrusting my spear into the air, and yelled at the top of my lungs, "FOR OLYMPUS!"

"FOR OLYMPUS!" the troops echoed. With renewed hope, the soldiers all around the edges of the meadow raised their weapons as well. Then we charged in unison toward the undead monsters in the center, our swords and spears glinting brightly under the electric sky. Admittedly, I had not seen the battles from the day before, but I had a strong feeling that this one was going to be the biggest and bloodiest.

The rain pelted us, drenched us, battered us as we sprinted farther into the storm, into the battle, and I couldn't help but hold my breath as my gold and silver shield collided with the first undead warrior's burning iron sword, the loud clang drowned out by the battle cries and thunder. Before the cloaked skeleton could take another swing at me, I slammed my shield as hard as I could into its rib cage, and it fell to the ground, dropping its sword. Before it could retrieve its blade, I stomped my boot down onto its brittle, yellowed spine, and the undead warrior crumbled to dust, mixing with the tiny pools of rainwater in the soil.

One undead down, a countless number to go, I thought to myself bitterly.

I looked up, boldly glaring down the next undead warrior in line to face me, and twirled the spear around in my hand once or twice. But I just gaped in surprise when, from behind, the tip of someone else's sword suddenly punched a good-sized hole through the undead's long cloak and then its spine. Finally, the undead warrior crumbled to dust as it fell forward onto its bony knees, thus revealing its killer: the mighty Alec, his sword still raised menacingly. Due to the torrential rainfall, his hair was plastered to his skull, hiding the brightness in his blue eyes, but his subtle sigh of relief was unmistakable and so was mine. To be honest, I wasn't quite sure what I would have done if he had died.

"You're here," he breathed gratefully, taking a few steps closer to me while temporarily loosening his grip on the hilt of his *kopis* sword. In that moment, I saw the fatigued hero find something to believe in, whether it was a greatly improved chance at winning the battle or just someone he could always count on.

Downplaying my significance to him, I simply rolled my eyes; he was acting like we were the only two people around. "Move," I grunted, keeping my face emotionless as I pushed him to the side and stabbed my spear into the rib cage of an undead that was about to slice at Alec from behind; it was killed instantly and cleanly. The main benefit of fighting undead warriors was that because they were made up of only bones, their deaths resulted in much less blood spatter and ruined articles of clothing.

"Pull yourself together, Alec. Now, where the hell have you been?" I demanded worriedly as the young hero whirled around to block with his shield the stab of yet another undead.

Alec smirked. "Well, *Lady* Athena," he began much more formally, almost mockingly, turning back around to whisper in my ear, "in case you didn't see, Nicholas just fell from the sky over there and has at least one broken leg. I hid him in the undergrowth because there was no one but the tree nymph Ella to help him get back to camp safely. Medusa provided a bit of a delay too."

"Thank the Fates you survived," I replied over my shoulder as Alec rested his back lightly against mine, slicing and stabbing at about seven undead warriors. Of course, Alec and I knew each other's fighting style so well by then that working together and covering each other's blind spots felt natural and somewhat refreshing, even under such great stress. Undead warriors fell with each blink of our eyes as we relentlessly sliced or stabbed their torsos and blocked or occasionally flipped out of the way of their blind jabs and thrusts, still keeping time to the steady rhythm of our heartbeats. Every once in a while, I would catch sight of a distracted Knowing Warrior gaping at Alec and me in amazement, only solidifying my guess as to the speedy rate at which we were killing Hades's servants. It was the kind of challenging fight that made the rest of the gods and I feel really powerful, the kind of fight worth reliving over and over again just to feel that compelling connection of instincts working together like magic. Frankly, anything that could kill us only made us feel more alive, not afraid.

Our long streak of kills was cruelly interrupted when our ears were filled with a loud thud, which was immediately followed by a man's scream of pure pain coming from right next to us. As soon as we spun around on our heels, I knew it was too late to save the poor Knowing Warrior. He was dead, obviously crushed by a gigantic rock that one of the Erinyes had dropped. His well-muscled arms and legs were splayed out at awkward angles, and half of his skull was smashed, caving inward toward his brain, which was luckily covered by the grass and his mop of long hair. The better half of the small boulder sat unmoving upon the man's torso, still squishing his dead body (his armor couldn't help much in this situation) and causing his lifeless brown eyes to bulge out of their sockets. I did not know who this particular Knowing Warrior was, but that fact didn't make the sight any less disturbing.

"I guess we'd better be watching the skies, too," Alec said with a gulp, raising his shiny bronze shield just in time to keep the burning tip of another undead's sword from scraping his shoulder. I simply nodded and glanced toward the flashing sky to look for any more of the dangerous flying women. There was no time to mourn deaths or pay attention to how well the other soldiers were doing; we had to keep moving forward.

With each passing minute, the rain fell harder, decreasing the visibility even further. I used my ears to pinpoint the exact place that each undead warrior was and listened carefully for the *whoosh* of each undead's sizzling iron blade cutting through the frigid air and pouring rain. I knew that the clouds were completely covering the sun so it should have been nearly pitch black, but Zeus, still riding Pegasus, was throwing bright, almost blinding bolts of lightning every couple of seconds, some through the sky toward the Erinyes and some down to the dozens of undead warriors. I just prayed that Zeus wouldn't accidentally hit one of our own soldiers since we were already badly outnumbered.

Eventually, Alec and I managed to kill all of the undead warriors that had been surrounding us and were able to rest for a brief moment. I thought it was past lunchtime, but I couldn't be sure because I had lost my appetite long ago, after seeing the first few soldiers fall, and the comforting light of day was nonexistent. We were in the dark both literally and figuratively.

"This is crazy," I shouted at Alec over the thunder, rain, and screams. "I can barely even see you. I know this is a war, but Zeus is out of control."

"Did somebody call my name?" I heard the overconfident, booming sound of our king's voice come from behind me and turned around to see him sitting atop Pegasus, a bright white spot in a field of darkness. Zeus was panting like a dog and his dark golden hair was so wet that it now looked brown, but for some reason he still had a playful smirk written across his handsome face. Like I said, crazy.

The resounding thunder quieted for a moment, so I knew the lord of the skies was about to speak again. His voice *was* the thunder this time. "Would you like to join me, Athena?" he asked politely, holding out his rough hand for me to take.

I raised my eyebrows in question and glanced at Alec to make sure he was going to be okay on his own. "I'll be fine," he confirmed, though I thought I saw a flicker of worry pass through his eyes, which had abruptly turned as deep and murky as the churning sea. With a short nod, he added, "Good luck. And please don't die up there."

"I'll try not to," I mimicked Alec as I gave him a soft punch on his arm and received a small but wary smile in return.

"Ready?" Zeus said eagerly. With an indifferent shrug, I grabbed my godly father's hand, and he used his superhuman strength to pull me up behind him on Pegasus. When we took off at a gallop, I knew my extra weight would not bother the strongest horse in the world.

Muttering to myself, I gripped the wet, heaving barrel of Pegasus with my legs as he launched himself up into the stormy sky and spread out his enormous wings. My breath caught in my throat as I started to slip a few inches down

Pegasus's smooth back. To save myself from plummeting to earth, I quickly slid my arms around Zeus's armored midsection, feeling the ridges of the six-pack abs that were carefully chiseled into his chestplate. Even though all of the gods and most of the male soldiers had real six-pack abs, it was traditional to wear muscle armor to try to intimidate enemies in battle. I wasn't sure the undead warriors cared one bit, however.

As soon as Zeus and I flew up into the thick, moist clouds, my jaw dropped. The Erinyes had now been joined by a few Stymphalian birds and their three screeching harpy friends who, like the Erinyes, were also half-bird, half-women, though the harpies were mostly made of bird parts. Four monsters circled around Pegasus, who laid his ears back and let out a piercing whinny, while the other two Erinyes kept dropping giant stones on the soldiers on the ground. I realized that Zeus needed Apollo or Artemis with him, an archer who could shoot down these beasts, not me with my short spear, but maybe the twins were still more valuable on the ground.

"I know you're not an archer, but see if you can use your spear to redirect the lightning toward the other harpies and I'll try not to electrocute you," Zeus yelled over his shoulder, sensing my doubts. "I swear I've been killing these stupid things, but Hades releases them from the Underworld again just as fast."

I simply nodded in understanding, keeping a tight hold on Zeus with one arm as I readjusted the spear in my right hand. When Pegasus suddenly banked to the left, I recognized just how difficult staying on during the fight was going to be. Before I could even prepare myself to redirect the lightning, Zeus had extricated one of his hands from Pegasus's mane, and it crackled with hot, blinding electricity that jumped from finger to finger before it was released, stretching out to our left toward the familiar harpy with wild black hair and pale skin. But, unfortunately, the harpy just rolled over in midair to avoid the blow, though one side of her feathered bird body did look a bit charred.

Refocusing, I took a deep breath and waited for Zeus to throw the next lightning bolt. The second I saw Zeus's hand light up again, I held out my spear, pointing it at the same black-haired harpy. The deafening thunder that followed the first bolt of lightning had just faded away when Zeus threw out his second fistful of electricity. This time, however, the blazing hot bolt split into two jagged branches, one heading toward an Erinye and one zapping the harpy's left wing. I smirked victoriously as my nose filled with the smell of smoke and gravity pulled the harpy's ashes down to the meadow like black snow. The Erinye had also disappeared for the time being, hopefully making her own way to the Underworld. Unfortunately (but not unexpectedly), another harpy flew into my view almost immediately.

This one was a brunette, and her long hair whipped around her face as she rapidly flapped her dark wings, trying not to be pushed by the strong winds into one of her monster allies. Aiming my spear at the second harpy, I waited for Zeus's hand to light up again and when it did, the static immediately skipped to the pointed tip of my spear then shot the harpy square in the chest. I just hoped she wouldn't return from the dead as fast as she had the last time.

But while I watched her ashes fade into the dark clouds below me, an Erinye suddenly flew up from under the neighing Pegasus. I gasped as her giant, black wings beat in my face and when she turned to face me, I could see that her narrow eyes were dripping with blood. As her thin arms entwined with shimmering green snakes reached out to pull me off of Pegasus, I whipped my spear over my head, careful not to hit Zeus, and jabbed the spear into her stomach with a solid thunk before she could touch me with her bony hands and long, claw-like fingernails. Golden-green monster blood slowly trickled down the smooth shaft of my spear and onto my hand as the Erinye let out one last, low moan and tumbled away, slowly disintegrating.

I let out a quick sigh of relief before tightening my hold on the spear and electrocuting a humungous Stymphalian bird, but that was when our walkie-talkies burst to life with Hermes's voice. Anxious to hear the full report, Zeus urged Pegasus to fly farther up and away from the monsters for the time being. Honestly, I was just glad to have a short break; my hands were burning and my skin was boiling thanks to Zeus's energy.

"This is Hermes calling to inform you all that Hades has both Cole and Persephone locked up. Repeat: Hades has Cole tied up and unconscious, and Persephone is locked in her room," Hermes muttered breathlessly, and I heard Zeus curse under his breath in front of me. "I'm sorry, guys, I—I couldn't free them—Hades wouldn't even say a word to me—but it's lucky I got out alive because, well, there's a large hole in my arm . . . ."

Wishing someone could have been down in the Underworld with Hermes for support, I shut my eyes and let out a long, tired sigh. Zeus only stiffened at the feeling of my warm breath rolling down his neck and ordered, "Alec, head back to the army camp and meet Hermes there. Hermes, when you're all patched up, you and Alec are going down to the Underworld again to get them back, no excuses."

"Okay, I'm headed back to camp now," Alec answered uncertainly but obediently. I could tell by his voice that he, like me, had a very bad feeling about this plan.

Chapter 10

A BIT OF DUMB LUCK

A s soon as Alec let everyone know that he was heading back to the army camp to meet Hermes, Zeus peeked over his shoulder, his stormy eyes meeting mine. "I want to drop you off by Main Street with Hestia and Hephaestus," he said, practically shouting over the thunder while trying to steer Pegasus through the pounding rain.

"Affirmative," I replied loudly, slipping my black walkie-talkie off my belt loop, one arm still locked around his armored torso. Then, speaking into the device, I asked, "This is Athena calling Hestia and Hephaestus. What is your position?"

I strained my ears as I waited for the response, thinking that the heavy-duty, waterproof walkie-talkies had proved to be a good investment when Hestia's calm voice came on the line. She was speaking Greek, but her voice was low so I knew she was with some Sightless humans. "Hephaestus and I are sort of trapped in the Fire Pit along with the rest of the town. Thanks to the storm, the power's out, and this is the only place with a generator. Just say the word and we'll be in the forest right away." Hestia paused for a second before continuing, "But

Hephaestus just told me that he made a bunch of new weapons, so we'll have to drop by his house first to pick them up."

"All right, meet me at the east edge of the woods where we keep our armor in precisely ten minutes," I ordered. "Zeus wants me to help you two bring the weapons in safely. With any luck, we won't run into too many monsters."

After Hestia agreed to the plan, the walkie-talkies went quiet once again until Zeus asked for everyone to check in. Since Alec, Zeus, and I had all left the small meadow, our troops there were struggling again, but at least they had the archers for help. At the same time, Poseidon, Hera, Demeter, and Pan were defending the army camp against a kraken residing in the deepest part of the river. A tree nymph then added that a troop of undead warriors was supposedly on its way to the camp. On the bright side, Pan had received word from another satyr that the centaurs were winning a battle in their territory on the west side of the river. To the north, Ares, Aphrodite, and Dionysus seemed to be in control of their battle too.

When everyone with a walkie-talkie had given an update, Zeus gave Pegasus a kick in the sides and we flew even higher into the black clouds, away from the flying monsters. Grasping Pegasus with only his strong legs, Zeus twisted around and started to fling lightning bolts in the general direction of where he thought the Erinyes and harpies were, just in case they had foolishly decided to follow us. I cringed as my ears were filled with the extremely loud sound of rolling thunder, and I felt the heat of the electricity when the bolts whizzed by me, mere inches away from my arms. Slowly, Pegasus leveled off and made a wide turn to our left somewhere above the meadow, heading us toward Main Street, and Zeus turned back around, his hands no longer crackling with electricity.

Meanwhile, I blinked my eyes rapidly, attempting to clear my vision of the large raindrops, which were falling nonstop. I had to squint my eyes in order to see ahead and look for the tiny town standing tall and nearly silent below us. The temperature had dropped quite a bit since the rain had started so I decided that I wouldn't be surprised if any gods or soldiers ended up with a cold or even pneumonia by the end of the war. If any of them survived, of course.

A few minutes later, Zeus claimed that he could see the town ahead. I didn't see it myself, but I obviously trusted Zeus with my life so that was that. Without another word, Zeus calmly urged Pegasus to fly lower, and the horse's powerful hooves lightly skimmed the treetops, like a bird flying over a lake. However, mere seconds had passed when Zeus suddenly stopped in midair.

"Jump off here," Zeus ordered firmly as we hovered a few feet above the pine trees that were rooted about fifty yards from the edge of the forest. "I don't want anyone in town to see us or Pegasus. They'll just make us go inside to explain ourselves, and if we don't, they'll get themselves killed trying to come after us."

I nodded, frowning down at the trees through which I was about to reluctantly crash. I was almost certain that a regular human would have been seriously injured after a fall from that great height, if not killed. At least I was going to be slowed down by the branches, though they would also scratch me like thousands of cat claws.

"I guess I'll see you later," I muttered under my breath, disgruntled. I didn't even glance back at Zeus as I tightened my grip on the cold spear in my right hand and forcefully pushed off Pegasus with my shield, which was still strapped onto my left arm.

I couldn't help but hold my breath as I felt myself slip, feet first, off of Pegasus's smooth, slippery back then plummeted through the rain, the rushing wind filling my ears. Shutting my eyes, I winced as I suddenly slammed into the first bushy treetop and was knocked sideways, losing my helmet almost immediately. Even though the wind had just been slapped out of me, I curled up instinctively, bringing my knees to my chest, and covered my vulnerable skull with my shield as I crashed through more branches encrusted in prickly pine needles. I blinked rapidly, trying to ignore the stinging sensation that seared through my whole body and to keep my head clear at the same time. After all, I still needed to land somehow.

Realizing that I could hit the ground at any second, I took my spear and pushed it out to the side of me as hard as I could. My efforts were rewarded when the sharp tip of the spear conveniently stuck in a tree branch that seemed to support my weight, although my arm had been violently jerked in the process and the branch was creaking a little bit. Wasting no time at all, I heaved myself up onto the thick branch, straddling it like a horse, and yanked out my short spear from the rough bark. I then swiftly proceeded to clamber down the rest of the tall tree, which was only a couple of yards to the forest floor.

Relieved to be standing on solid ground, I subconsciously readjusted my armor and simultaneously glanced around for my fallen helmet. My eyes lit up when I saw the familiar blue plume sticking out from a bush, and I raced over and placed the helmet back on my head. I then grabbed the walkie-talkie off my belt loop, amazed that it hadn't fallen from my hip during the fall, and called into it, "Hestia and Hephaestus, what's taking you so long?"

I was just beginning to worry because they hadn't answered me yet, but then I heard a rustling in the bushes behind me and turned around to see the two drenched, humbled gods. I immediately hurried over to help them, seeing that they were both weighed down with large trash bags full of new armor and more weapons. Hephaestus in particular was struggling to remain upright, and his dark hair with gray flecks was already covered in sweat, not just rainwater. His trusty wooden cane was doing almost nothing to help him walk since his already mangled leg was still broken and in a cast, though it wasn't bothering him quite as much as the days before.

"Sorry for the wait," Hephaestus began breathlessly as I took the heavy trash bag from him and flung it over my own shoulder. "We were held up by the Minotaur and a few Stymphalian birds near my house, but, luckily, Zeus managed to electrocute them before they did any damage."

I shrugged as the three of us began to head west at a slow pace. "It's no big deal." After all, a Minotaur trespassing in town required much more immediate attention than me. "So how is everything in town? Hectic?"

"You guessed it," Hestia said with a sigh, her voice cracking with fatigue and sadness. "The adults think most of the other gods are taking shelter at the mall or something like that, but your mom is really worried, of course. Apparently, your dad told her that the Monster Watch went camping in this weather. He didn't seem to care, though."

I nodded, as that was exactly what I had expected to hear. But as we trudged through the undergrowth, I silently wondered whether or not my human father would have been freaking out as well if he didn't know Alec was with us. Meeting Alec seemed to have a strange calming effect on my father and I hoped it would last for a while. Both my human mother and I could benefit from his supposedly cheerful new attitude.

"You look awful, by the way," Hestia spoke up a minute later, waggling her eyebrows at me in a disapproving fashion. "You do realize that you have blood all over, right? And leaves in your hair."

Raising my eyebrows, I looked down at my torso and realized that Hestia was, indeed, correct. Some golden blood was seeping out from under my bronze breastplate, smearing over my sides, although there wasn't enough to be *too* worried about. Bits of green pine needles were entangled in my wavy ponytail so I quickly brushed them out with my freshly cut, numb fingers. I had been so busy that I hadn't even noticed my bedraggled appearance, not to mention the fact that my body was probably in a state of shock.

"Well, I did just fall through the trees from the freaking sky—I'd like to see *you* try that—and I probably have some pieces of shrapnel still stuck in my sides. You know, from *your* explosion," I hissed at Hestia dryly, feeling stressed. "I think I'm allowed to look like a mess."

"Yes, and I'm sure that Alec wouldn't mind," she mused softly, a slight smirk on her face.

"What's that supposed to mean?" I retorted, glaring at the winding path ahead. I didn't like the tone of her voice one bit. "There's nothing going on between Alec and me."

Hephaestus let out a hearty laugh, and I narrowed my eyes at him until he finally decided to shut up. Hestia just smiled wider and said quickly, "Oh, I know. It's quite a shame, really. You two would look so good together, and he obviously loves you. At least that's what Aphrodite thinks—"

"I don't give a damn about what Aphrodite thinks," I interrupted, shaking my head and suddenly feeling annoyed. "Even if I do feel the same way Alec does, it's not going to happen, Hestia. It can't. How many times do I have to say it? He's a hero and I'm a virgin goddess. End of story. A relationship would just be a distraction anyway."

"So you would rather go out with Cole? A regular, un-Knowing human?" Hestia raised her voice accusingly, looking at me in disbelief. I stared back at her in a similar way, but angrier.

"I would rather date no one. Where the hell did you get that idea?"

Realizing she'd made a huge mistake, she continued, "In the Fire Pit, your father was talking about how Cole gave you a necklace so I guess I just assumed . . ."

Hestia's voice trailed off as she waited for me to explain, but I just flashed back in my mind to when Alec and I had first walked into my house. My human father must have seen the necklace in my hand then, although he hadn't mentioned it to me. Since I left the necklace on my desk in my bedroom, my father probably figured Alec wasn't the one who had given it to me; otherwise, I would have been wearing it. And Cole was one of the only boys in town ignorant enough to offer me, of all people, a necklace, so I supposed my father would have no reason not to mention it in front of everyone at the restaurant. I just wished he hadn't said anything at all.

"I never wanted to go out with Cole," I muttered bitterly. "And I don't even wear necklaces."

Hestia gasped and whipped out her walkie-talkie in mock horror, interrupting my explanation. Either she didn't sense the frustrated edge to my voice, or she was blatantly ignoring it. "Aphrodite," she called into the device for someone she knew would take her side in our debate. "Athena just said she won't wear necklaces—not even the one that Cole gave her!"

I only rolled my eyes at her and irritably muttered some profanities as Aphrodite's shocked voice asked, "Why not? Athena, are you *trying* to avoid all things feminine?"

Am I missing something? Why is a necklace so important?

I smacked my forehead in frustration, about to start explaining, but then Alec jumped into the conversation. "She's just being practical," he defended me, a sharp, impatient edge to his voice. "Come on, think about it. Someone could sneak up from behind you, and bang! If the chain on the necklace were strong enough, you'd be choked to death."

At first, I grinned at his answer, but when Hestia and Hephaestus glanced at me suggestively, I quickly changed my expression to a frown again. *I don't care. I don't care,* I repeated to myself, staring down at my combat boots.

Meanwhile, Apollo broke in, "Alec, choking someone doesn't make a 'bang' sound." As if that actually mattered.

"Why are you even a part of this conversation right now?" Alec's befuddled voice echoed my exact thoughts.

"Fine then. You guys talk, and I'll just drink my lemonade over here by myself," Apollo's voice trailed off.

"Hey! How do you have lemonade in the middle of a battle?" Ares suddenly exclaimed over the walkie-talkie. "I want some!"

Next, Dionysus piped up, "And I could use a glass of Greek wine if you have any of that. We clearly have plenty of water to dilute the stuff, *Zeus*."

I only shook my head at Hestia, blaming her for distracting everyone from their battles. More and more gods kept butting into the conversation, and the very last thing we needed was a drunken one fighting; Dionysus must have had a death wish. Plus, he should have known that no one in the forest even had Greek wine (unless the Knowing had brought some along on their journey) since the ingredients weren't indigenous to our forest and climate.

"I don't *actually* have lemonade. It was just an expression, guys," Apollo sighed, as if it should have been obvious, and I snorted. Leave it to the gods to be so insensitive as to start making jokes in the middle of war.

"Since when is drinking lemonade an expression?" Ares wondered aloud, sounding dubious. "Are you messing with me? Because if you are, then *I'm* going to mess *you* up."

"Stop it! Just do everyone a favor and shut up, all of you," I ordered harshly through the walkie-talkie.

Ignoring Dionysus, Apollo, and Ares's further irrelevant comments, Aphrodite answered Alec and me in defeat, "Ugh, why do you two always have to spoil the fun? An argument over a necklace? Seriously . . ." I imagined her throwing up her hands into the air with an exasperated sigh, deciding that trying to deal with Alec and me was hopeless. Which it was. I just smiled to myself victoriously, refraining from pointing out that she and Hestia were the ones who had started the argument to begin with.

When the conversation finally died out over the walkie-talkies, I turned back to face Hestia and Hephaestus. "Anyway," I started over a bit frostily with what I had been trying to say earlier. "Aphrodite was the one who told me to go on the date with Cole in the first place and all it caused was trouble. That's just what love is—trouble."

"You've been watching Zeus too closely. Love isn't always trouble," Hestia whispered, the tone of her voice getting softer and more empathetic again. "It makes people happy, like how Alec is always happier when he's with you."

"I was just as happy before Alec came here," I argued hoarsely, trying to convince and remind myself as well as the two of them. "And I will be happy again someday, when this war is over." Before either Hestia or Hephaestus could respond, I lengthened my stride and moved ahead of them, not in the mood to talk anymore. If only they had known what the cost of the whole prophecy really was, had known about that godforsaken arrow, then they might have understood the way I was acting.

A few minutes later, the walkie-talkie burst to life with Alec's voice again, and Hestia, Hephaestus, and I stopped to listen. "This is Alec. I just wanted to let you all know that Hermes and I are about to go down into the Underworld, so this is the last time you'll hear from us until we come back out—well, if we come back out." He didn't exactly wait for someone to respond, but there was a slight, hesitant pause before he said one simple word, "Athena?" The underlying question in his hopeful but shaky voice was unmistakable.

I shut my eyes with a sigh, but was vaguely aware of Hestia and Hephaestus holding their breaths behind me, waiting to see what I would do next. Actually, all of the gods and Alec were probably stark still, anticipating my proud proclamation of love for the young hero, which was what they had been secretly wishing for all along. But the stiff moment of deafening silence ended abruptly when I ordered into the walkie-talkie, my voice tight, determined not to show any emotion, "Just go, Alec. You'll be fine."

I know; I was a little bit heartless.

But please, hear me out: I would have been even crueler if I had let Alec go down to Hades distracted, thinking about our bright future together when I knew there wasn't even a real future to speak of. There was only one way for this war to end, for this prophecy to be fulfilled, and it had to happen soon; school started in less than three weeks.

As I silently cursed myself over and over again, Hestia, Hephaestus, and I trudged on through the thick trees. Thankfully, Hestia and Hephaestus knew better than to talk to me when I was so lost in thought, though I probably would have ignored them either way. Then again, perhaps they were too shocked at my sudden heartlessness to say anything at all. In the meantime, my head was painfully pounding with thoughts about the prophecy and my ears seemed extra sensitive, every rustling bush sounding like a roaring waterfall. Taking deep breaths, I tried unsuccessfully to calm my thoughts, but my head only seemed to spin even faster.

Therefore, it should have been no surprise to either god that when only a half hour later a small troop of undead warriors popped out of the foliage in front of me, I was eager to jump into the fight and clear my head. At the first sight of the hooded skeletons, I dropped the bag of new weapons that I had been carrying and raced forward aggressively. The sheer impact with my shield, *aegis*, killed the first undead warrior in line, and the next was impaled by my spear before it even had the chance to raise its own deadly weapon. I ducked to the right just as the third undead brought down its iron blade and whirled around to stab it from behind, its dust falling slowly onto my combat boots as the fourth stepped up to face me. This undead warrior managed to knock me off balance, but only for a moment. Within the next minute or so, the last two undead had crumpled to the earth, and their ugly gray remains sank into the soft soil.

"Whoa," Hephaestus breathed as I turned around, his voice excited and his brown eyes wide. "You sure know how to make a god feel useless. Amazing work."

I simply shrugged, wiping the tip of my spear on the wet grass. I was still feeling quite conflicted over what I had said—or rather, what I *hadn't* said to Alec. I wordlessly picked up the bag of weapons again and started to walk forward, but stopped when I realized that the other two gods were still frozen in place behind me.

"You can go back to the meadow if you want," Hestia said calmly, her steady gaze meeting mine. She stood with her head held high and her chin up, as if she were confronting someone she didn't trust, someone she didn't know very well.

I wasn't sure if I should have been offended or not, but perhaps my grumpy attitude in the past hour had scared her and Hephaestus more than I thought.

It was dead quiet for a moment, like the entire forest was a giant jury, judging my innocence and looking down on me, the defendant, with a strange mixture of disappointment and amazement, and I felt almost as if I had done something wrong. Maybe it was just the guilt of keeping such large secrets starting to affect me. Maybe I was crazy. Nevertheless, it suddenly occurred to me just how similar the golden blood on my hands (on all of the gods' hands, I supposed) was to the greenish-gold blood of monsters. In a certain light, the two sticky substances appeared to be exactly the same.

But then again, maybe I was crazy.

When I didn't answer her right away, Hestia continued, "The soldiers probably need you more than we do at the moment, and we're only a few minutes away from the camp. You look like you would rather fight right now anyway."

She was completely correct; I didn't even have to weigh my options. So, glancing back and forth between the two of them, I asked seriously, "Are you sure you'll be okay?"

Hestia nodded, flashing me a wary smile. "I'll blast some good old Greek fire at any monsters we see. Just promise me that you'll come back soon and get your wounds treated." With a shrug, I looked back down at the smeared, dried blood on my torso and reluctantly agreed to her terms. A minute later, we went our separate ways.

I walked much faster alone since I wasn't being slowed down by the injured Hephaestus or having to carry that heavy trash bag, so I made good time as I headed back northeast to meet the troops. The forest was strangely quiet and I had not seen a monster since I fought the undead warriors by Hestia and Hephaestus. I knew that things were much worse somewhere else in the woods, however, so I just put on my game face and hurried along the beaten path, not particularly worried if my footsteps were unusually noisy; the pattering sound of rain assaulting the canopy of treetops was much louder.

I estimated that I was about ten minutes away from the small meadow when I heard a noise in the ferns ahead of me. I stopped dead in my tracks, standing as still as the tall trees surrounding me with my spear poised above my head and ready to be thrown. Searching for the source of the mysterious sound, I narrowed my eyes as I carefully examined each bush and tree in my peripheral vision, waiting for something or someone to suddenly pop out at me.

I was met with only silence. Shrugging to myself, I was just about to give up and start walking again when the unexpected happened. About ten yards in front of me, none other than Hades stepped out from behind a tree. Obviously not paying much attention to what was going on around him, he whistled softly to himself as he walked along and studied the ground under his feet. I couldn't help but notice that one cheek was swollen and had three ugly scars running down it, and I felt satisfaction knowing I had done that to him only the night before. His jet-black hair and clothes were plastered to his pearly white skin by the cold rain, but he did not appear to be bothered by it. In one hand, Hades was lazily twirling around his black staff, but under his other arm was the bronze helm of invisibility, glistening with pellucid raindrops.

There it is! one part of my brain screamed to the other. With a gulp, I tightened my grip on my spear, realizing this would be my one chance to redeem myself by getting back the helm of invisibility I once had in my clutches. I was sure that Hades's ignorance and arrogance would be his downfall this time. I would make it so.

But Hades chose that exact moment to look up, and his black eyes widened when they met my gray ones. He was apparently just as dumbfounded and speechless as I was. Taking the time to size each other up, we just stood still for a moment then I slowly raised one questioning eyebrow at him. After all, if Hades knew that Hermes and Alec were on their way down to his dark palace to retrieve Cole and Persephone, would he really have been strutting around the forest like a carefree king? I didn't think so.

Smirking, I took one confident step toward him. When he took one cautious step backward, I shrugged him off nonchalantly, raising my spear again in response. Hesitantly, Hades stated, "There's something going on, isn't there? You're planning something, I think." He narrowed his black eyes out of suspicion and waited for me to break eye contact, to give him a sign. But I didn't.

"Care to stay around and find out? It always seems like you have something to say to me anyway," I said lightly, hoping to delay his return to the Underworld for as long as I possibly could.

"I think I'll have to pass on that offer," Hades grunted, shaking his head. Suddenly, he slammed the blunt end of his staff into the ground with the force of a swinging wrecking ball. Hoping I wouldn't accidentally kill him, I took a risk and hurled my spear at him just as a crack opened up in the grass, and Hades stumbled as he tried to dive to avoid the spear, which landed somewhere in the bushes behind him. Hurriedly, he jumped into the large, gaping crack without looking back, and the earth swallowed him whole, resealing itself with a terrible grinding sound. It all happened so fast.

But contrary to what you might think, I hadn't really lost much at all. Because, during the great commotion, Hades had accidentally *dropped* the helm of invisibility. Just like I had hoped. Oh, yes, it was about time that my side of the war received a bit of dumb luck, and I couldn't help but smile in pure ecstasy as I sprinted forward without hesitation, knowing I had finally beaten the lord of the Underworld.

Still feeling overconfident, I raced at top speed away from the scene once the helm, along with my spear, was back in my hands. I was long gone by the time Hades could even begin to think about reappearing to claim what was rightfully his. But I was no longer heading northeast to the small meadow; instead, I was running west toward a very familiar boulder.

"Has anyone seen Demeter lately?" Poseidon's worried voice burst out of the walkie-talkie less than five minutes later, momentarily interrupting the formulation of my plan. "Hera and I don't know where she went."

"Demeter's with me," I quickly lied in response since I didn't want anyone to worry about the goddess of harvest and fertility. Now I knew exactly where she was and what she was trying to do.

You see, when we had that enlightening conversation with the Oracle, Demeter hinted at what she felt needed to be done above all else, but Zeus waved her off without a second thought and her problem had since been left unresolved. I guessed she finally decided that this was the perfect time to carry out the hideously desperate plan to save her daughter, even if she had to do it on her own. I could only hope that Alec and Hermes were already down in the Underworld to meet her, but so was Hades, with an army of bloodthirsty monsters at his side, no doubt. My good friends would be in dire need of some help.

So what did I do next, you ask? I took off my helmet. Then, of course, I put on Hades's infamous helm of invisibility.

Chapter 11

A WAR OF WORDS . . .
AND OTHER STUFF

I lost track of time as I raced through the forest as fast as I could; all I could think about were the different strategies I could use down in the Underworld. I knew I was going to be at a disadvantage, having never been down there before, so I had to do everything perfectly if I was going to help Alec and Hermes get Demeter, Persephone, and Cole out of the Underworld alive. The entire war could be lost or won with this unannounced visit, so I wasn't about to go down there without a plan in mind.

I tried to ignore all the prayers of the soldiers that had started echoing through my head again and wondered if they knew how distracting and maddening it was to the other gods and me. But at the same time, I knew the first generations of the Greek gods had had it even worse because they had hundreds of thousands of people worshipping them back then, not just a couple thousand spread thin around the world.

Speaking of past generations, this was only the second time in history that Athena had worn the helm of invisibility, and this was going to be the very first time that Athena ventured into the Underworld, as far as I knew. I had not had any visions or memories of my past lives doing anything like what I was about to do. Normally, only Hermes the messenger could travel between the different realms of the gods, though I figured the war gave me probable cause.

Concentrate, Athena, I told myself.

When I reached the giant, cave-like boulder where the rest of the gods and I had first come face-to-face with Hades, I slowed to a stop and glanced around, surprised that Hades didn't have any monsters guarding that particular entrance to his realm. It was a big mistake on his part. But perhaps all of the monsters were guarding his prisoners or wreaking havoc on my tired troops around the forest. I didn't really like either of those ideas.

Staying as quiet as possible just in case there really was a monster lurking around nearby, I strode up to the boulder and ran my hand over its cool, rough surface. I was trying to find a trigger that would open the entrance when I stepped on a fallen branch and it cracked, triggering a dark hole to open beneath me. I squealed as I felt my stomach drop then cringed when I hit the hard earth not a second later. Apparently, I had only fallen a few feet underground, though I was now covered in a fine layer of reddish-brown dirt.

I squinted my eyes as I studied my surroundings, but I couldn't see much. In front of me, an earthy staircase descended into the blackness below, but besides that, I was walled in. I took a deep breath, wishing I had brought a flashlight, then set down my own helmet, spear, and shield, still keeping the helm of invisibility on my head. Shivering from the cold air, I slowly began to strip off my shoes, along with nearly all of my clothes, which were soaking wet from the rain and dripping all over the ground. After all, I couldn't sneak into the palace very well if I was leaving a trail of water behind me and making weird squishing noises in my wet boots.

It took a few minutes for me to wring out my shirt and jeans while I kept a close eye and ear out for monsters, but I knew my efforts would be worth it. Had there been another being in that tunnel, he or she would have witnessed only my sopping clothes seeming to levitate, though, thankfully, I was able to see myself. Once I had re-dressed, thus rendering my clothes invisible to another's eye again, I started to put on my shoes but stopped when I realized that they were still full of water. I made the executive decision to leave my shoes there and go barefoot since I couldn't risk being heard by anyone or anything in the palace and didn't have time to wait hours for them to dry out. I also left my armor and shield behind to avoid dealing with the loud noise of clanging metal and to be able to move more freely. I just hoped that I wouldn't accidentally step on anything sharp on my way down to Hades and that I wouldn't get into a bloody battle later on down there.

Alone with my thoughts, I began to silently walk down the stairs. It got darker and darker as I moved away from the hole through which I had fallen and, soon enough, I couldn't see a thing. I had to move much more slowly than I originally expected, using one hand to brace myself against the walls of the tunnel and my spear as a walking stick, but the uneven, rocky steps made my descent even more difficult. However, in about ten minutes or so, I had gotten used to the darkness and was moving a bit faster.

But the farther I went on, the more frustrated I became. I couldn't stand the silence, the never-ending darkness through which I was trudging. I worried endlessly about my friends since I felt certain that I had been walking for at least an hour, yet there was no change in the scenery whatsoever. I thought I was finally starting to understand Hades's bitterness, though at the same time it was no reason to start a war, for I was sure that his life in the palace was a breeze.

Over time, I became more and more desperate to find the end of the dark tunnel, and was practically running down the rocky steps. I rounded a couple of corners, expecting to see the opening to the cavern through which the River Styx ran, but each time I was disappointed. Needless to say, my thoughts became even more pessimistic than usual. My walkie-talkie was well out of range by then so, for all I knew, the rescue mission could have been a success and my friends had already returned to camp. Or Hades had somehow managed to capture all of them.

Expecting the worst, I ran faster.

And then I tripped. I just barely managed to keep my mouth shut as I tumbled down the hard staircase, curling up defensively. I closed my eyes and winced every time my back, sides, or legs slammed into the edge of a stair, hoping that I would stop rolling and reach flat ground sooner rather than later. It was the only time so far that I wished I hadn't left my armor behind, but at least I knew my head was relatively safe from harm.

Thankfully, I managed to direct myself toward the side of the rocky tunnel which prevented me from rolling down the steps any farther. Holding back a groan, I stood up again and glanced over my body to make sure I hadn't been too seriously injured, but it was hard to see through the darkness. Luckily, it appeared that I had only received some new (very ugly) bruises on my sides and scars on my ankles, although my older, larger scratches made by the shrapnel from Hestia's explosion were starting to bleed again, not unexpectedly. Knowing I shouldn't waste any more time, I shook off the throbbing pain with a sigh and continued around the next dark corner.

I let out another sigh, but this one was in relief as I gazed below me at the one and only River Styx. Its dark, stagnant waters stretched as far as I could see in either direction in the cavern, and large masses of souls, which were almost transparent, lined both rocky riverbanks. One small lantern at the front of Charon's gondola on the water, coupled with the dim light emanating from the souls, was enough to light up the whole underground area. Now, I could see that across from the long staircase on which I stood, hugging the wall, was the similar staircase Alec had used on his first trip to the Underworld. Thinking back on how long it took me to reach the gigantic cavern, I realized that the way he had come must have been about three or four times faster than this one.

Shrugging to myself, I rushed down the rest of the staircase and started to weave my way through the groups of poor souls who didn't have the money to pay the fare for Charon's gondola ride across the wide river. I quickly realized, however, that although I was invisible, the ghostly souls could sense someone pushing right through them. They knew something was amiss and if Charon noticed this as well and had a monster report his suspicions to Hades, I knew I would be caught within seconds.

Therefore, I quickened my pace and mere moments later I was standing next to the hooded, gray-skinned Charon on his little black gondola. Luckily, there was a tiny group of souls trying to get a ride across the river at the same time I was, so I carefully hopped on board alongside of them as the last couple paid Charon. I made sure to sit very still for the entire time, so as not to accidentally rock the boat and risk the chance of being caught. I could only hope that Charon and the souls had no sense of smell since I probably smelled strongly of dirt and pine trees, whereas the Underworld smelled more like a wet dog. But despite the possible issues, everything was going okay until I looked closer at the faces of the souls with whom I was sitting.

My heart dropped when I recognized all four of them, though I should have expected to. After all, few people still believed in the ancient myths, which meant that few were buried with money to pay the fare and almost all of them were fighting in the war.

I swallowed down a lump in my throat, forcing myself to look away from the four of them and over at Charon's unnaturally bony hands, but it was too late. The sorrowful images of the twelve-year-old archer named Ben, a friendly water nymph, a petite tree nymph, and the scrawny Knowing boy with whom Alec had fought back in Kentucky were all burned into my brain permanently. Part of me couldn't help but wonder where they had been when they were killed and which monsters were responsible. I wanted to declare vengeance in their names as well as for all the others who had died so far and who had yet to die. But to do that, I had to first make it to Hades's palace.

As soon as the long, thin boat reached the other side of the bluish-black river, I hopped off gracefully, landing on solid rock once again. Before I continued forward, however, I took one last glance behind me at the four sad souls, which floated right by me impassively. Unfortunately, Charon noticed the way that the ghosts had moved around a pocket of seemingly empty space, and my breath caught in my throat for a second. Even though his large hood completely covered his unearthly face, I felt as if Charon were staring right through me, as if he knew I was standing right under his nose.

Realizing I was wasting precious time, I whirled around and started to run through even more souls of dead people, which were waiting in three different mile-long lines for Cerberus to assess them. I did not even pause in front of the giant, black and brown Rottweiler, although he started to bark and yelp angrily as soon as I passed under his tall legs. It appeared that the helm of invisibility had a drawback much like the master bolt and Poseidon's golden trident. All three inanimate objects seemed to radiate power that could be felt subconsciously by those nearby, yet none of those who felt it seemed able to determine the source of the odd feeling so they just carried on with whatever they had been doing beforehand.

I slowed to a stop in front of the looming Corinthian palace a few minutes later, having run through huge fields of grass that looked like the color had been drained out of them. I paused for a moment, waiting for the tall iron gates to open like they did for Alec weeks before, and when they didn't, I was forced to start climbing while trying to keep hold of my spear. Although my hands were sweaty, my strength and tree-climbing skills paid off and, soon, I lowered myself onto the ground on the other side of the twenty-foot-high fence.

Next, I walked right up to the two monster guards standing on either side of the black double doors and jabbed my spear through each of their stomachs before either one could sound an alarm. I stopped to dust off my scarred bare feet, making sure I wouldn't leave dirty tracks in the palace. With that done, I crept inside Hades's castle, shutting the doors behind me as quietly as possible. I did not dare to stop to admire the colorful, classical-era paintings that hung on the pastel walls even though I really wanted to because I was certain I could name all of them. Instead, I followed a hunch and walked along the musty-smelling red carpet that wound its way through all of the different rooms until I heard two familiar voices ahead of me.

As soon as I rounded the corner, my hands flew to my mouth, stifling a gasp. In the center of the marble floor was a shirtless and bleeding Alec, kneeling with his hands tied to two posts and his head hanging low just like when he had been whipped at the Knowing camp. This time, however, Hades was the one standing over him, a small knife glinting in his pale fist. I desperately fought off the urge to drive my spear straight through his ice cold heart when he bent over and slowly dragged the tip of his knife through the skin on Alec's back, reopening the wounds from the hero's whipping. As more red blood dribbled in thin streams down Alec's spine and mixed with stinging beads of sweat, causing him to stiffen, I forced myself to stop shaking and assess the entire situation.

In the left corner of the room nearest to me, Hermes and Demeter sat tied to chairs with gags in their mouths and were helplessly watching, wide-eyed, as Alec was tortured. The rosy pink color had long since drained from Demeter's face and she sat still, as if in a trance. I knew she had put up a tough fight, however, because she had a few new scratches and her blonde hair was messy. Hermes, too, was in no condition to escape on his own since one of his arms was gushing golden blood, which I assumed was the wound he had mentioned over the walkie-talkies.

But at least they were both conscious, unlike Cole who was splayed out in the far corner of the room, his hair covering his face. I sighed inwardly, tightening my white-knuckled grip on the shaft of my spear and wishing yet again that he had never been brought into this merciless world. Cole didn't deserve to live a life plagued by death and destruction; he was far too innocent.

When a loud bang suddenly sounded from behind a closed wooden door off to my right, I jumped and Hades shouted in Greek, "Persephone, be quiet. You're fine!"

"No, she's not fine," Alec growled angrily, in a somewhat raspy voice. "She'll be fine once she's away from *you*!"

Then Hades's black eyes narrowed and he slapped Alec across the face as hard as he could, leaving a bright red mark on the hero's cheek. Alec just laughed, though he still sounded very tired and defeated. "Is that the best you can do? Athena hits me harder than that all the time."

I couldn't help but smirk to myself; it was good to see that Alec hadn't given up hope. I knew he would go down fighting no matter what.

"You would be wise not to make me any angrier, *little hero*," Hades sneered, his eyes flashing as he placed the blade of the knife back on Alec's skin. "I'm sure that your precious Athena would agree, given your unfortunate situation."

If only to prove his point, Hades put pressure on the blade and dragged it along another old scar on Alec's back just below the black owl tattoo, causing Alec to groan and gasp in pain as his muscles rippled in waves of tension. My mouth went dry with worry as Hades finished loudly, "Like I said before, Alec, you just have to tell me your battle plans and this can stop."

"You'll kill me either way," Alec said between clenched teeth, trying to stifle a groan and ignore the sweat dripping down his brow, the back of his neck, and even his dark hair. "I'm not telling you anything."

"HADES!" I heard Persephone scream from behind the door again, louder this time. "LET ME OUT! LEAVE ALEC ALONE!" She pounded on the locked door in a panic, and I heard her begin to sob. "Let me out! I—I'll do anything. Just stop this. Please, Hades. Just stop."

Hades stood still for a moment, glaring at the door while debating his options. He then grumbled some profanities under his breath and reluctantly made his way into the adjacent room that housed his lover, taking the bloody knife with him. Knowing this would be my only chance to engineer an escape attempt, I ran over to Alec and knelt down on the cold marble floor in front of him. I had to glance around to make sure there weren't any monsters or souls in the vicinity.

"Alec," I whispered in his ear and he froze instantly, his blue eyes wildly darting around the room. "I'm right here, Alec. I'm right here," I comforted him, hesitantly placing a hand on his sweaty shoulder, and he relaxed a little bit.

"You're invisible," Alec whispered back quietly in realization and Demeter and Hermes seemed to perk up behind him, noticing his sudden calmness. Meanwhile, Alec closed his eyes and took a long, deep breath, his dark eyebrows knitting together as if he were trying to picture me in front of him. For a moment, the only sound I could hear was of his labored breathing until he stated blandly, "You smell like the forest."

"Is that a good thing?" I asked him quizzically. My heart raced faster and faster as I took a closer look at the deep cuts on his back from which blood seeped out very slowly like red-hot lava from a volcano. The fact that I was there distracting him was probably the only reason Alec wasn't either screaming or unconscious. As I felt my own body begin to shake uncontrollably, I gulped and wondered if Alec knew that he was one of the few in the world who could cause me to panic like this.

"You are always a good thing," he replied under his breath, lowering his head sheepishly, and I blushed even though I knew no one could see me. His jaw was set in a hard line as he tried not to quake from pain or appear too weak in front of me, but I hoped he knew that he didn't have to pretend for me; he was still the bravest and most loyal human I had ever met.

"But at this rate," he added in a more playful tone, "you will without question be the death of me and if I go down . . . well, I hope you're coming too. I wouldn't want you to have to struggle to live without me, after all." I only smirked at his attempt at cockiness, but I had to admit to myself that I didn't want to die any other way.

Then a loud bang came from the direction of Persephone's room and I slid my hand off of Alec's shoulder. He tensed up again and stayed that way even when I started to loosen the rope around his reddening wrists. "You'll be fine," I told him. "Just follow my lead."

Alec nodded and I raced over to Cole, shaking him awake. I figured that if I tried to tell Cole the plans right away, he would just start freaking out because I was invisible and end up giving away my position. So, as soon as he opened his soft brown eyes in confusion, I stood up and moved on to Demeter and Hermes in the opposite corner of the room. "It's me, Athena," I informed them in a hushed voice as I began to loosen the ropes that bound their arms to the old wooden chairs. "I've got a plan to get you all out of here."

"Well, that's a relief," Hermes muttered gratefully once I had removed his gag. He opened his mouth to say more, but just then, Hades stormed into the room, slamming the heavy door behind him.

"Now . . . where were we?" Hades mused to himself as he strode over to Alec again, twirling the small knife around in his hand like it was a child's toy. He wore an awful smirk which made me despise him a thousand times more so I decided it was about time to escape that hellhole for real.

"We were right at the part where you surrender," I announced brazenly, tearing off the helm of invisibility with a confident smirk and thus allowing my long, wavy hair to ripple in wet, matted strands down my back. Hades whirled around and glared at me furiously, but he, as well as everyone else in the room, was slightly taken aback at the sight of my many bruises, bloody tank top, armor-free torso, and bare feet. He was confused just long enough for Demeter, Hermes, and Alec to break free of their remaining restraints, and Hermes shot off into the next room faster than a rocket. Meanwhile, Cole was still sitting on the floor in a daze. Poor kid.

"Well, I have to admit I was wondering when you'd show up," Hades growled at me with a shrug, completely ignoring Alec and Demeter as they raced over to retrieve their bronze armor from a large pile near the empty hallway. Hermes returned to the scene moments later, he and the abused Persephone leaning heavily against each other for support.

They all looked at me expectantly, ready to sprint out of the palace right away, but I knew they needed a head start since they were all beat up pretty badly and would be much slower together. Plus, I wanted to talk to Hades alone. "Just go without me," I ordered over my shoulder, keeping my eyes on Hades in case he tried to attack me when I wasn't ready. "I'll take Cole and meet you guys up there. I've got this. But if I'm not back at camp by later tonight, you have permission to worry."

I heard Demeter, Hermes, Persephone, and Alec grumble together in a quick discussion, trying to decide whether or not leaving me behind was really the best idea. However, I heard the sound of running footsteps fade away less than a minute later after Alec told me to stay safe then silence ensued. I could only hope that Hades didn't have a troop of bloodthirsty monsters on their heels already.

"So, this entire war's come down to just you and me again," Hades began smugly, wiping off Alec's blood from the knife using his own T-shirt. I frowned, not sure if Hades was really that disgusting or if he was just trying to intimidate me. Personally, I was betting both were true.

"I knew it would eventually," I responded impassively, pretending to be more interested in picking at the tip of my spear than in anything else. The first one of us to show fear would be the first to break.

Hades just frowned impatiently, though, and drummed his fingers against his chin. Getting straight to the point, I said, "I have a proposition to make. I want to end this war, Hades. We all do—"

Hades laughed, interrupting my speech. "*I* don't mind continuing the war. It's not like *my* side is suffering any casualties, since . . . well, my soldiers are already dead."

I rolled my eyes and let out a fatigued sigh. "Sometimes I think you're more selfish than Aphrodite," I murmured, more to myself than to Hades. Then I pointed out, "You know, you should be more careful. One of these days when you're strutting around in the forest, you might get wounded accidentally. In fact, I almost killed you once today already."

Tucking the knife under his arm, Hades crossed his arms over his chest and hissed defiantly, "Death is not the worst thing that can happen to men."

I raised my eyebrows in surprise and scratched my head. "You just quoted Plato," I observed, an idea already formulating in my mind, though Hades simply shrugged, as if this fact was insignificant. But it proved to me that he might actually have a slight soft spot or an interest for something besides Persephone, who didn't even love him back. If he wasn't going to listen to me, maybe he would listen to his literary hero.

"Ashley? What's going on?" I heard Cole's shaky voice, speaking in English, come from somewhere behind me. But I just ignored him for now.

"The real tragedy of life is when men are afraid of the light," I quickly quipped in Greek, in response to Hades. "Plato said that too. So are you afraid of the light, Lord Hades? Are you afraid that I'm correct in believing this war is a complete waste of time? That things will just go back to the way they were before? Because Plato also wrote, 'courage is knowing what not to fear.' And right now, you should be fearing whether or not you've dug a hole too deep for yourself to climb out of."

I met Hades's gaze and held it for as long as I could, knowing I had almost convinced him. He gulped and rubbed the back of his neck self-consciously, realizing he had been beaten in our little war of words before he could even respond with a counterattack. But I was the all-knowing goddess of wisdom, so what did he expect? Besides, I wasn't even sure *he* knew the specifics of what he was actually fighting for.

When Hades didn't say anything, I declared confidently, "Anyway, my proposition is this: you stop sending out so many monsters." Hades immediately opened his mouth to object, but I threw one hand into the air, signaling for him to wait for me to finish. "Leave everyone alone except for us gods. Let them return to their camps. Zeus and I were wrong to involve the Knowing. I've realized that while the Knowing have an inalienable right to their homes and must protect them from being annexed by your monsters, you and I are really arguing over who has the right to reign, something far more debatable and intangible. This war is just between you and the Olympian Council, and we don't need any more lives lost. That being said, feel free to send as many monsters as you'd like to attack the rest of the gods and me until either you or Zeus surrenders. Fair enough?"

Hades tilted his head sideways, mulling over the idea in his head. After a moment of silence, he asked, raising his voice, "And what do I get if I win? Because I know I'll win." His voice cracked slightly so he sounded a lot less confident than he meant to.

"Well," I began. "That depends on how everything plays out. You obviously can't take over the entire world—"

"No!" Hades interrupted firmly, almost shouting. He sounded like a child throwing a tantrum. "If I win and beat all of the other gods, I should get everything I fought for, fair and square! You yourself said we're fighting over reign. So, no, I won't accept your stupid proposition. You can leave now." He crossed his arms over his chest, glaring at me with his cold eyes. Impatiently, he started tapping his foot on the floor, but I didn't move a muscle. Now growling, Hades pointed the knife at me and threatened, "Get out of here now or I'll throw this knife at your stupid friend and I promise I won't miss."

"Hades, if you get everything, the world will be thrown out of balance," I calmly started over yet again, but Hades continued grumbling so I raised my voice. "You'll lose control. Trust me; I know. It's happened over and over throughout history, even to Zeus, and this time will be no different. As far as we can tell, the Council's had control for thousands upon thousands of years so why change it now? Why let Chaos return?"

"You have fifteen seconds to compromise with me. If not, take your friend with you and get the hell out of here before I send fifty monsters to this location, Athena. Even *you* aren't good enough to beat those odds," Hades hissed, raising the knife, and my mind began to race at top speed, searching for a quick, temporary solution to the problem. "No? Then your time starts now. Fifteen, fourteen, thirteen, twelve, eleven, ten . . . ."

"FINE!" I yelled desperately, throwing my hands into the air. "Fine. You'll get the forest, okay? If you win, you'll get the forest and the rest of the gods and I will never go in again." My voice, as well as my hands, shook violently as I wagered my true home with a mere promise. Just thinking about my life without the woods made my mouth go dry and my head start to hurt. There would be no more swimming in the river, no more playing reverse hide-and-seek, no more of anything involving the beautiful forest. I watched my life flash before my eyes; to be honest, I felt like I had just sold my soul to the devil. Unfortunately, that wasn't far from the truth.

"I'll have to think about it . . . but that was a much better offer," Hades said reluctantly as he lowered the knife and his chapped lips triumphantly peeled back into a grin that was both hideous and handsome. After all, it wouldn't really matter if he had the entire world because everyone who actually believed in the myths lived right there in the woods or at various Knowing camps. More important, however, was that taking away the rest of the gods' happiness by closing off the forest would only add to his own satisfaction.

Determined to get in the last word after what I had just done, I grumbled unhappily, "Meet Zeus and I by the cave where we first saw you at noon tomorrow. We'll discuss whatever you decide then. But don't bring more than two monsters for backup unless you want to be severely punished." Hades nodded in agreement, though he was also frowning doubtfully.

Then, after a moment of tense silence, he gave a small cough and motioned to the invisibility helmet, which I was still gripping with sweaty hands. "You still have something that belongs to me," he whispered quietly.

Realizing what I had to do, I sighed and reluctantly tossed the bronze helm back to its owner. After all, the archers and swordfighters would be spread out all over the forest the next day and if they saw Hades wandering about, their first instinct would be to shoot, possibly to kill. I wanted to keep the meeting a secret from everyone except the gods and Alec just in case something went horribly wrong. And on the other hand, even if Hades didn't show up at the meeting, nothing about the war would really change.

"No funny business, Hades. Just get to the cave without being seen, and maybe then we can all put away our weapons long enough to agree on peace terms," I said seriously. I wasn't sure he heard me, however, because he only grinned down at his reflection on the shiny metal helm in his hands. Before

Hades could say anything more, I spun around on my heel and dragged the confused Cole out of the dark palace.

———————————

I have to admit it was lucky that Cole was friends with Hermes—well, Josh—because he was fit from running everywhere around town and, therefore, was able to keep up while I ran as fast as I could to get out of the Underworld. Thankfully, Hades had opened the iron gates of his palace for us this time, which was good because I really wasn't in the mood to climb all the way up and over them again.

As we sprinted through the dull Fields of Asphodel filled with wandering souls and headed for the rocky shore of the River Styx, I noticed Cole looking around wildly and could tell he was struggling to understand exactly what he was seeing. Even though he had been unconscious for most of the time, he was down in the Underworld surrounded by mythical beings long enough for the thick fog in his head to clear, for his Sight to be uncovered. In other words, he no longer had the rigid mindset of regular humans in which monsters didn't exist so he saw the mythical creatures clearly now, in their true forms.

Sure enough, he asked, "Where are we, Ashley? What's going on? And who was that guy with the knife? He looked like he was seriously ready to kill someone."

I sighed and squeezed my eyes shut for a moment, trying to decide the best way to explain everything to him. "Cole, do you remember anything we learned about the Greek myths in ninth grade?"

"I think so," he said slowly, his eyebrows knitting together as he tried to recall the information. "There were a bunch of different gods and monsters and heroes and stuff, right?"

"Yes," I answered him as we slowed to a stop near the barking Cerberus. "So the short version of this story is that the myths are true and a bunch of kids from school are reincarnations of the gods, including Josh and me. That guy in the palace was Lord Hades, the ruler of the Underworld. The rest of the gods and I are in a war against him."

Cole's expression was blank, but I knew he was in a state of utter shock, which tends to happen when someone finds out everything he or she previously believed was a lie. "Th—that's impossible . . . but you're not kidding are you?" he whimpered after a minute or two. "Wait—does that mean there really *are* monsters in the forest? Is that why only the Monster Watch survived? Because you're all gods?"

I nodded, relieved (and quite surprised) to see that he was catching on remarkably well. "And the war . . . that's why Hades was torturing Josh's cousin. What's his name again? Alex?"

"*Alec*," I corrected Cole. "But he's not a god. He's a hero. And he's not really Josh's cousin, either. We just made up that lie so he wouldn't look too suspicious wandering around the Woods. It's a long story." I let my voice trail off since I didn't particularly want to tell Cole all the details about what Alec and I had been through together.

Cole frowned, but he didn't say anything more as we stepped up to Charon and his little boat. I wasn't really surprised at Cole's silence because Alec had been a touchy subject ever since I had picked up his phone call in the middle of my conversation with Cole at the Fire Pit. Plus, Cole was acting a bit fidgety under the blank gaze of the creepy Charon. Still, the peace and quiet gave my brain a much-needed rest and, even better, Charon didn't make me pay the fare for bringing us across the river. I thought his small act of kindness was very strange, but I didn't complain.

As soon as we landed on the opposite side of the river, Cole and I hopped off the small black gondola and he followed me up the long, rocky staircase I had come down earlier. Although the other staircase was a lot shorter, my armor and shoes were at the end of this one so we didn't really have a choice. Hopefully, the other gods weren't panicking too much because I was gone for so long.

"Be prepared for the darkness," I muttered to Cole. "I forgot to bring a flashlight." He just nodded as we climbed up the final steps, leaving behind the colossal cavern lit up by the lone lantern, and were forced to slow our pace when we could no longer see what was ahead. At least I still had my spear to use as a walking stick, but Cole didn't have anything.

A little more than half an hour later, Cole finally broke the awkward silence and said, "So you said you were a goddess. Which one?"

"Athena, goddess of wisdom, war, and skills," I stated emotionlessly. "But I suppose you can still call me Ashley, if you prefer. I know it's hard, trying to understand all of this."

I heard Cole chuckle weakly from behind me. "Yeah, just a little bit," he replied sarcastically, and I smirked. Cole then proceeded to ask me about all of the other gods and I did my best to explain who was who. He didn't bring up Alec again, and I was glad. Cole did, however, ask me how he got down to the Underworld in the first place, but I could only guess that Hades had a few of his monsters knock Cole out and kidnap him earlier in the day or perhaps after he had left my house the night before.

Time seemed to pass much quicker now that we were talking a little bit and the only bad part was that I kept accidentally stubbing my toes. Even better, Cole and I could see a bit of dim light up ahead, signifying the end of the tunnel. Not ten minutes later, we came across my combat boots, armor, and shield right where I had left them under the small hole in the ground.

After I had put on my shoes and armor once again, Cole and I managed to muster the strength to start climbing out of the hole even though we were dead tired from walking and running so far. As I gave Cole a leg up, the walkie-talkie suddenly crackled to life so I knew we were no longer out of range of the others'. Unsurprisingly, Zeus's and Alec's worried voices were already calling though the speakers in Greek, "Athena, are you there? Answer us. Athena, are you okay? Can you hear us? Are you safe? Is Cole safe? Are you out of the Underworld yet?"

Their pestering went unanswered as I stood up on the grassy forest floor next to Cole and breathed in the comforting smell of pine trees, but the sound of their voices was ruining my moment of gratitude. Annoyed, I yanked the walkie-talkie off my belt loop and snapped into it, "Can you guys just shut up for a second? You're giving me a headache."

"Oh my gods . . . Athena? You're okay!" The other gods seemed to ignore my request to keep quiet and continued to babble excitedly, so I just shut off the walkie-talkie completely. I would reach them soon enough.

It was pretty dark, especially since we were under the cover of the trees, and I estimated it to be around six o'clock at night, maybe even later. Although I didn't hear any thunder, I realized Zeus's storm was still brewing because a few large raindrops splashed onto my head and face. The heavy rain had, indeed, been going on almost all day so part of me wondered with worry if the entire town was flooded yet. What a mess.

I handed my round shield to Cole so he would have some protection in case a monster attacked us from out of nowhere, although it was a little too heavy for his liking. Then we silently started to trudge southwest toward the river and tiny army camp. Thankfully, we didn't run into any monsters, which led me to assume that Hades was giving us a break until we made final decisions on peace or war the next day.

A few minutes later, however, we passed through one area of the forest that was littered with a dozen dead bodies of centaurs and Knowing warriors alike. But these bodies weren't bleeding out—they were steel gray in color and rock solid, still wearing their last expressions of fear. I immediately recognized the frozen bodies, either lying on the ground or standing in a battle stance with swords raised, as the infamous handiwork of my old enemy Medusa. Knowing the frightful gorgon with eyes that turned people to stone could have been nearby, I turned to Cole and ordered, "If you hear any movement in the bushes, close your eyes."

"Okay, but a—are these real people?" he wondered aloud, his voice shaking as he rudely tapped a dead Knowing man on the head. I just nodded gravely and kept moving along the overgrown path since we needed to get back to the camp as soon as possible. Cole followed me closely and didn't say anything more.

Finally, after we rounded a sharp curve in the trail, I spotted a mass of nymphs, satyrs, Knowing warriors, and even a couple centaurs wandering about. Looking closer, I could make out the outlines of the camouflaged tents covered in dirt and branches. With a sigh of relief, I quickened my pace with renewed strength as the tired Cole scurried along after me, practically dragging my beautiful shield on the ground. Only my excitement to join the other gods helped me restrain myself from giving Cole an austere lecture.

There was one armored soldier, a satyr, standing guard about ten yards away from the actual camp, but he instantly recognized me and kindly waved me through along with Cole. Unlike me, however, Cole was not yet accustomed to seeing such creatures since he had become Knowing only an hour earlier. Therefore, I was not surprised when an open-mouthed stare at the guard's furry goat legs earned him a cold glare and a threatening growl from the satyr. I quickly apologized to the guard for the boy's ignorance then dragged Cole into the middle of the circle of tents, past all of the staring soldiers who had suddenly gone quiet with great interest. They were obviously very surprised to see another human, but they didn't dare to speak up about it.

"Jan!" I shouted for the plump Knowing nurse as I forcefully pushed back the tent flap of the infirmary. But I stopped immediately and my jaw dropped, for the large tent was completely filled with sad, groaning, wounded soldiers. The unlucky ones didn't even get to sit on cots; instead, they just lay on the flattened grass, clutching their various wounds in vain to try to stop the bleeding. Shirts were soaked through with the substance, while beads of blood slid slowly down the smooth armored torsos of those who were still wearing their chestplates. The soldiers' forlorn faces were streaked with dirt, blood, and grime, and a few of them were even missing half of an arm or a leg. Small pools of dark red and golden blood sat stagnant in the grass under their severed limbs, and various pieces of armor and weapons were scattered on the ground.

"Yes, Lady Athena?" Jan the head nurse asked as she anxiously trotted up to me and bowed.

Grunting, I pushed Cole forward once he returned my shield to me and ordered Jan to watch over him and possibly even direct him in helping to care for the soldiers. But after seeing the amount of gold and red blood on her blue apron and everywhere else in the tent, Cole began to protest in anguish, begging me to stay with him. I could tell that the gravity of the war was finally starting to hit him and he wasn't the least bit prepared.

"Cole, listen to me," I said in English, raising my voice and ignoring the fact that every single being in the room was watching us. "You'll be fine. Don't worry; you're in capable hands and I'll be right back."

Although Cole's lips quivered as Jan forced him to sit down on a small cot next to a tree nymph and a blond Knowing archer whose names I didn't know, he stayed silent and the nurse began dabbing his face with a wet cloth. "The other gods are all in their private tent, my lady, and I'm sure they'll want to talk to you right away, but is there anything else you need before you go?" Jan said in Greek, looking pointedly at my blood-smeared torso and bruised arms.

I knew I should have stayed and had Jan treat my many minor wounds, but I felt like meeting with the gods was much more important. So I simply shook my head and replied firmly in Greek, "No, thank you. That will be all for now." Then I acknowledged the brave soldiers in the room with a short nod and walked out of the infirmary, now heading for the similar tent at the other end of the circle, the one Zeus, Alec, and I had slept in two nights before.

Sighing, I took a short pause right outside the tent in order to prepare myself for all of the shouting and fighting I would face inside, the kind of arguments that could actually turn into a hurricane. I could already hear the worried voices of the gods trying to talk over each other at once and couldn't help but roll my eyes as I stepped into the confines of the tent. They would never learn to take turns.

But the gods hardly even noticed me at first, as they were all crowded around Zeus at the far side of the tent still arguing about what to do about me. Finally, Apollo looked up when I pulled off my bronze helmet and smoothed down my wavy hair, and his hazel eyes widened in utter shock as they met my piercing gray ones. "She's back," he said quietly, obviously noticing my dilapidated appearance, and the other gods whirled around.

I barely even had time to open my mouth before a shirtless and very bloody Alec broke away from the crowd, pushing over Hera, Dionysus, and Ares in the process. "You're such an idiot!" he exclaimed as he raced over, a mixture of desperation and relief in his starry blue eyes. I couldn't even fight back as he dragged me in closer with the force of a tornado then gently cupped my face in his warm hands and, suddenly, his soft lips crashed into mine.

To be honest, I shouldn't have been surprised. Not at all. But I was, so I ended up dropping my helmet immediately and it fell to the ground with a dull thud. *Damn*, I thought to myself, knowing I probably should have stopped this from happening somehow. But then, *Oh, why not?* And so I kissed him back, permitting myself to sink even deeper into his strong arms, his velvety lips. Because let's face it; that would certainly be my first and last kiss so it was only right to make it worthwhile.

Mere seconds later and much too soon, I pulled away from Alec, both of us gasping for breath. Out of the corner of my eye, I saw most of the gods either raise their eyebrows or smile collectively, and Aphrodite threw her hands into the air as she shouted passionately, "Well, it's about time!" Ares let out a long, high-pitched whistle in agreement, and Hera appeared especially pleased, though she was probably just glad that I wasn't latched onto Zeus.

Ignoring the other gods' excitement, I stayed silent and looked down at the grass under my feet then at the blood on my hands—both Alec's and mine. I was still shocked and slightly embarrassed at what I had done and apparently so was Alec. "You kissed me back," he whispered, sounding stunned—but clearly in a good way—because he hadn't expected me to hang on.

"Like you said, I'm an idiot," I responded dryly, my mind clouded with mixed, out of control emotions. Part of me meant that as a joke, and part of me didn't.

Quickly, I tore off each part of my armor and hurled them onto my small cot, one after another. I just wanted to have full control over my own feelings again. Half of my time spent with Alec felt as if Aphrodite was inside my head, encouraging me to surrender in my seemingly endless fight against love. And I was not one who surrendered easily.

But then Alec grabbed my arm just before I could throw my spear into the cluttered pile of armor and out of annoyance with my erratic behavior, he pulled me back to him. "Hey, calm down," he told me in a low but commanding voice, and I simply raised my eyebrows at him. I found it slightly ironic that the only guy I ever loved as more than a friend was the only one who would ever call me an idiot or try to push me around. But then again, maybe someone like that was what I really needed. Throughout my entire life, no one had ever questioned me or ordered me around, though it was mostly because I had never actually needed to be told to calm down before. Usually, I was able to settle these problems by myself, but love was definitely uncharted territory.

It seemed like hours passed as Alec and I stared each other down, neither of us giving in, until I glanced back at his bandaged hand, which was still possessively gripping my arm. He let go immediately and cleared his throat awkwardly as a bright red color began to rise to his cheeks again, but I, on the other hand, managed to keep a straight face. We then stiffly turned in unison to face the rest of the gods who were just grinning at us as if there wasn't anything else in the world to be worried about. So, crossing my arms, I rolled my eyes and proclaimed seriously, "I have some stuff to report."

"Yes," Zeus replied, still smirking somewhat proudly. "Yes, you do."

Chapter 12

A PHILOSOPHICAL PARTY

I sat on the nearest cot and let Persephone clean off my visible wounds with a damp cloth as I recounted my story of what had happened down in the Underworld with Hades. I'm sure Alec would have happily sat next to me, but on the other side of the tent Apollo was currently taping bandages to his bleeding back. Nevertheless, Alec didn't take his eyes off me once and I was certain that he was still thinking about our kiss. Hell, *I* was still thinking about the kiss.

And the prophecy, of course. You can't forget that.

When I had finished telling the story, Ares exclaimed angrily in Greek, "So you just *gave* the helm to Hades?! What on earth were you thinking?"

"I have to agree with Ares on this one," Poseidon murmured, running his fingers through his jet-black hair. "How do you know for sure that Hades will even come to this meeting tomorrow? I can't say I would be surprised if he screwed us over."

"Trust me, he'll show up," I responded confidently, clenching my fists in my lap. "Let's just say I gave him an offer he couldn't refuse." Thinking again about what it would be like to leave the forest forever, I gulped, but when Zeus raised one eyebrow questioningly, I quickly shrugged it off.

Breaking the short moment of silence, he announced vaguely, "Well, what's done is done." And after a few last orders were handed out, most of the gods left the tent in a hurry, heading back in a large group toward Main Street. Yes, even after a full day of saving the world from being taken over, some of the gods still had curfews to meet and lies to tell. So after a few minutes, only Alec, Persephone, Pan, and the Monster Watch remained.

When Persephone had finished cleaning up and bandaging my wounds, I muttered a quick thank-you and began polishing my armor so it wouldn't rust. Out of the corner of my eye, I saw that everyone but Persephone, who didn't even have armor, was doing the same, and I simply ignored them as they chatted nonchalantly about who had died and which monsters they had killed that day. I wasn't in the mood to talk and, frankly, I just didn't have the energy to socialize.

I'm not sure how much time passed, but eventually Alec strode over to his cot next to mine. I didn't even have to look up to know it was him so I continued to scrub my breastplate as I asked him seriously, "Are you actually going to have a conversation with me this time, or are you just going to try to kiss me again?"

Alec smirked sheepishly, but I avoided his gaze and kept picking at the dirt on my armor as I waited for him to speak up. When he finally realized I wasn't joking, he cleared his throat and said firmly, "Athena, I'm not sorry for kissing you so I'm not going to apologize."

"I know," I whispered, squeezing my eyes shut, and Alec patiently waited for me to continue. I paused to take a few deep breaths and then, with a shaking voice, I finally admitted, "I'm not sorry either. I'm just . . . confused."

Alec chewed his lip thoughtfully. "I'm sure you'll figure something out. You always do," he told me, trying his best to comfort me. "You're just lucky you don't get confused as often as the average person."

He sat down on the cot across from me, pausing to brush a stray piece of dark hair out of my dirty face and to wipe off a tiny smudge of blood, and then he smirked again. "Damn, you look absolutely gorgeous."

I honestly couldn't tell if he was joking or not so I simply rolled my eyes at him. "Why did you come over here again? I hope it wasn't just to tease me."

"Oh, right, that reminds me . . . I brought you some food," he said. I glanced up and narrowed my eyes in slight disappointment as he set down some berries, a few nuts, and a single piece of bread in front of me. Reading my less-than-thrilled expression, Alec explained with a sigh, "I know it's not much, but the troops already ate the food we brought from your house."

"It's fine. I've had to live off of less food before," I assured him, picking up a berry and popping it into my mouth. "So how is your back?"

Alec's expression darkened, and he looked down at his worn-out shoes. "Hades is a jerk" was all he said as he clenched his fists in his lap.

"How long had Hades been cutting you before I got to the palace?" I asked softly, swallowing down a pang of guilt. But Alec just shut his eyes and shook his head silently so I knew that Hades had been torturing him for a long time—too long to measure and too long to want to think about. Woefully, I took a shaky breath and put my head in my hands. "I'm sorry I couldn't get there sooner, Alec."

Alec shook his head. "Athena, it's not your fault. I'm just glad you got there when you did. Remembering how powerful and alive I felt when I was destroying those monsters with you earlier today and patrolling with the A Team a couple of weeks ago—that's what got me through the pain. I knew that if I survived to see the gods again, everything would be fine again or at least I would *feel* fine. And I was right."

But for how long will you feel fine? I thought to myself guiltily, though deep down I already knew the answer. *How long until the prophecy is finally fulfilled?*

Seemingly oblivious to my personal emotional struggles, Alec paused for a moment to eat a few berries before he questioned me in an equally grave tone, "Now, how are your own injuries? I have to admit you scared me quite a bit when you showed up looking so bloodied."

I just shrugged indifferently in response, seeing as neither of us was willing to complain about the amount of pain we were suffering; we both viewed whining as weak. After all, there was no point in dwelling on what could have happened, what the results could have been. Preparing for future battles was much more important at the time.

"Maybe we should talk about something else," I suggested, tugging aimlessly at the end of my ponytail.

Alec nodded in agreement, passing me half of the piece of bread. "Are you going to tell me about that letter now? You promised you would," he said, hesitantly reaching for the piece of paper sticking out of the pocket on my leather jacket.

I ducked out of Alec's reach as I quickly stuffed the paper farther down in my pocket. To be honest, I had almost forgotten that I had actually written it. And when Alec glanced at me suspiciously, I gulped, trying to decide on the best way to handle this. "I'll show it to you tomorrow," I replied firmly, thinking about the meeting with Hades the next day. I couldn't think of any better time to explain it to him, although "better" wasn't quite the right word.

"Okay, I guess. But speaking of tomorrow, do you want to fight alongside me? I think Zeus will have me stationed in the small meadow again," he asked in a lighter tone, and I couldn't help but giggle. "What is it?" Alec's dark eyebrows knit together in confusion.

"My life," I responded, rolling my eyes playfully. "Most girls get asked out to dances, but I get asked out to go to battle. Crazy, huh?"

Alec just grinned hopefully. "So is that a yes? Don't tell me you'd rather go to a dance, Athena, because I am definitely *not* taking you to another one with the Knowing."

"Never in a million years would I willingly pass up the chance to kick the enemy's ass, little hero. You know that. So, yes, I will *gladly* fight with you," I answered him with a sly smile. Then I finished polishing my armor and pushed all of the different pieces under my cot, looking up just in time to catch Alec's eye, and he blushed, slightly embarrassed to be caught staring.

I opened my mouth to reprimand him, but was suddenly sandwiched on my cot by Zeus and Apollo on one side, Poseidon on the other. "Whoa, is this a date? Can we crash it?" Apollo asked, a goofy smile on his face and his blond hair sticking out all over the place, a common result of wearing a helmet for almost the entire day.

Unamused, I retorted, "First of all, you can't 'crash' an event if you ask for permission. And second of all, we're eating berries and nuts over an old cot—in an army camp, no less! Does this look anything like a date to you?"

"No, but it looks like *your* idea of a perfect date," Zeus pointed out smartly, raising his eyebrows, and I tried my best to keep myself from blushing, settling instead for a glare in his direction. Meanwhile, Poseidon and Apollo both started cracking up and Alec just smiled; they all knew it was true.

"But no worries," Zeus continued, patting my shoulder lovingly. "We'll join you anyway. We're all on a date tonight, boys!"

"Ew! I don't want to go on a date with Athena!" Poseidon exclaimed in mock disgust.

"Your loss," Alec replied to the lord of the sea, eagerly sticking up for me. He winked at me jokingly, but I just rolled my eyes again and stood up.

"Well, I'll leave you guys to flirt with each other while I go talk to Cole. He's probably freaking out," I told them as I ate another berry, and Alec frowned. Poseidon and Apollo didn't seem to care, as they were currently stuffing their faces with the food, but Zeus said he would come along with me.

We left the tent together and started to slowly make our way over to the infirmary, where we thanked the nurses (specifically Jan) for their services and picked up Cole, who had been listening to the older blond man sitting next to him tell stories from the battles. Unsurprisingly, Cole seemed to relax a little bit as we left the tent full of strange creatures and sat down on the riverbank about thirty yards from the camp, looking out over the rushing waters. Other than the noises coming from the camp behind us and from the river, it was quiet. Zeus had stopped the rain for the time being, although silver mist hung low and heavy in the air.

"So how are you, Cole?" Zeus asked in English, breaking our state of awkward silence. I thought that he sounded a little too optimistic given our circumstances, but he was probably just trying to make Cole feel better.

"Okay," Cole replied vaguely. He avoided eye contact, looking down at his shoes and picking at the lush grass instead. Ever since we had passed through the section of the forest with Medusa's kills, Cole had been on edge, like he hadn't expected any of this. I had tried to warn him, but maybe he hadn't taken me seriously until then.

"My parents are probably worried sick about me," Cole added a moment later, hinting at the fact that he wanted to go home.

Zeus sighed and replied quietly, "Sorry, man, but it's not safe for you to go back into town without protection. You're a target for monsters now, just like the rest of us. But don't worry, I'll tell someone to make up a cover story for you." Then he muttered some orders into his walkie-talkie and a minute later, Hermes agreed to talk to Cole's parents.

"When will I be able to go home?" Cole asked, hugging his knees. He sounded a lot like a lost child and, in a way, he really was.

Zeus looked over to me, figuring that my guess would be better than his, and I thought silently to myself for a moment. "Probably tomorrow, later in the day," I told Cole with a shrug. "With any luck, the war will have ended by then."

"You really think so?" Zeus looked at me, mild surprise in his blue eyes, and I nodded. I knew that most of the Knowing had expected the war to run on for at least two more weeks, if not months, though I'm not sure how well they thought it would continue once the gods started school again. If it did, we would be forced to abandon our regular human lifestyles completely, which was never part of the gods' plan.

Scratching my head, I pondered aloud, "Do you think it's wrong that we haven't told the Knowing everything about the war? Why they're fighting, how this whole thing really started and all that."

Again, Zeus raised one eyebrow at me, probably wondering why I would ask such an indicative question, the answer to which had the potential to make us gods look too secretive and untrustworthy or possibly even unfit to rule. His expression was deadly serious, however, as he answered me without the slightest indication of hesitancy, "No, they know enough."

Frowning, he clenched his fists in his lap and glared at them. I wanted to ask, *Do you think they would actually fight for us if they knew the whole truth?* But I knew another provocative question would only upset the king of the gods, who was already on edge, so I kept the thought to myself.

Uncomfortably, the three of us plunged into another silence, listening to the rushing river, the wind rustling through the tree branches, and the murmurs coming from the camp. Silver dapples of reflected moonlight seeping through the thick tree cover danced across the strong currents of dark waters in front of us, and the only other light emanated dully from the flickering orange campfire behind us. But then I heard a more noticeable sound that didn't quite belong with the rest—the low rustling of a bush nearby—and I rolled my eyes immediately.

"Stop spying and get over here, Alec," I called over my shoulder and heard the rebellious hero sigh for dramatic effect as he emerged from the thick foliage. When Alec pointedly took a seat a few inches closer to me than Cole had, Cole narrowed his eyes at him. Alec didn't seem to notice, but he still sat stiff and rigid, his fists clenched, his muscles taut. I, meanwhile, exchanged amused glances with Zeus, who just grinned at me teasingly and rolled his eyes as well. *Boys will be boys*, I supposed.

"So what are you guys talking about?" Alec asked me in Greek, as if he didn't know already, though he was probably just trying to make Cole jealous. And judging by Cole's sudden restlessness, the plan was working. Plus, Alec was shirtless, showing off his well-defined abs and bandaged back, so he probably looked pretty intimidating. Having Zeus, who was even better looking and more intimidating than Alec, splayed out in the grass probably didn't help much either.

"Tomorrow," I answered Alec, also in Greek. "Do you want to come with Zeus and me to meet with Hades? I think it would be beneficial." He just nodded eagerly.

"He speaks English, right?" Cole suddenly interrupted.

"Yes, you idiot," Alec rudely snarled back in English, and I shot him a warning glare. I also heard a snicker come from the other side of Cole where Zeus was sitting, but then Alec changed the subject, still speaking English. "Anyway, I thought you might want to know that Pan just updated the map. A scout spotted a huge troop of undead warriors camped out on the east edge of the forest, close to town. It sure seems like Hades isn't slowing his additions to his army."

Zeus let out a stressed sigh, running his fingers through his dark blond hair. "As long as they don't make a move tonight, everyone should be fine. I'll just send Ares, Apollo, and a bunch of sword fighters in that direction tomorrow."

"How can you guys deal with this life? You could die any day, but you keep coming into the woods, and now you've gotten yourselves caught up in a war," Cole butted in as he shook his head in disbelief. "You're only fifteen years old, for crying out loud! Why are you doing this? How could you let this happen? I thought you all were *smart.*"

Again, Zeus looked to me to give the moral support. (Why was that not surprising?) In the meantime, Alec was staring blankly off into the trees on my other side, doing his best to completely ignore Cole as I explained, "Well, we—and that includes Hades—probably did rush into war too quickly. Now we just have to finish it, rather than let it drag on forever. Adding more and more soldiers isn't the best way to do that, but Hades is forcing our hand, which is partly why we're meeting with him tomorrow. I want to get rid of as much extraneous damage as possible. So I'll tell you the same thing I told Alec when I was training him: it's better to die a hero than a monster. I'd rather not leave any more trouble behind than I already have. And on a shallower note, being a hero is a hell of a lot more fun than being a lonely villain."

Zeus and Alec chuckled in agreement, exchanging a fist bump, but Cole only mumbled glumly, "You must be crazy."

"Well, I like crazy. Crazy can be good sometimes," Alec spoke up, playfully nudging me in the side with his elbow, and I winced as he accidentally hit a bruise. It occurred to me that I might have cracked a rib or two during my tumble down the steps to the Underworld. When Alec raised one eyebrow at me out of concern, I waved him off, knowing I would heal soon enough. He continued brightly, "After all, you can't have a philosophical party without a little insanity. Everyone knows the truth is just as insane as the lie." Both Zeus and I snorted at his bumptious tone, but he was still right.

"A philosophical party, huh? Well, I guess this is a good time to vent about how much my life sucks," Cole mused halfheartedly, more to himself than anyone else, but it was enough to set Alec off on a rant, to switch his mood in the blink of an eye.

"You think *you* have it bad?" Alec stood up abruptly and gave a short, hollow laugh. "Really? You haven't even done anything yet! Try being persecuted for your beliefs, beaten by your own family, and tortured by Hades!" By the time Alec had stopped shouting, his blue eyes were angry and cold.

"Well, sorry—" Cole started, not sounding very sorry at all as he lazily picked at a clump of dirt stuck to his old, white T-shirt. I wished he would've been a little more sympathetic, even though he had been unconscious for the most terrorizing part of our visit to the Underworld and being kidnapped was definitely stressful too.

Fuming, Alec interrupted, "You're just ignorant and innocent, and you know absolutely nothing about suffering! Forget this. I'm done."

Without another word, he turned on his heel and stalked off toward our tent, the crowds parting for him like the sea. I couldn't help but think that I was finally catching a glimpse of what Alec was like before he met the gods. Or maybe he had just been spending too much time around Hera; it seemed her jealous nature was rubbing off on him. Actually, with a temper like Poseidon's, bloodlust like Ares's, leadership like Zeus's, love like Aphrodite's, optimism like Apollo's, strategies like mine, and more, it seemed Alec really did have a little bit of each god inside of him. I also knew that in the long run these attributes would unfortunately cause both physical and mental problems for us, the gods, and most importantly, for the hero himself.

As I watched the disgruntled hero disappear into the crowded circle of tents, I suggested quietly, "Maybe we should all just go to bed now. It's getting late."

Zeus nodded in agreement, stood up, and then followed Alec's path to the tent, making sure to stop and wink flirtatiously at each of the most beautiful nymphs and Knowing members. I got up next and Cole followed suit, but he grabbed my arm and whispered suggestively, "Maybe you and I could stay out here a little longer? You know, *alone.*"

"Oh." My mouth went dry, not sure how to let him down without sounding like a jerk. "Sorry, Cole, but I shouldn't. Athena can't date. She's supposed to be a virgin and never marry and all that, so . . ." I let my voice trail off, but when I saw Cole narrow his eyes dubiously, I added curtly, "That means I can't date Alec either, you know. I was never cheating on you, if that's what you're thinking." Obviously, I didn't mention the kiss I had shared with Alec just an hour earlier.

Cole brightened up again, but only slightly. We then returned to camp, and I felt the eyes of the many different soldiers boring into the backs of our necks as I led him into the large tent to sleep with the rest of the gods. I simply exchanged nods with Pan, Persephone, Poseidon, and Apollo on the other side of the tent, bidding them goodnight before I settled down on my own little cot while Cole took his place on the other side of Zeus. Alec didn't say anything, but he caught my hand and kissed it lightly before hastily rolling over on his side, and I heard Cole mutter some profanities under his breath in annoyance.

Next, I squeezed my eyes shut, hoping that sleep would come easily to me, but of course, it did not. My mind was too alert and busy thinking over the terrible prophecy to allow me to rest so, instead, I fretfully tossed and turned on my cot all night long. Nevertheless, morning came much, much too soon.

The soldiers and all of the other gods had a light breakfast of nuts and berries, but I ate nothing. If I had, I was certain I would have just vomited so I only watched as the troops split up around eight, each heading toward a different part of the forest, each led by a different god. After thirty minutes, Zeus, Alec, and I were the only gods left in camp (besides Hestia and the injured Hephaestus, who were helping out in the infirmary with Cole), busy coming up with a battle strategy for the day and waiting for the time when we would meet Hades. Together we monitored the chatter on the walkie-talkies, changed the map and its figures accordingly, then ordered the troops' movements based on those changes—a true exercise of strategy, a chess match with real-life consequences.

"Alec, how long has it been since you've heard from Jason back in Kentucky?" I asked when there was a pause in radio communications.

He furrowed his brow. "A couple of days, maybe? Base camp was under siege at the time."

Zeus inhaled sharply and held my gaze. Although his expression was stoic, his silence told me his aggravation was mounting. When he finally exhaled, temporarily letting go of his anger in favor of maintaining self-control in front of two friends, he looked back to Alec.

"Well, you'd better call him now. I don't know what you're waiting for," Zeus ordered, his voice tight. "Hopefully the Knowing haven't been starved to insuperable weakness already."

The king turned swiftly on his heel and headed toward the infirmary, his stress level obviously increasing by the minute. He was no doubt going to tell Hephaestus and Hestia it was time for us to leave and meet Hades, so Alec and I quickly suited up in our armor.

"Make sure you ask about the other Knowing camps as well," I added to Alec as he stepped away to call Jason. "Don't let up about New York."

The hero just nodded, and a few minutes later both he and Zeus returned to my side. The news wasn't good; the Knowing base camp had lost a lot of men, and Jason had lost contact with two of the other, smaller camps around the world, presumably due to destruction by monsters. Evidently, we were losing the war on more than one front.

There wasn't a moment to lose. We walked at a faster pace than the day before since most of the wounds Zeus and I had received had healed overnight and Alec didn't have any injuries except the ugly gashes on his back. We ran into a couple of undead warriors, but Zeus electrocuted them all with a single bolt of lightning, and they crumbled to dust before Alec and I could do anything to help out. About half an hour later, we descended a small hill and found ourselves next to the entrance to the Underworld I had used the night before, the place we had first met Hades.

While we waited for the lord of the dead to show up, Zeus, Alec, and I stood as silent and still as the gray boulder in front of us, keeping a close ear out for anyone or anything coming our way. I was sure that I heard the loud crack of a tree branch behind me, and I was just about to turn around when the buff Minotaur and golden Nemean Lion walked out in front of the boulder together, keeping just enough distance between them to fit one person: the invisible Hades.

Zeus glanced over at me quizzically, and I just nodded at him, as if to answer his unspoken question. Two guards—Hades had held up his end of the bargain so far, which was a very good sign. I was almost certain that he would agree to my terms of continuing the war only among the gods.

The lion and Minotaur stopped a few feet in front of us, staring hungrily with their yellow and red eyes until Hades gave a commanding cough. Immediately, the lion sat down on his haunches and, out of respect, bowed his head in unison with the Minotaur. Hades chose that moment to nonchalantly slip off his helm of invisibility, revealing his pearl-white body and messy hair that was as black as night—features with which I'd recently become all too familiar. I gulped.

"Nice to see you again," Hades began coldly, gripping the bronze helmet under his arm very tightly and nodding in turn to each of us. "Let's get right down to business. I've thought a lot about your proposition, Lady Athena, and I'm going to—"

I squeezed my eyes shut, bracing myself. *Sometimes I hate being right all the time.*

An arrow pierced Hades's vulnerable forehead before he even got the chance to finish his sentence. Suddenly out of breath, both Zeus and I fell to our knees and watched Hades helplessly crumble to dust in front of us. *Just like a monster,* I thought bitterly. The only difference was that if you looked closely, you could see his almost transparent soul rise out of the gray ashes and disappear into the treetops, on its way to inhabit the body of the next generation Hades. *What a way to die.*

"NO!" Alec screamed, reaching out for me. Neither Zeus nor I had the strength to move toward him.

I only panicked more when out of the corner of my eye I saw Hades's shimmering spirit suddenly dive back down through the forest canopy as if pulled by some powerful outside force toward Alec, *into* Alec. And the spirit didn't come back out. I automatically glanced at Zeus, but he didn't appear to have seen what I had. For Alec's sake, I hoped that I really was crazy, that I really hadn't seen what I thought I did.

Simultaneously, the Nemean lion let out a great roar and leaped over Zeus and me, landing heavily on the grass behind us. Without hesitation, the lion lunged for the throat of the clueless archer, who had stepped out from behind a pine tree in order to take the deadly shot. I could only let out a shaky sigh when I recognized him as the man Cole had been talking to in the infirmary. Then the body collapsed and dark red beads of blood sprayed everywhere when the lion latched onto the Knowing Warrior's neck with its powerful jaws and shook its head vigorously.

With blurry vision, I saw the Warrior's severed head roll away from the lion, which then started to devour the rest of the man's muscular body, clawing off his armor in the process. Blood pooled, turning the man's blond hair red. A swollen tongue stuck out of the head's open mouth, and its lifeless brown eyes were ripped out of their sockets, hanging only by thin, pink strands of soft tissue. I noticed that his mouth was still open and his facial muscles were still taut in an expression of horror at what he had done, but at least he didn't have to live on with the guilt of knowing he had killed the gods. The lion was angry, so angry, yet so merciful. I wished I had been merciful to Alec.

As I was lifted up from the damp forest floor, I could only feel relief that the disturbing sights of the dead man and the lion's furry face speckled with blood were not the last things I would see.

Meanwhile, the Minotaur bounded off in the opposite direction, presumably to spread word that the gods were dying, that the war was over. The monsters had no true purpose for fighting anymore, except to fill their insatiable hunger.

I gasped for air, feeling as if something had just died inside of me, and clung desperately to Alec as he just barely managed to throw me over one shoulder and Zeus over the other. With a sudden burst of superhuman strength, Alec ran through the forest as fast as he could while carrying Zeus and me, repeating over and over under his breath, "No, no, no."

"You'll be okay, Alec," I whispered to him shakily, trying not to cry. "You'll be okay."

Alec did not say anything more as we crashed noisily through bushes and ferns, but I felt his body quivering slightly so I gave his shoulder a reassuring squeeze, although I knew very well that it wouldn't be enough to comfort him. Nothing would ever be enough for him after the deaths of the gods. My heart had this irrational hope that Alec would recover emotionally, at least somewhat, but my brain—my better half—knew he would ultimately choose to live a lonely life filled with sadness, punishing himself for not stopping our deaths even though the prophecy had always been out of his control.

I glanced over at Zeus, who looked like his troubled breathing equaled mine, and he gave me a weak smile before mouthing sadly, *I love you.* Our matching stormy gray eyes swelled up with tears as we silently relived our past together, but somehow we managed to keep from breaking down completely. We couldn't let our worshippers see us bawling our eyes out.

It was about ten minutes later that we came upon the camp, and I heard scared whispers from all around us as Alec broke through the crowds. Ahead of us, a limp Demeter was being carried into the tent by the black centaur Anton, and I saw Pan use his strong arms to drag himself through the long grass toward the tent, his furry goat legs failing to support him.

"MOVE!" Alec shouted in despair, racing for our tent at the other end of the circle, and the crowds parted nervously, though they surged forward afterward and tried to follow us into the tent. Enraged, Alec dropped Zeus and me from his shoulders, but still kept an arm around each of us for support as he whirled around and ordered to the crowd, his voice hoarse, "No one comes in here. Get it? Absolutely no one."

Silence ensued until Cole stepped forward and cleared his throat. "Let me come in. I'm their friend too," he begged Alec worriedly, not quite sure what was happening.

"No," Alec snarled maliciously, his eyes flashing like some kind of warning alarm. "You're friends with *humans*, not gods."

The unforgiving hero turned around to lead Zeus and me into the tent, but Cole suddenly took hold of his blue T-shirt and yanked him backward, finishing with a swift punch to Alec's jaw. Needless to say, Cole had made a huge mistake.

Before Cole could even prepare himself, Alec temporarily let go of Zeus and me—we simply clung to each other in an effort to stay standing—and tackled Cole in one graceful motion. Cole then received a brutal punch to the nose, which broke it, no doubt, and blood began to gush out of his nostrils like two red rivers. I did not have the energy to tell Alec to stop and knew he wouldn't have listened to me anyway, though I was more than slightly ashamed to admit that I didn't even try, that I felt nothing. Therefore, the punches continued relentlessly, leaving Cole no chance to fight back, and Alec only stopped his ruthless campaign when Cole went limp—unconscious, not quite dead.

Without saying another word, Alec picked us up again and closed the flap of the tent behind him before laying us down on our small, green cots. I struggled to keep breathing as I glanced around the tent, seeing that Persephone, Hestia, Demeter, Pan, Hermes, Poseidon, Artemis, Aphrodite, Hephaestus, and Hera were on their cots as well. Obviously having heard Alec and Cole's fight, Anton, Jan, and two water nymphs acting as nurses abruptly put down their bandages and cloths to hurry out of the tent. A few minutes later, Dionysus, Ares, and Apollo were also brought in.

At last, the tent was filled with only the sounds of the gods gasping for air or sobbing violently. This was the end for us. Even Alec, who was usually so strong, had tears welling in his eyes as he held onto my hand, begging me to stay with him. "You should have up to twenty-four hours left here, r—right?" he clarified hopefully.

I shook my head sadly. "We are already tired and weak from the war, Alec. We won't be able to hold on much longer," I croaked softly, running my fingers through his hair with my free hand.

As if to prove my point, the Oracle rushed in at that exact moment, carrying the little Eros in her arms. As soon as she sat him down next to Aphrodite, the winged god of love turned his small head full of golden curls toward me, gave a nod as if silently confirming the prophecy, then crumbled to dust without uttering a single word. Aphrodite just sobbed harder, covering her beautiful face with her frail hands. As my stomach began to cramp up, I winced and silently wondered if I would be the next god to die.

"You knew this would happen, didn't you?" Zeus asked from beside me, noticing my unusual calmness, and as the Oracle sat down cross-legged on the grass, all of the other gods turned their heads toward me.

My slight hesitation gave them the answer, and they responded with only a chorus of sighs. When my forlorn gray eyes met the Oracle's solemn green ones, she nodded in encouragement, so I monotonously recited the prophecy that had been haunting me for years, "Still you must listen, for the goddess of wisdom will no longer be free of that blasted curse called love. Her beloved hero is great, but he is only bait for the man who will decide this mighty one's tragic fate."

Between all the sobs and sadness, the other gods and Alec exchanged confused glances. I took a short pause to let the words sink in before I admitted, "That was the second part of the prophecy. Hades, Eros, and I were the only gods who knew about it."

"The 'mighty one' referred to your entire generation of gods, not just one person," the Oracle concluded blandly, as if it wasn't obvious by then, and I nodded.

"I guess the Oracle and I were the only ones who realized the gods would die. Hades always seemed to think the 'mighty one' would be Alec," I added, meeting my hero's deep blue eyes once again.

"Well, this explains a lot," he muttered darkly, apparently flashing back to when Hades had tortured him only the night before and when Eros had confronted us a few days earlier.

Then the Oracle cleared her throat and all eyes turned toward her for the second time as she whispered, "And the man who killed you—Jerome, if I'm not mistaken—was one of Alec's old acquaintances. He was loyal, just following you to protect you, I think. Unfortunately, he did his job too well."

Staying quiet, Alec did not look too concerned over the death of Jerome; his sad eyes were focused solely on me, one of few he was really worried about.

"I'm sorry," I whispered in distress to everyone in the room, "but telling you all about the second part of the prophecy would have had no benefits. I—I didn't want to hurt you."

Depressed silence ensued, and I felt a few hot tears run down my face, if only because I was leaving Alec to fix the corrupted Knowing society and the chaos that would rage on after we died—things someone should never have to face by oneself, things we should have been able to fix while we had the chance. In truth, he wouldn't have to face them completely alone, but I knew he would want to.

It was the very first time I had cried, really cried, since I was little, which, of course, caused me to think of my human family. Sighing, I let go of Alec's hand for a moment and pulled out the crinkled paper from my jacket pocket. "Alec, I want you to post this letter on the DANGER sign outside the forest and make sure someone finds it. Can you do that for me?"

Alec gulped as he took the letter from my shaking hands, finally realizing why I had hidden it from him earlier. "Th—this is a suicide letter, isn't it?" he said, his voice cracking with emotion.

I wiped my eyes. "Well, technically it's not *suicide,* but yes. I figured that the people in town deserve to know something about what happened to us."

I watched him hesitate for only a heartbeat before stuffing the letter into his jeans pocket, his woeful eyes meeting mine for less than a second, but it was plenty long enough to make my heart race. He left my side for just a minute in order to bring a few other gods some cool water and wet cloths for their foreheads to try to control their rapidly rising fevers—a result from both fighting in the rain for long hours on end and our internal organs finally beginning to fail us.

All of a sudden, the tent was once again filled up with a bright light.

When we had all regained our vision, our generation's Aphrodite was dust. Then Ares, flashing out with a frustrated war cry, was instantly followed by Dionysus and Hephaestus. Feeling as if some other vital organ had stopped working inside of each one of our bodies, we remaining gods let out a collective gasp. I couldn't breathe, let alone shout out, as I helplessly watched sweet Hestia's soul rise up out of her ashes in another flash.

Alec, meanwhile, raced around like a madman, unsuccessfully trying to deter the deaths of each one of us, and our old friend Pan crumbled to dust in his arms. Everything was happening so fast. Unfortunately, I had yet to see a god's spirit make it safely out of the tent and soar on to inhabit another baby human somewhere else in the world. In other words, their spirits, like Hades's, were still among us in the tent, in a different body, and they probably weren't going to leave.

"A—Alec," I was just barely able to gasp, and my little hero whirled around, bits of Pan's gray ashes still slipping through his fingers, panic in his wild eyes. I couldn't speak any more words as my head exploded with searing pain and my stomach twisted in knots, making me feel as if my whole body might burst into flames at any second.

But simultaneously, Persephone and Demeter began having the same issues on the other side of the tent and they too cried out to Alec for help. Not knowing which way to turn because he knew he couldn't save all of us, he froze up like a lost puppy, and a tear leaked from one eye as the other bedridden gods looked on powerlessly. "Alec, go to her," Persephone finally whispered, a pained smile on her face and love in her soft, brown eyes.

Then she grabbed her ailing mother's hand and their bodies were reduced to ashes.

Sniffling, Alec raced to my side and gripped my hand once again. "Hang on, Athena," he pleaded and gently kissed my forehead before slipping outside for a moment.

As my mind continued to race at full speed, I turned my head to face the Oracle and beckoned for her to come closer. Sensing that what I was about to say was important, she scrambled over to me immediately and put her head near my quivering lips. "Alec. When I look at him, I see . . ." I tried to whisper my confession to her, but my voice trailed off when I started to cough up golden blood with so much force that I was sure my ribs were cracking.

"Yourself?" the Oracle guessed, her eyes boring knowingly into mine.

I nodded. "Yes, and the other gods. It worries me for more than one reason."

"As it should."

"He will never be happy. A long time will pass before his work fixing the Knowing is done and our world can regulate itself again."

The Oracle smiled. "Hearing that from you, I'm not sure if it's an understatement or an exaggeration. But I know. I promise to keep an eye on him for you."

"Thank you," I whispered to her, closing my eyes and sighing. I felt strangely at peace now, but I wished the pain would go away.

When Alec returned mere seconds later, my leather journal, which would later become this book, was in his rough hands. I forced myself to ignore the fact that Cole's dried blood was still smeared over them. Apparently on a mission, Alec swiftly opened the journal, placed it in my lap, held out a pen for me, then told me hoarsely, "You have to finish this. It's what you wanted."

Still incapable of transforming my thoughts into coherent speech, I simply nodded and took the pen from Alec's warm, blood-covered hands. That was when I finished this book, and these are the last words I shall ever write:

As I watch my closest friends and fellow gods vaporize around me, I think about the prophecy one last time. Before the war, I constantly worried about when and how we would die; I was not afraid of death or the pain that would come with it, but I worried about the timing most of all. What would happen to the human families of the gods? What if our deaths caused even more terrible things to happen?

But lying on my deathbed, I just worry that I haven't prepared enough for our passing. Maybe I should have left something besides a letter for the citizens of the Woods, and maybe I should have made certain that every Knowing member knew all of the gods would die at once. My biggest regret, however, is that maybe I should have confided in someone else about the entire prophecy, rather than take sole responsibility for their lives. But I see that it didn't matter anymore, and it probably never really mattered because the ending would have been the same either way. Our fates were sealed immediately with the revealing of the prophecy, and nothing could have stopped our deaths from happening at one time or another.

Now, if you are actually reading this, you might be wondering how on earth I knew that my generation of gods was the "mighty one" referred to in the prophecy. Well, it was obvious to me for many reasons, the first being that this ending made the most sense. Honestly, how much longer could we have kept our powers and true identities as gods a secret from the tight-knit families in our tiny town? As I mentioned briefly, many of the other gods' human parents (besides those of the Monster Watch) were starting to be suspicious of how their children seemed to disappear almost every day and why they always came back with scars. In short, lies about going to the mall in Pine Grove were no longer believable.

And what were we all supposed to do when we were older? Outside of our hometown, it would have been awfully hard to get normal jobs and try to stick together at the same time and, going off of my argument above, we definitely couldn't stay in the Woods for much longer. I suppose we could have fled to the Knowing base camp, but I am positive that none of us would have been able to stand the nonstop worship from the people there for very long. We would become wanderers then, though even a seemingly simple group of good-looking people would be closely watched by others.

This is one of the many troubles with being a god: you're always going to be noticed, but you can't just hide away because somebody somewhere will find you eventually, whether it happens by accident or due to a prophecy, like what happened with Alec. Plus, you're always going to have things to do and people to care for, no matter how much you hate your job or would rather be doing something else. Ignorance causes more problems than it's worth. Perhaps my generation of gods, the Forest Gods, as the Knowing called us, figured this out too late and should have tried to establish contact with Hades years earlier. Or perhaps, deep down inside ourselves, we just liked to cause problems. After all, problems need attention and so do gods. I told Alec and Cole that it is always better to die a hero than a monster, but I should have followed my own advice a little more closely all along and tried harder to prevent the war in the first place; causing problems is not in the least bit heroic.

Secondly (and I promise I'm not trying to be snobby or anything), the gods were probably the only ones worthy of dying in the prophecy, besides the man who would ultimately kill us. In Alec, we would have lost a great fighter and the only person I ever loved as more than a friend or family member, but, theoretically, his death would not have had a huge effect on anything, except for causing sadness and pain amongst the gods, his only friends. And apart from Alec, there weren't many other significant people in our lives who could be even remotely considered as having to do with the prophecy.

Therefore, the whole prophecy was about us. It always was, and I knew that. I knew what was coming, but that didn't mean I was completely prepared. Sadly, it took me six years to realize that accepting all of our fates alone might not have been the fairest reaction to the prophecy. Would it have been better to tell the others and probably cause the war to start sooner and last longer? Would it have been better to suffer together than alone? There are no right answers. Possibly, the rest of the gods and I could have stayed in the forest for years and years without even bothering to come out, trapped in a constant loop of wars against Hades and his giant army, wars fought over disagreements that would never be completely settled until we were all dead anyway. Possibly, you could say that I sacrificed all of the gods' lives sooner than was absolutely necessary. It was about time for our remarkable reign over the forest (and the rest of the world, I supposed) to come to an end.

Now, I would love to say that I deserve more time in this world, but I don't. Overall, I had a fulfilling life; I did all I needed to do and had everything I ever wanted or required, except for more time with Alec. One summer was simply not enough, but perhaps he can read this story over and over again to remind himself that he actually was happy once, that the Fates aren't totally merciless.

All of this reflection brings me to the original reason I wrote this book, something you should understand. The truth is, most people worship gods for two reasons: hope and blame. The wisest people, however, view gods as examples and know that they too have the ability to be better than the gods, at least in character. After reading this book, I hope you all can learn from my tips and from the mistakes made, whether you believe in the Greek myths or not. I always thought G. K. Chesterton said it best: "Fairy tales are more than true—not because they tell us dragons exist, but because they tell us dragons can be beaten."

Who knows? Maybe one of you out there will read this book and say, "Hey, these kids and their powers remind me of my friends and me." Well, congratulations; you and your friends may be members of the next generation of Greek gods. If so, my final piece of advice to you is this: don't get too excited, for being a god takes a lot of work and is not as fun as it seems. Please, remember the Hades of my generation, whose hunger for power caused a horrific war. Remember me and how a single choice ensured all of our downfalls. You probably wouldn't want to meet the same "tragic fate" so early on in your own lives.

At last, here is where I put down my pen permanently, for the pain crushing my chest suddenly becomes too much to bear and my hands shake uncontrollably. But thank you for reading.

Chapter 13

CONCLUSIONS

By Alec

Athena asked me to write down what happened next, so I did. Here it is: She handed her worn, leather journal back to me, hands shaking violently. That defeated look in her pretty gray eyes . . . it killed me. Another tear leaked out of my eye because I really didn't want her (or any of the others) to die, and I knew she didn't want to either. The gods, my friends, were all I ever wanted and all I ever needed. How was I supposed to go on living without them?

"D—don't cry, Alec," Athena stuttered in Greek, choking on her own words. But she started to cry with me again, so I did my best to stop myself, seeing that it was upsetting her.

Sighing, I set the journal down on the ground and wiped my eyes with my bloody hands. "But I love you. You can't leave now, babe. I only got to kiss you once," I said in a shaky but lighter voice, hoping to cheer her up.

Athena just gave me a ghost of a smile in return, her skin losing that amazing golden tone and becoming slightly gray in color right before my eyes. The other gods were suffering the same symptoms, and their skin appeared to sag slightly, their faces sunken in. They were still the inexplicably gorgeous figures everyone pictures in their heads when thinking of Greek gods, but now they looked tired and defeated, lacking the energy to live on.

Sniffling, I quickly took a glance around the tent just in time to see a flash of light a few cots over and a small pile of dust where the handsome Hermes had been lying not a moment earlier. *Six gods left*, I thought hopelessly.

My attention was brought back to Athena when she suddenly gasped in pain, her eyes still locked on Hermes's cot as if she was searching for something. But she obviously didn't see whatever she was looking for, because her eyes only darted back and forth across the tent, and her breathing quickened. She whimpered. Was that fear, sadness, pity, or pain in her voice? I couldn't tell. Admittedly, I had never seen her truly afraid, but there was something different about her in this moment. She just looked back at me, eyes watering, shaking her head, as if to silently apologize for something I didn't know about.

It was all four of those emotions, I decided. And it meant bad news, bad news that must have had something to do with me.

Worrying even more than before, I held on to her hands to try to stop her from quaking, but it wasn't really helping much. "Breathe," I ordered in a low voice, carefully undoing her signature ponytail and running my fingers through her long, wavy, dark hair.

Next, I lifted Athena's head up so she might be able to breathe a bit easier and slipped one arm around her slim waist, pulling her closer to me. Our wet, bronze breastplates were the only tangible things separating us, and I could still feel her rising body heat radiating through her armor, which highlighted the shape of her small breasts and the athletic curve in her sides. She had never let me hold her at all before and I knew that even if she had survived the war, she probably never would have let me hold her so intimately again. She preferred punches to hugs, indifference to love, and I was okay with that. In fact, I was usually the same way, but for some reason I wanted her more than anything.

Savoring the once-in-a-lifetime moment, I breathed in the pungent scents of sweat, blood, and pine trees. She smelled like home. I wanted to stay there forever.

"See you on the other side, everyone," Poseidon's voice suddenly called out from behind me, interrupting my thoughts, and I whirled around in my seat, meeting his sea green eyes only a second before I was blinded by another flash of white light.

"No," I croaked helplessly, knowing that his death would hurt the remaining gods even worse because he was one of the more powerful and most prominent in this generation.

Sure enough, Hera started to violently cough up blood from a cot across the tent. "Zeus, are you ready to go?" the queen asked in a scratchy voice, clutching her pained stomach.

"Go without me, love. It will be fine," Zeus responded between coughs, and Hera was gone seconds later, her soul fading away into thin air too fast for me to follow its path. I found myself wondering if she had known he had cheated on her only the day before.

Meanwhile, next to Apollo, Artemis was groaning in agony, trying to hang on to her life just a little longer. I glanced back down at Athena, who was biting her lip so hard that it had started to bleed, and a single golden bead of blood rested on her pale lips. They were all on the brink of death.

"You have to let go now, Alec," Zeus whispered. "Our time has come."

I shook my head stubbornly, in denial. The Oracle, however, left the tent calmly. I had to admit that sometimes her indifferent actions angered me, even though she was just obeying orders this time.

"I won't get to see you again," I told them all sadly, although I kept my eyes solely on Athena. You see, even though the gods would be immediately reincarnated once again, they would be babies, probably reborn somewhere far away. It would be many years before they would discover their powers. Most likely, I would die before I found them again, and even if I did somehow manage to find them, there was no telling whether or not they would remember me. The next Athena might have flashes of good memories, but she would be a different Athena (if that makes any sense to you), so I wasn't sure if I would be able to love her in the same way again and vice versa.

"Alec, you'll always remember us. You can see us in your head and in your dreams whenever you want. I promise I'll be there," Athena told me softly, letting out a shaky breath. I opened my mouth to retort, but Athena answered my question before I could even ask it. "Alec, you'll be fine. You lived without the gods once and you'll do it again now."

"But I don't *want* to live without you guys," I protested, blinking away the tears. "You're all I have left."

And it was true; I would be alone after their deaths. No family, no friends left in the Knowing. There were a few nymphs and satyrs I liked well enough, but no one could compare to the gods. No matter what I did, those thoughts would always be at the back of my mind, preventing me from getting close to anyone ever again.

Plus, my late father already seemed to be forgotten; upon my return with Athena, no one at the Knowing base camp had even bothered to ask about what had happened to him. None of the gods had even mentioned him after the day we'd met, except for one time during training with Athena when I admitted that I wasn't as saddened by his death as I expected to be. Beforehand, I had felt guilty about his death, but later I felt nothing toward him at all. To be honest, I had found much better company, people who actually wanted to support and be friends with me without a different motive. After all, the only reason my father had come to the Woods with me was to meet the gods.

I didn't really care about my mother at that moment; she could do absolutely nothing to help or comfort me. She never could, nor did she really want to. My mother could've gone straight to Tartarus, the worst part of the Underworld, and I wouldn't have given a damn after her actions during my whipping. The rest of the Knowing could go as well. They never cared either. Their supposedly selfless motto was valuing the gods over family, but they really valued their own sorry lives over anything else.

Then again, the Knowing members couldn't all die at once, and I was only one person. Better me than them.

Athena knew my thoughts on all of this, of course, and she tightened her grip on my hands. "Alec, promise me you won't commit suicide," she begged, shaking her head. I hesitated. How did she always manage to see straight through me? "Please, Alec. Please. I know you didn't really want to be considered a hero for your people because you thought they didn't deserve one, but you're the best hope they have for change. And they *desperately* need to change their ways. I didn't have enough time with them, but you do. This war is finished now, but I know there will be plenty of battles left to fight back at the base camp, battles only you can win. So please, Alec, don't kill yourself. This isn't over yet. *We* aren't over yet."

"Okay, okay. I promise I won't," I finally told her, wondering what the hell her last sentence meant, and her tears slowed to a stop. Studying her face carefully, I asked, "What do you want me to do then? Go back to the Knowing camp?"

"Do what you think is right. I believe I trained you well—not just as a fighter, but also as a leader—so here's your chance to really prove it. Even though you can't be a hero *for* the gods anymore, you can still be a hero *in memory* of all of them," Athena said firmly, meeting my eyes as if giving me an unspoken message as well. When she exchanged a quiet nod with Zeus, I could tell for certain that I was losing her. With every second, she slipped further and further away from me. Her body, her voice, everything about her was shaking as she looked deep into my eyes for the last time. "Sir Alec, first official hero of Mount Olympus of the twenty-first century and unofficial knight of the Woods, I probably should've told you this earlier, but I just want to say that I love—"

Her voice stopped, and I could see panic suddenly flash through her stormy eyes like a lightning bolt. *You*, I thought, desperately hoping she would be able to finish her sentence. I wanted to hear the words I'd always dreamed of her saying to me come from her own mouth. *Come on, you can do it, babe. Just say the word. Come on!*

But she couldn't finish. We both needed more time, even if it was only a few seconds. Unfortunately, the Fates wouldn't give it to us.

A flash of white light so bright that it blinded me suddenly emanated from all around me, not just from where Athena lay, so I knew all of the other gods would be gone by the time I opened my eyes. Sure enough, when I regained the ability to see, Athena was just dust in my hands and the other gods were piles of tiny gray particles on their own respective cots. I hadn't even gotten to see their souls float away from me.

"NO!" I screamed as if it would help somehow. Out of frustration, I sank to my knees and punched the ground as hard as I could, scraping the skin off my knuckles. *Damn the Fates!* Tears were streaming down my face and I couldn't stop them. I gave up. But, collapsed on the grass, I caught sight of Athena's black pocketknife a few inches away. She must have dropped it while I was carrying her into the tent.

Without really thinking, I grabbed her knife and opened it. I thought the blade was shiny, beautiful even, just like the gods, and I had made three long slits on my left wrist before I truly realized what I was doing. "No, no," I repeated to myself angrily, my voice shaky. I was such an idiot. "You have to stay alive, Alec. Live for the gods. Live."

I stuffed the knife into my pocket. A keepsake to help me remember her.

Now what? I asked myself once I had calmed down as much as I possibly could, but I knew the answer immediately. Ignoring the blood that dribbled down my left arm, I rose from the ground and went to the middle of the tent where a small table full of medical supplies stood. I quickly dumped the bandages out of a large glass jar then collected all of the gods' ashes, pile by pile. In a rush, I wiped my eyes and headed out of the tent. I didn't even think of bandaging my wrist.

"ATTENTION!" I shouted at the top of my lungs as soon as I stepped outside, and at least a hundred centaurs, nymphs, satyrs, and Knowing members instantly whirled around to face me. It was dead quiet until I continued, "The gods are dead. They are being reincarnated somewhere else as we speak."

Gasps and sobs from the crowd momentarily distracted me, but I still searched the sea of faces until I found a satyr and centaur I recognized. "You two, tell any remaining troops on the battlefield to retreat. All Knowing members, start packing up because you'll leave for Kentucky tonight. Centaurs, prepare to go back to your own territory. No stalling."

There were a few unhappy murmurs from the crowd, but everyone dispersed for the most part. I didn't know what else there was to say. So, without wasting another second, I started sprinting east toward Main Street with Athena's letter and the jar of ashes in hand. I ran about forty-five minutes before I came to the edge of the woods, but even though the light hadn't really changed, the forest felt much darker than normal—even darker than it had seemed during the actual war. Perhaps it was just that I no longer felt empowered or excited to fight. I had nothing worth fighting for anymore.

Therefore, I guessed the one lucky part of my frantic sprint was that I didn't come across any monsters. Since their leader had died, the mythical beasts were probably retreating into the Underworld and trying to sort themselves out.

I poked my head out from under the thick tree cover by Main Street to find that it was still raining a little bit and that the street was more like a rushing river, with dirty rainwater flowing along the slippery pavement. Anxiously, I sat down on the damp grass behind a tree and waited for the rain to stop so I could post the letter without it being ruined. With nothing else to do, I reluctantly pulled the folded piece of paper out of my pocket and started to read it.

Two hours later, I was still numb and in shock, feeling empty and alone. But the rain had stopped temporarily and I decided to post the letter. With shaking hands, I made my way to the red and white DANGER, DO NOT ENTER sign, after looking both ways to make sure no one was watching me. A random guy dressed in Greek armor would seem pretty suspicious so I waited until I was fully hidden by foliage again before I yelled in English, "HEY! Look over here! There's a message on the sign!"

My heart raced faster and faster as I waited for someone to emerge from one of the tiny shops. What was only a minute seemed like an eternity, but when I saw Athena's human father, Henry, emerge from the Fire Pit first, I wished time had passed even slower. Feeling even more awful than before, I fell to my knees.

I was supposed to protect his daughter, after all, and I hadn't. I knew he would never forgive me, never even think of me as more than a measly monster after this. I was not sure why his opinion mattered to me so much since he was always drunk and I'd only ever talked to him for five minutes. But I still cared. I really did. Maybe it was just because he knew Athena and loved her too.

Taking deep breaths, I tried to force myself to watch as the town slowly gathered to read the note, but I couldn't do it. Instead, I just sat in the long grass with my eyes shut, clutching the glass jar full of ashes as if my life depended on it. No matter how hard I tried, I couldn't stop rereading the letter in my mind; I had subconsciously memorized the damned thing. This is what it said:

Dear humble citizens of the Woods,

If you are reading this, Alicia, Maddie, Matt, Jack, Josh, Rebecca, Camille, Haley, Shane, and the Monster Watch (Zach, Luke, Connor, and I, Ashley) are dead. This is not a joke, although I wish it were.

To answer the questions I know everyone is currently wondering, yes, we were killed in the forest—ironically, I'd like to think, since we were the first to survive the terrible things in there. (So, yes, your suspicions were correct if you thought that the Monster Watch might have occasionally brought friends along on its journeys.) Why then, after all of these years, did we die now, you ask? Well, it's hard to explain, but I suppose we had cheated Death for far too long and he finally caught up to us. That being said, our tired bodies will soon be disposed of, if they haven't been already, so do not go into the forest to look for them. You will only get yourselves killed as well, and we definitely wouldn't want that.

I truly wish I could tell you more about what happened in our beloved yet horrifying woods, but I cannot bring myself to place the burden of this knowledge upon you. It would be quite cruel of me, to tell the truth, for Zach once observed that if you knew about the things in the forest, you would probably wish you didn't. You should understand, however, that although the Monster Watch had many great times gallivanting throughout the haunted forest, I regret that we grew up much too fast as a result of the things we saw. We were thousands of years old in mind, yet we acted like regular teenaged fools. We partied, dated (admittedly, some of us more than others), and played our own versions of childish games just to try to feel young again—this I do not regret, although thinking of it now saddens me greatly.

In conclusion, you must realize that if you can help it, you should never go into the forest, whether it is the physical one in front of you or the metaphorical one, which might not even be a forest at all in your case. Why not? Firstly, the physical one is simply too dangerous and deadly, but the metaphorical one will steal something from you that is arguably far more valuable than a short spell of bravery: your innocence and immaturity, which must not be taken for granted. I cannot stress this enough.

Overall, I had a wonderful life in the town of the Woods, and I know my friends would agree. I can only hope that you realize what you have here is amazing—a stable economy, friendly relations, a beautiful setting, et cetera—and I do not want *you to leave it all behind just because a bunch of people died here. After all, people die everywhere and people die every day. We just happened to die here, on this day.*

So, if you still feel the need to take some sort of action as a result of our deaths, you may as well fulfill our last wish: Stay here and keep the town of the Woods alive, but do not tear down the forest, for it really does share a home with you, whether you like it or not. As long as people don't disturb it, the creatures inside won't disturb you. Hopefully, you still have many more years left to live, and those years should not be wasted fretting over the fate of a natural habitat, a fate which may very well be intertwined with yours.

Lastly, I want to thank you, every single one of you, for the Woods would not have been so wonderful without you. I must go now, but I wish you good luck in all of your adventures to come.

—Ashley

How she managed to write in a tone that was so emotionless but sorrowful at the same time was beyond me. That girl was a genius.

Suddenly determined to get away from all the sadness in the town so as to keep from breaking down again, I pushed myself off the ground and headed west. I planned on returning to Main Street later to see how the townspeople were faring, but I had something else I needed to do now.

I knew the gods had loved the Woods—the forest in particular—and I knew that if they had survived the war, they would've wanted to stay in their isolated hometown as long as possible. This is why I had collected their ashes.

For Poseidon, I threw some in the river. For Pan, a handful of ashes was placed on his small throne of rock and moss, and for Hestia, ashes were added to the fire pit in the center of the army camp. For Persephone and Demeter, I threw two handfuls over the large boulder, the entrance to the Underworld where mother and daughter were first reunited in this generation. For Artemis, I spread some ashes around her preferred part of the forest for hunting, near the Oracle's camp to the northwest, and for Apollo, I dumped dust around the small meadow, his favorite place in the forest, one of the few spots you could actually see the sky. Finally, for the great Zeus and Hera, I threw ashes into the air, and the wind carried them up into the silvery clouds floating around their heavens.

I scattered the rest of the ashes at random around the forest in honor of the other gods, since I didn't have any specific ideas for them. I thought about putting some for Athena on the roof of her house, but I didn't want to risk getting caught by her father and I couldn't wait until nightfall for the cover of darkness. I didn't know what to do with the glass jar either, so I simply tossed it into the thick bushes, hoping it would be lost in time forever, or maybe a nymph would find a good use for it sometime in the future.

After that, I returned to the army camp. I didn't want to talk to anyone, but without the gods and Jason, who had been running the Knowing base camp in Kentucky, I was left in charge. Lucky me.

I looked down and avoided everyone's gaze as I made my way through the crowd, not exactly sure where I was going. I wasn't sure it really mattered. Everyone around me was busy packing up their belongings and saying good-bye to new friends. All of the centaurs had already left the camp and had jumped across the rushing river, back into their own territory. Most of the satyrs and nymphs were staying in the forest, but I was surprised to see a couple of them starting to head out with the Knowing. I was a little bit disappointed, to tell the truth.

There was only one person—the outsider—who was not doing anything to aid in the packing.

With a grim look on his face, Cole hobbled over to me, gasping for air and clutching his sides in pain. His face was bruised in shades of blue and purple I didn't even know existed, and blood from his broken nose was smeared across his cheeks and mouth in a way that could have been considered artistic if the colors were on an actual canvas. I had to remind myself that I was the artist. As his whole body began to shake, he said, "N—no hard feelings?"

I could tell that, like everyone else, Cole had been crying since his eyes were still puffy and red. He stuck out his hand for me to shake, but I chose not to respond. Instead, I settled with an exasperated sigh for dramatic effect and after a moment of tense silence, he continued anyway, "Because . . . well, you should know that I never really had a chance with Ashley. I realize that now. The two of us together . . . it wouldn't have worked."

"Athena," I corrected him gravely, flashing back to a moment on her rooftop on the Fourth of July. "Her name was Athena. She didn't like Ashley very much."

Cole gulped and nodded. "See? I didn't know that. But you did. I bet she always liked you, because you actually knew these things about her. You understood her better than anyone, except maybe Zach. You never needed to worry about me getting in the way of you two," he told me truthfully yet cautiously, as if he were expecting me to blow up at him again.

But I stayed silent, thinking quietly to myself. This was the first time in a while that I felt even remotely like a normal teenager, arguing over a girl instead of who gets to kill the next monster that wandered by. With the gods, everything had been so serious and backward, including games. Sure, we would tease each other a bit, but we were always sarcastic, joking in a crude manner. And our jokes never lasted very long. Within seconds, our discussion would return to more serious topics, like monsters or the war. Whenever there really was "regular" drama of some kind, a fight of words often turned into a raging storm, a dangerous physical battle, or even a war, and none of those were even fun to watch.

At the same time, however, I knew Cole felt older than he had ever felt before. He had never experienced so much death, and it was definitely affecting him. Here he was, being a good person and trying to make up with his enemy, sort of. I just wished his life hadn't come to this. I knew he was carefree at one point in his life, but he never would be again. The gods, Knowing about the monsters, and the Sighted life in general tend to have that effect on people.

Once he realized I wasn't going to respond, Cole cleared his throat and nervously scratched his head. "Um, have you seen Jerome? I should probably thank him."

I froze up immediately and echoed him in confusion, "Jerome?"

"Yeah. You know, the blond archer, probably around thirty?" Cole said with a shrug. "I sort of told him to follow you this morning and look for anything romantic going on between you and Ash—I mean, Athena. I know it was wrong, but—"

"Jerome is dead," I cut off Cole angrily, realizing what all of this meant. I really had been "bait," just like the prophecy had foretold.

But when Cole's face went pale, I clenched my fists and started to quake involuntarily, fighting to refrain from placing even more guilt on his shoulders by telling him that the death of the gods was his entire fault. Frankly, I was surprised with myself for cutting him so much slack when he had caused me so much pain. Now, I just wanted him out of my life. I never wanted to set my eyes on him again.

"You're going back to town now," I told him harshly. "You're going to forget all of this ever happened, and you're going to continue living your life like you were before."

"How can I go back and forget all of this? I just learned about it last night!" he exclaimed. "My parents will put me in a mental hospital! I'm sure of it."

Cole paused to wipe blood off his nose, and I smirked, glad I had caused him pain. There was something about him that really set my teeth on edge. It was probably the fact that he killed all of my best friends. Indirectly, of course.

"Would you rather die instead?" I asked him emotionlessly. "I can do it quickly and painlessly. Athena trained me herself, you know, but I'm not sure this is what she would have wanted for you."

Cole's jaw dropped and his brown eyes were unblinking. "Dude, you are seriously messed up. Haven't you already beaten me enough?" he questioned, and I shrugged; I was just being straightforward, practical even, and I hoped Athena might have offered him the same thing. After all, I had considered doing it to myself only hours earlier. Death was a simple and inevitable thing, often an act of loyalty, to the gods and me.

"Maybe you could just knock me out again and leave me by Main Street," Cole suggested reluctantly. "Hopefully when I wake up, I won't remember anything." And after a bit more arguing, I agreed and enlisted the help of the Oracle.

Together, we headed east a few minutes later and when we finally reached Main Street, Cole asked, "Hey, one last thing before I forget all of this—have you ever thought about just shooting the monsters? Like with a gun. I'm sure it would be much easier than using a sword, and I know Ashley's dad, Henry, has a couple." The curious look on his innocent face told me that he had been waiting to ask this specific question ever since he had developed the Sight.

I frowned, glancing down at my sword in its leather sheath on my hip. "I'm not sure if that would work. Monsters are weird that way," I mused slowly, scratching my head. "Besides, sword fighting is a Greek tradition and I love a challenge." I finished with a nod, thinking that Athena would have said something along the same lines.

"There is a little bit of magic involved in the myths," the Oracle agreed thoughtfully, a mysterious smile playing across her lips.

Two hours later, she and I had grilled Cole with so many questions at once that he didn't even remember the gods and was convinced he had imagined almost all of the monsters. One swift punch and he was out like a light. Then I waited just inside the tree line for someone to pick Cole up and only a minute or two later, someone did. I bet you can guess who it was.

Henry, of course. (Apparently, the universe hadn't finished torturing me.) But he didn't just drag Cole back into the Fire Pit—he left an empty beer bottle at the base of the DANGER sign. There was a message inside.

As soon as he and Cole were gone, I quickly retrieved the bottle and sprinted away from any prying eyes of un-Knowing humans, back inside the forest for safety. Silently vowing to steer clear of alcohol for the rest of my life, I crinkled my nose at the terrible smell of the beer before I pulled out the tiny note to read it. *Meet me in Ashley's room at 5:00.* Sounded okay to me; I had nothing to lose.

Since I wasn't sure exactly what time it was but I knew it was relatively late, I decided to go meet Henry right away. Staying hidden, I followed the edge of the trees that ran along the flooded streets and arrived at Athena's house just before sundown. I then took off my armor, stuffed the pieces in a hollow log, sprinted across the yard, and climbed up to her balcony like I used to do almost every night. Only this time I dreaded what awaited me.

For a while, I just stood outside, staring at the door and contemplating whether I should actually go in or not. I would reach out for the door handle, but then I'd pull my hand back abruptly. Over and over again. *Why the hell is this so hard?* I asked myself out of confusion, but I knew deep inside that I was really just scared of what Athena's human father would say to me. I couldn't even remember the last time I had been truly afraid like this. But, finally, I jerked open the door, knowing Athena would have wanted me to face him. I was supposed to be a hero, after all.

"Took you long enough to open that door," her father's gruff voice said, and I jumped, surprised to see him waiting for me, sitting on the edge of his daughter's bed.

"I know. I'm so sorry, sir." I knelt on my knees in front of him, bowing my head and avoiding his cold gaze as I fought back tears. I was determined to appear strong in front of him, to keep my last shreds of dignity after completely breaking down earlier. "I'm such an idiot. I should've—"

"You're not an idiot," he interrupted me, putting his hand on my shoulder. I was shaking so much. Why couldn't I stop? "It's okay, son. It's not your fault."

"But it is!" I exclaimed desperately. Why couldn't he just admit that I was to blame? "You told me to protect her and I didn't. I—I should've tried harder to help all of them."

I tried to take deep breaths, but I just started to cough instead. Then I tried to wipe my eyes, but I accidentally smeared thick, red blood from my arm all over my face, and I slammed my fist against the bed frame in frustration. Her father saw the blood trickling down my arm and raised his eyebrows so he might have guessed I had been cutting myself, but he still didn't say a word about it. I was grateful.

"Look, Alec," Henry began, running his fingers through his light brown hair. "I haven't known you for very long, but I can see that you're tough and I can tell that you did everything you possibly could to save her. I mean, you're covered in blood—and whatever that gold stuff is—so I *know* you put up a fight. You shouldn't be ashamed of yourself. Now, you just need a little help before you bleed to death."

"No, sir," I argued, glaring at my shoes. "I'll be fine. The blood on my back is . . . old."

Okay, so maybe the blood seeping through my shirt actually *was* fresh from my reopened scars, but he didn't need to know that. Henry still looked dubious, though, so I held up my arm and slowly ran my finger right over the three burning slits, keeping my face straight so as not to show my pain. "Only my arm is cut, and it doesn't even hurt anymore. See?"

I finally looked up to meet his puffy eyes, and I could immediately tell that he had been crying, too. "Can I ask you something?" he asked, once he realized that trying to help me was a waste of time, and I nodded. "Did you love her?" I nodded again self-consciously, chewing my lip and wondering what he would say next. Would he be mad? Disappointed?

Henry let out a long, sad sigh. Stroking the stubble of a beard on his chin, tears welling in his eyes, he said, "She loved you too, kid. She loved you too—more than she loved me, at least." He paused to guiltily cover his face in his hands, but I stayed silent because I knew now that what he said was true. "Besides the Monster Watch, you were the only boy she ever really brought home. That's how I knew—knew she loved you, that is. I guess that's why I sort of liked you. But my God. . . one day later and this happens?"

"I know, I know." I was sniffling again. I couldn't help it. "I saw her writing something in here, but I sh—should've stopped her and asked her about it. I never expected this, but for years, *years*, she knew. Way before she even met me, she knew something like this would happen. And she didn't tell anyone."

Damn the Fates, I thought to myself yet again since I couldn't really blame the Oracle for simply delivering their plans in the form of a stupid prophecy. And I just couldn't bring myself to be angry with Athena, either, for not telling me her biggest secret, because if I had been in her shoes, I probably would have done the exact same thing she did: let events play out the way they were meant to be.

It was quiet for a long time as both of us seemed frozen in time and place. Finally, her father stood up and whispered shakily, "Take anything you want from here—books, pictures, anything. It's not like anyone else will use her stuff." As if suddenly remembering something, he paused and strode over to Athena's desk against the wall. There were papers strewn all over the place, and her supply of bandages was sticking out of the lower drawer, but somehow her desk still looked organized.

Her human father went straight for the top drawer and pulled out five leather journals exactly like the one Athena had been working on all summer. "You should take these. Maybe you can decipher them." Henry handed me the journals and I opened them one at a time to find that they were all written in Greek, with dates on each page ranging from when she found out at age nine that she was a goddess to the days just before this summer. They were diary entries from the lost years of the Forest Gods, the years not mentioned in this book.

"Wow, this is amazing," I said, mystified. I had no idea that those other journals even existed. "Thank you, sir. I could use these." Hundreds of pages of her advice—ten times as much as she could fit in this one book—and happy stories from their golden days. Her journals were the greatest gifts I'd ever received, the best things to help me remember my friends.

"Anything else?" her father asked, and I quickly glanced around the room at the tall bookcases that completely covered each wall.

I was about to say no and just leave when a small photograph on one shelf caught my eye. It was a class picture from the gods' last year of school in the next town over, Pine Grove. Only eighteen kids in the entire tenth grade and thirteen of them were gods. Talk about small towns.

In two rows, each god stood strong and proud and handsome, but the six other kids looked like fragile wimps in comparison. It was spooky, really, how the camera had managed to capture each god's different personality in one shot. While Zeus, front and center next to Hera, had his head held high like a leader, Apollo was grinning playfully next to an overexcited Hermes. Aphrodite looked like she was posing for a magazine cover shoot, and Ares was daring someone to mess with him, his arms crossed. But most impressive to me was Athena, staring straight into the camera, now straight at me, with her steel gray eyes peeking out from under her cute side bangs, slightly narrowed in her signature intimidating fashion as if she knew exactly what I was thinking. Like I said, spooky.

I took the photo out of the frame, folded it up, and slid it into my pocket. "Thank you, sir," I said yet again to Athena's human father, and he nodded solemnly.

He then walked over to the window and looked out toward the lush, green forest on the other side of the street, his hunched back facing me. "Don't mention it. Are you going to go back to where you came from now?" he asked sternly. He seemed genuinely concerned about me and I was quite surprised.

"It's complicated," I admitted, thinking about my dysfunctional family and the rest of the Knowing. "I don't really have anyone to go back to, so I'll probably stay in the forest for at least a little while longer."

"Well," Henry began, scratching his head, "if you ever need anything, you can come to me. I'll leave the door unlocked—people in the Woods don't usually lock them anyway—and if you ever need bandages or a safer place to sleep, come on in. Just make sure my wife doesn't catch you here." He paused again before he added under his breath, "And I'm going to try to stop drinking too—for Ashley—so you don't have to worry about that."

I gulped and hesitated before I assured him, "Ashley would've been very proud of you, sir." It was true.

He chuckled halfheartedly, still facing away from me. "I guess that forest really does make one more mature," he mused, more to himself than to me. "You know, I always thought there were weird, bad things in there. I could swear I used to hear screams every once in a while, but lately I haven't heard anything over these damn storms . . . I mean, you'd think all of those kids would've been smart enough to come inside when the lightning started flashing right over that wretched forest, right over their heads. Oh, do you see something else you like?" He had turned around again to find me pulling out two newspapers in glass frames, which had been hidden behind a bookcase.

"These are from the first week the Monster Watch went in?" It wasn't really a question, though, as I was studying the headlines. "Out of the Woods," "The Woods Gets a Monster Watch," and "Monster Watch Sparks New Week of Tragedy" were among the front-page stories. But it wasn't the cute pictures of them as kids that caught my eye—it was the ages of two people in the list of missing persons from that terrible week when more people tried to beat the odds but couldn't.

The two youngest on the list were a boy and a girl, both aged six, the same age as the Monster Watch had been at that time. For some reason, a thought of Hades and Persephone automatically popped into my mind. I remembered when Athena said that all of the gods had found out they were gods within twenty-four hours (at age nine), but the very first time they had come into memorable, direct contact with Hades and Persephone inside the forest was just earlier this summer. This meant that the two had run away together and lived deep inside the woods for three full years before someone—probably the Oracle, after she first delivered the prophecy—told them they were gods, when they would have been forced into the Underworld.

There had to be more to the story then, for Persephone wouldn't have let Hades drag her along into the forest and force her to live with him for three whole years if she hadn't had any feelings for him—she would have escaped eventually, if she had wanted to. But this summer, Persephone seemed to despise him more than anything. She loved the lord of the dead once, so what went wrong in those lost years? I had a feeling the answers were somewhere in Athena's journals.

"Thanks again, sir," I said awkwardly, hiding the newspaper articles behind the bookcase once again. "I—I should probably go now." He just nodded silently and, without another word, I quickly backed out of the room and jumped off the balcony, with Athena's journals and the class picture tucked safely under my arm.

After I stopped to put on my armor again, I made my way back to camp slowly, very slowly. The monsters still seemed to be MIA, so I made it safely back to camp and hid my new keepsakes by the river in a dry spot behind a rock. The tents and cots were taken down and the fire was already put out, although I thought about lighting it up again. Almost all of the Knowing members were gone, and the nymphs and satyrs were splitting off into various groups to go back to their own corners of the forest. I would have said things were returning to normal, but the gods were gone.

"Let me wrap up your arm for you," Jan ordered sweetly as she unexpectedly walked up behind me. Still in a state of shock, I turned away from the river reluctantly and held out my bleeding arm for her to bandage. I watched the plump woman carefully, not trusting her, as she began to put gauze around the slits in my left arm. To be honest, I thought it was kind of disturbing that she did not seem nervous around me at all, unlike the other Knowing members.

"Don't think I don't know where these cuts came from, boy. You shouldn't have done this to yourself," she whispered to me, shaking her head back and forth.

"I deserved it," I hissed back.

Jan sighed, pausing to tuck a stray piece of brown hair back under her bonnet. "You couldn't have stopped the Fates' plan, Alec."

"But I should've *tried!* You just don't understand." I jerked my injured arm away from her, and she started to cluck her tongue softly at me in disappointment. "You can leave now. You're done here," I told her coldly, raising my voice a little.

Jan gulped and I knew I had scared her, but she didn't back down. She simply smoothed out her tattered blue dress and placed her hands on her hips, looking me straight in the eye. "Alec, you need help." I had to admit that she was persistent.

"Go away," I growled, standing up a little taller. "I'm fine on my own. I always have been."

Jan sighed again and lowered her voice so no one else could hear her abruptly switch topics. "Alec, I know you loved her. Lady Athena, I mean."

Now *that* got my attention.

"Don't deny it. I watched you two together in the tent, after your whipping."

I glared at her menacingly, clenching my fists by my side. "That was never supposed to happen between us. It shouldn't have happened. She didn't want it to. You can't tell anyone."

"I wasn't going to, boy. I'm just letting you know that you can trust me, if there's no one else," Jan told me. She paused to look around and check on some Knowing Warriors packing up the last few bags then asked quietly, "Now, are you coming back home with us or not? We're about to leave."

Then it was my turn to sigh, thinking about all the things Athena had said to me that summer. What did she expect me to do? I knew she had to have left me clues somewhere . . . *I believe I trained you well—not just as a fighter, but also as a leader . . . .*

Suddenly, I knew exactly what to do and that was when I confessed my plans to Jan. But, for some reason, Athena thought that you might want to know them as well.

On the night of my whipping, I had asked her if I could stay in the Woods after the war was over, and Athena had said yes, even though she already knew the gods would die. But right before she died, she told me that it was time to prove myself as a leader. She meant as leader of the Knowing.

So I decided I was going to do both, in a way. I planned on living in the forest—there was no denying that it was my true home now since I cared about no one in the Knowing and they had never cared for me. I would be alone for the most part, besides a few wandering nymphs and satyrs, but it was the right thing for me; I deserved to be sad and alone for not deterring the deaths of the gods. I should have just stepped in front of Hades, and the gods would have been okay. Simple, really.

But anyway, I also planned on visiting the Knowing about once a month for the time being, maybe less often later on. (I was sure I could find the money for a plane ticket somewhere, but I would just walk if I had to. Walking is a good way to kill time.) I couldn't just ditch that part of my life completely, especially since the Knowing mark was tattooed onto the back of my neck and the base camp was so corrupt. As a hero, it was my job to help protect future Knowing generations by fixing what was broken now. Which was pretty much everything, in my opinion. Since Athena was only at the camp for about twenty-four hours, she never really saw the extent of the corruption for herself, but I think she had a pretty good idea of what things were like for me. She must have, since her last words were ones of warning. "*We* aren't over yet," she had said. Again, I pondered what that really meant.

I knew for a fact that dealing with the Knowing would be the hardest part of my life from then on. You see, that's the trouble with being a hero—you always have to do the right thing, such as helping your least favorite people no matter how much you hate the idea. I certainly didn't feel like a hero. Now that Athena and the rest of the gods were gone, I didn't even want to be one. Other than to uphold certain morals, there was just no point, in my opinion. I didn't really have anyone left in my life to make proud, to impress, or to love.

I honestly did not expect to live much longer, but I was going to try nonetheless. As you can probably guess, heroes don't tend to have very long lifespans, especially ones who live on their own. One day in the near future, a monster (or monsters) would track me down as usual, but it would take only one second for me to make one wrong move and then I would die. So perhaps you could say that I knew what my "tragic fate" would be ahead of time, just like Athena did.

Speaking of Athena, I wasn't sure I would ever get over the deaths of the gods. People say that you should let go of the past and move on, but what if the past is all you have, all you want to remember? I felt like it was my personal duty to remember and honor the gods. Before that beautiful, tragic, painful summer, I was definitely a loner and a troublemaker, but later on, I was treated like an outsider and sometimes a criminal by my own family. Meeting the gods had been the greatest thing that ever happened to me and I had finally felt like I belonged somewhere, but now I was left alone again, this time with guilt to carry around. (Though, little did I know, I was carrying around a lot more than guilt.)

However, even though the gods were great company and always kept life interesting, I hope you realize that the gods and I weren't perfect people; we were often ruthless and insensitive, sometimes cocky too. To be honest, Athena and I were not exactly proud of all of our actions, such as treating innocent people with hostility or toying around like animals with certain monsters before we killed them. But, just like Athena wrote in the last chapter, maybe you can learn from us to better yourselves.

Now, since Athena hid pieces of advice in each of her chapters, I figured I should get to tell you a piece of mine: Whatever you do, don't fall in love with a god. And if you can help it, don't even become friends with the gods, for there is simply too much to lose once you get attached. Please, just walk away or worship them from afar. Don't let them get to you. They'll completely turn your life around and, before you know it, you won't be able to go back to the way things were before. I can't bear to see that happen to you. It may have seemed like a good thing in my case (and I still think it was), but just look at me in this chapter; I am a mess.

Anyway, it's about time for you to put down this book and move on in your own lives. Hopefully you learned something from Athena's book, from the most recent story in a long list of Greek tragedies, but if not, maybe you just enjoyed reading it. Maybe you'll even go back and reread this book to try to catch all the metaphors and life lessons if you overlooked them the first time. But, whatever happens, I wish you—as Athena always said—good luck. Try not to die.

Printed in the USA
CPSIA information can be obtained
at www.ICGtesting.com
JSHW022329140824
68134JS00019B/1376